*continued . . .*

*Berkley Sensation Titles by Sandra Hill*

ROUGH AND READY
DOWN AND DIRTY
VIKING UNCHAINED
VIKING HEAT

# Viking Heat

## Sandra Hill

BERKLEY SENSATION, NEW YORK

**THE BERKLEY PUBLISHING GROUP**
**Published by the Penguin Group**
**Penguin Group (USA) Inc.**
**375 Hudson Street, New York, New York 10014, USA**
Penguin Group (Canada), 90 Eglinton Avenue East, Suite 700, Toronto, Ontario M4P 2Y3, Canada
(a division of Pearson Penguin Canada Inc.)
Penguin Books Ltd., 80 Strand, London WC2R 0RL, England
Penguin Group Ireland, 25 St. Stephen's Green, Dublin 2, Ireland (a division of Penguin Books Ltd.)
Penguin Group (Australia), 250 Camberwell Road, Camberwell, Victoria 3124, Australia
(a division of Pearson Australia Group Pty. Ltd.)
Penguin Books India Pvt. Ltd., 11 Community Centre, Panchsheel Park, New Delhi—110 017, India
Penguin Group (NZ), 67 Apollo Drive, Rosedale, North Shore 0632, New Zealand
(a division of Pearson New Zealand Ltd.)
Penguin Books (South Africa) (Pty.) Ltd., 24 Sturdee Avenue, Rosebank, Johannesburg 2196,
South Africa

Penguin Books Ltd., Registered Offices: 80 Strand, London WC2R 0RL, England

This is a work of fiction. Names, characters, places, and incidents either are the product of the author's imagination or are used fictitiously, and any resemblance to actual persons, living or dead, business establishments, events, or locales is entirely coincidental. The publisher does not have any control over and does not assume any responsibility for author or third-party websites or their content.

VIKING HEAT

A Berkley Sensation Book / published by arrangement with the author

PRINTING HISTORY
Berkley Sensation mass-market edition / September 2009

Copyright © 2009 by Sandra Hill.
Excerpt from *Even Vikings Get the Blues* copyright © Sandra Hill.
Cover art by Phil Heffernan.
Cover design by Rich Hasselberger.
Interior text design by Stacy Irwin.

ISBN: 978-0-425-23067-1

BERKLEY® SENSATION
Berkley Sensation Books are published by The Berkley Publishing Group,
a division of Penguin Group (USA) Inc.,
375 Hudson Street, New York, New York 10014.
BERKLEY® SENSATION and the "B" design are trademarks of Penguin Group (USA) Inc.

PRINTED IN THE UNITED STATES OF AMERICA

10  9  8  7  6  5  4  3

This novel is dedicated to book lovers everywhere.

In an age of computers, eReaders, iPods, high-tech video games, BlackBerrys, GPS devices, and telephones that can do everything except bake bread (and maybe that is coming soon), the gurus would have you believe that books are going out of style, that one day they will be relics of the past.

Bah! Humbug!

That's nothing against eBooks or even reading books online, but is that anything like having an actual book in hand? Curled up in bed, in the tub, in front of a fireplace? The joy of opening to that first page? The excitement of staying up all night because you couldn't put the book down?

So, while I applaud all the modern technology and am thankful that my books are in those formats, I must say, God bless books and the people who read them!

# Chapter 1

**Testosterone made her do it . . .**

She had no one to blame but herself.

Joy Nelson, a seemingly intelligent woman with a master's degree in psychology, about to start a doctorate program at Yale, had made some dumb choices in her life, mostly because she had spent way too much of her twenty-six years competing with her three older brothers or doing incredibly stupid things after being egged on by the Three Muska-dopes, as she'd called them.

But this one beat the cake.

And it broke her heart thinking about why she'd done it.

Here she was in mud up to her eyeballs on San Clemente Island, one grueling year into her training program to become a female Navy SEAL. *And doesn't that fall into the category of "What was I thinking?"*

It all began when she was about twelve years old and well on her way to her eventual five foot ten, towering over all her classmates. What girl in the throes of puberty wants to have boys looking up at her, making tall jokes? Not to mention three older jock brothers, Matt, Jerry, and Tom, who were not shy about their observations, even after they had gone on to be an Air Force pilot, Wall Street hotshot broker, and NFL football player, respectively.

Also, it hadn't helped that she had curly red hair. *Bright* curly red hair. Think Orphan Annie but not so cute.

"I dare you" had been a common refrain around their house. And "I double-dog dare you" had been the worst challenge of all to a little girl trying to keep up with three young Rambos.

"I dare you to climb that tree," her oldest brother Matt had challenged her. "The one outside the principal's office."

The jerks had even taken pictures of that incident and loved to bring them out on the most embarrassing occasions. Her hanging from the limb, Barbie underpants exposed, with Mr. Clemmons yelling up at her.

"I dare you to try this hair toner," Jerry had suggested one day. "My girlfriend says it will give you gold highlights."

Her hair had turned green. There were photos of that disaster, too.

"If you want to lose your butt," Tom had suggested. *Who knew I even had a butt then?* "Why not try competitive weight lifting . . . you know, body building? I double-dog dare you."

She did, and in the process gained some manly shoulders and lost most of her breasts. *No kidding! No boobs.* But she still had a butt.

They were still laughing over that one.

Well, two of them were.

While her brothers had excelled in sports from elementary school through college, she'd felt compelled to do the same. Therefore, she'd been an all-American tennis player, softball pitcher, basketball forward, and marathon runner. For every trophy they won, she earned two. She didn't have to be a psychologist to understand the subliminal dynamics that had been going on there.

Despite all the teasing and competition, they had been the best brothers in the world. In fact, they pretty much raised her, even before their dad, an Army lifer, died when she was eighteen. Their mother had passed years earlier of cancer when Joy had been only eight.

Matt especially had been her anchor, filling in when their father had been away on duty billets around the world. Matt had been the one who'd explained menstruation to her and purchased her first pads. He'd been the one whose shoulder she cried on after being dumped by her first boyfriend. He'd been the one who told her about birth control and warned her about fast boys and their smooth lines, from experience, no doubt. He was the one she called first with good news or bad.

But she was getting ahead of herself.

Fast forward to her twenty-fifth year and the day that changed her life forever. And, yes, it was related to her brothers.

### Oh, Brother, where art thou . . . ?

She was an intern at the Meadows, a psychiatric clinic in rural Pennsylvania, about to finish up her last group therapy session of the day. With her master's thesis completed and approved at nearby Penn State, she would be moving to New Haven in two weeks for doctoral studies at Yale.

The group today was one labeled Self Esteem: Only You Can Determine Your Worth. Although the facility included adults and children as young as five, on both an inpatient and outpatient basis, those here today were all young teenagers . . . three girls and one boy.

"So, Cindy, tell us how you've done this week."

Cindy, a fifteen-year-old recovering anorexic, replied, "I gained two pounds."

"Well, that's good news." Joy applauded, encouraging the others to follow suit. "But you don't appear happy."

"I'm getting fat." Cindy sank down into her folding chair as only a teenager could and pressed out her lower lip, sulkily.

If only she could see herself as others did. Little more than a skeleton.

"What's your total weight, honey?"

Cindy's gaunt face bloomed pink. Reluctantly, she admitted, "Ninety-eight pounds." When she'd been admitted two months ago, she'd been dying at an alarming eighty pounds.

"You know you can't be discharged until you're up to a hundred and ten? You're five foot seven, for goodness' sake. Even at that weight, you'll still be slim."

"I'll look like a pig," she disagreed.

"Remember my promise. If you get up to one hundred and two before I leave in two weeks, I'll bring a makeup consultant in here to show you just how beautiful you are. I've seen her case of samples. Wow!"

Her face brightened. Was there ever a teenage girl who didn't love makeup?

"I think you look good," Andy Barlow said from Cindy's other side. They were sitting in a small circle in her office.

Cindy flashed him a glare of disgust.

Which of course embarrassed Andy, who was one screwed-up sixteen-year-old. The product of sexual and physical abuse from a young age, he was addicted to cocaine and into tattoos, which covered most of his body.

"Cindy! You know better than that," Joy chided.

"I'm sorry," Cindy told Andy.

But, of course, the damage was done. Andy got up abruptly, knocking over his chair, and rushed from the room.

"I'm sorry," Cindy repeated to the rest of them, tears brimming in her eyes.

Joy brought the other two girls into the discussion then. Alicia, a high school sophomore who continued to blame herself for being gang-raped at a party, and Larise, who was failing academically in senior high, despite having a very high IQ, no doubt due to some undisclosed home issues. She'd been caught cutting herself on more than one occasion.

Joy was concluding the counseling session when she glanced up and saw two of her brothers standing in the doorway.

"Jerry? Tom? What's up? You told me you couldn't make it for graduation."

After the girls left the room, giggling at the sight of the good-looking visitors, they came in, shutting the door behind them, each giving her a big hug and a kiss.

She smiled, not having seen them in person for months.

Her brothers did not smile back.

"What? What's happened?" Fear suddenly riddled her body. Light-headed, she leaned against a chair. "It's Matt, isn't it?"

Jerry nodded and tried to take her hand.

She shoved the hand away.

"Tell me. Is he dead?" *Oh, God! Please don't let him be dead.*

"No," Tom said. "He's not dead."

But he said it in a way that was not hopeful.

A sob escaped her throat before she even knew the details. She knew, *she just knew* it was going to be bad.

"His plane was shot down over Afghanistan. Chuck Wiley, his copilot, died on impact. Matt was taken prisoner. He . . ." Jerry's voice broke, and his hazel eyes misted over with tears. She couldn't remember the last time she'd seen any of her brothers cry.

Tom was in just as bad shape, she soon realized.

"And?"

"The pictures . . . Al-Qaeda has him, and Al Jazeera is showing pictures. Oh, honey, they're bad." Jerry opened his arms, and she went into them.

She didn't ask for details. Her imagination was providing enough.

"They want us in D.C. . . . in case there's news," Tom told her a short time later. "We already went to your apartment and packed a bag for you."

Later that night they got the news. Captain Matthew Nelson was dead.

Joy, screaming hysterically, was immediately given a sedative that knocked her out. Just before she surrendered to unconsciousness, she wondered how she was ever going to face a world without her big brother. How?

In the middle of the night, she awakened, disoriented. She was in one of the two bedrooms in their hotel suite. Her brothers must be asleep, finally. She'd heard conversations and doors opening and closing for hours as she'd awakened, then went back to sleep, over and over throughout the day and evening.

Groggily, she made her way to the bathroom where she rinsed out her mouth and took two aspirin. Slowly, she walked into the living room, which was empty.

As if drawn by a magnet, she made her way to a laptop sitting on the coffee table. Logging on, she came to the main news page of AOL. And there it was, an announcement of Matt's death. A team of Navy SEALS had apparently gone in to rescue him, but they'd been too late.

The picture she saw broke her heart. Amidst a handful of armed men, crouched in a firing position . . . Navy SEALS, she assumed . . . was one particular SEAL carrying her brother. He wore a BDU uniform, and his face was cammied up, but through the black paint could be seen a single tear track stemming from haunted blue eyes.

She would never forget that poignant image.

And it would change her life forever.

## I double-dog dare you . . .

For the next two months, Joy succumbed to a mind-numbing grief, giving up her slot at Yale, rarely leaving her bed before noon. And she became obsessed with the picture of the Navy SEAL carrying her brother.

As a psychologist, she recognized all the signals. The grieving process was taking over her life. Academically, she was well-acquainted with all the counseling steps necessary for her to begin healing, but emotionally she was still not ready. Her brothers were probably just as grief-stricken, but they were back to work and managing to handle the stress. At least on the outside.

"What are you two doing here . . . again?" she asked when there was a knock on the door late one night.

"We're here to intervene . . . I mean, we're gonna do an intervention," Tom said.

"Whew!" She waved a hand in front of her face. "Just how much booze did you consume before coming up with this lame idea?"

"It's a kick-ass idea," Jerry disagreed, blowing an equal waft of liquor breath her way.

Turns out their goofball version of an intervention involved Vodka Stingers, photo albums, and Matt's hokey collection of country music CDs.

"I want to meet him," she told her brothers finally.

"Who?" Jerry slurred.

"That SEAL," she replied, taking out a computer printout of the TV photo.

Toby Keith was belting out "How Do You Like Me Now?" while Jerry and Tom studied the picture.

"Remember how Matt used to sing along with that song?" Tom reminded them.

"That, and 'Save a Horse, Ride a Cowboy,'" Jerry added.

"Yoo-hoo! Earth to bozos," Joy said, waving the picture in front of her brothers. "I want to meet him."

"I don't know, squirt," Jerry said. That's what her brothers had always called her. Some oxymoron! "The SEALs don't like any publicity."

She shrugged. "I need to ask him some questions . . . and to thank him."

"It's not necessary. He was already given some medal," Jerry said.

"I don't care. You want me to straighten out? Fine. Set up a meeting so I can meet the guy, dammit." She turned to Tom. "You know people who know people, Mr. Important Football Player. You can do it. I dare you."

Tom said something Important Football Players should not, a clear sign to Joy that she had won this challenge.

**Anchors aweigh, my dear, or some such nonsense . . .**

One week later, she, Jerry, and Tom were sitting in Commander MacLean's office at the Naval Special Warfare training command center in Coronado, California. Apparently some high muckety-muck in the Navy was a football fan, and Tom was one of his favorite players. The admiral had pulled some strings.

"This is highly irregular," the commander was continuing to argue, even after he'd sent for Lieutenant Luke Avenil, better known as Slick. Joy had learned on one of her Internet searches that all of the SEALs had nicknames, some more colorful than others, like Whiz, Shark, Easy, or Spider. "SEALs operate as teams," the commander continued to complain. "No individual is responsible for the success or failure of a mission."

"I know that. It's just that I need to put a face and a voice to my brother's rescuer," she started to explain.

"With all due respect, ma'am, there was no rescue, just a recovery."

She bristled. "His body wasn't left behind. As far as I'm concerned, that's a rescue. In any case, I was saying, I need to meet the man who carried my brother out of that hellhole. It will give me some closure."

"No offense, Ms. Nelson, but giving civilians closure, or any other psychobabble, is not my responsibility."

There was a sharp rap on the door.

"Enter," the commander snapped.

In came a good-looking, dark-haired man in his mid to late thirties, wearing a camouflage uniform and heavy lace-up boots, his Navy SEAL trident pin, known as a Budweiser, gleaming on his shirt, along with a bunch of stripes and badges that probably had some significance. His dark hair was cut military short in a style known as a high and tight, and he was very buff. He stood at attention until "At ease!" was barked out by his superior officer.

"Lieutenant Avenil, these folks have asked to meet with you. Jerry and Tom Nelson, and their sister, Joy Nelson," the commander said.

Lieutenant Avenil shook hands with her brothers, his eyes flickering for a second at seeing the famous Tom Nelson. While they were standing, she remained seated in front of the desk.

"The young man you rescued in Afghanistan was their brother."

Lieutenant Avenil's eyes connected with hers. The same haunted blue eyes she recognized from the picture. She couldn't help herself. She rose, walked over, and hugged him, whispering against his ear, "Thank you."

She could tell by the stiffness of his body, as well as his flushed face, that her gratitude embarrassed him. But then his arms wrapped around her waist, his hands giving a quick, soothing caress of her back, as if to show he understood.

"It's my job," Lieutenant Avenil said.

After that, the commander excused himself and allowed them time to visit more casually. They all sat down, and the men pulled their chairs closer to her.

He told them everything about the mission, from the moment they were called up, which he referred to as "boots off the ground," and on their way to the "insertion point" in the Middle East. They "put down" a half-dozens "tangos" to get into the stronghold—*tango* was the Navy SEAL term for terrorist—but her brother had been dead on their arrival. Lieutenant Avenil was able to tell them that Matt had been clutching a cross on a gold chain.

Joy choked up again. She'd given him that as a gift last Christmas.

Before they left, she asked Lieutenant Avenil, "Why do you do this?"

He seemed taken aback by her question, but then he replied, "There are a lot of bad people in the world, and if I can eliminate even one of them, then I've made a difference."

"A lot of men signed up after 9/11, didn't they?" Jerry remarked.

Lieutenant Avenil nodded. "There were SEALs before 9/11, of course, but the need is greater today because . . ."

". . . because terrorism is growing," Tom finished for him.

"Big-time," Lieutenant Avenil agreed.

"I wish there was something I could do to make up for Matt's life." She laughed, then kidded, "Too bad the SEALs don't take women."

"The SEALs don't, but the WEALS do," Commander MacLean inserted as he reentered the office, then went on to explain that Women on Earth, Air, Land and Sea was a female version of SEALs. "There have always been female military attached to the SEAL teams, but now they work with SEALs as equal partners."

"I don't know . . . women soldiers?" Jerry said.

She punched him in the arm. Jerry enjoyed goading her feminist leanings, and he had old-fashioned protective emotions about the female species.

"For a long time the military, all branches, resisted having women soldiers. A lot of them still do. Myself included," Commander MacLean admitted. "Researchers tell us that a woman of twenty has the lung power of a man of fifty. And they're not as strong, generally speaking. But mostly it's a nightmare trying to manage a sexy young sailorette in a base full of horny men."

Tom and Jerry chuckled.

"But they're here, right?" she argued. "Women in the military?"

"Yep, and they've proven most of the naysayers wrong."

"Yourself included?" she inquired sweetly.

"Definitely." His somber face relaxed into a grin. "You'd have to meet my wife, Madrene, to know why that was a politic answer."

"C'mon. I'll take you to the grinder where one of the WEALS classes is working out today," Lieutenant Avenil offered. "BUD/S, the latest SEAL training class, is just about finished."

They gave their thanks and said good-bye to the commander.

"BUD/S?" Tom asked as they followed Lieutenant Avenil down the corridor.

"Basic Underwater Demolition/Seals," the lieutenant explained as they exited the building. "In the old days, SEALs were primarily in the water; in fact, they called them frogmen or webfoot warriors. They're everywhere today, though . . . air, land, sea, but they kept the name."

The grinder was an asphalt area surrounded by several low buildings, almost like the exercise yard of a penitentiary. In the distance could be seen huge gray Navy warships lined up near the Naval Amphibious Base at the other end of Coronado. To one side was the cold blue Pacific Ocean, shimmering under the early morning sun, which would be relentless by afternoon. She could also see the red-tiled roof of the famous Hotel del Coronado, where she and her brothers would be having lunch before heading back home.

After spending a half hour watching two dozen women getting the most incredible workout on everything from climbing a high cargo net to gazillions of sit-ups, Jerry remarked to Lieutenant Avenil, "These women look especially fit. Are they, like, super-duper athletes? You know, wonder women with supersonic parts?"

Lieutenant Avenil laughed. "Nah. They have to be in good shape, of course. SEAL candidates do, too. But the program will hone them into the types of bodies they need. And, no, that doesn't mean muscle-bound masculine females. Don't tell anyone I said so, but some of them are pretty hot."

Her brothers looked at her in a funny way.

She recognized the look.

"Oh, no!" she exclaimed.

"I dare you," Jerry said.

"I double-dog dare you," Tom added. "Think of all the fun."

*Ha, ha, ha.*

"And, really, I bet there would be tons of opportunities for you to use your psychology skills." Tom was on a roll, or so he thought.

"The commander's sister is a Navy doctor assigned to the teams here in Coronado," Lieutenant Avenil added.

"A Navy SEAL psychologist . . . I mean, Navy WEALS

psychologist. Wow!" Tom batted his sinfully long, dark lashes at her. "Wouldn't that be *weally* great?"

"Just super."

"You could psychobabble the enemy to death."

"Tom, you are so not funny."

"It would be a breeze for you," Jerry promised, barely able to stifle his smile. "You're in great shape . . . except for your butt."

He ducked when she tried to whack him a good one.

So, that's how, a year later, she was here on San Clemente Island with a group of equally brain-dead WEALS wannabes. You could say hers was a classic case of *Private Benjamin* meets *Stripes*. At the moment, they were engaged in survival training. The goal was to evade the enemy . . . i.e., Navy SEAL instructors with sadist personalities and testosterone oozing out the yee haw. Her hiding place was under a slight ledge over an almost dry streambed . . . i.e., mud. The mosquitoes were the size of mothballs, the mud smelled, and she was pretty sure that was a spider in the long braid she had tucked under her cap.

Just then, Master Chief Justin LeBlanc, a Cajun SEAL better known as Cage, leaned over the ledge above her and drawled, "Peekaboo, darlin'," just before shooting her with a big yellow paintball.

In the butt.

# Chapter 2

**Men will be boys, always . . .**

Brandr Igorsson stood with hundreds of his Jomsviking comrades-in-arms, surveying the ritual initiation of six men into the brotherhood.

"Keep an eye on my brother Frode," his best friend Torkel said, his chin raised with pride. "Only sixteen, but there is no more fearless youthling in all the Norselands."

"Like you were, Tork?" Brandr grinned. He and Tork had joined the elite band of far-famed warriors, together, more than ten years past. In truth, they had been fighting men for closer to twenty years, since their selfsame thirteenth birthing day. In more battles than he could count, they had fought side by side, watching each other's backs.

"Just like," Tork agreed, humility never being one of his virtues.

Horns of ale were raised as a wave of shouting erupted around them . . . cheers of encouragement and hoots of ridicule. A large neck-ring of turf had been cut from the ground in such a way that two of the sides were still intact. In various places underneath stood sharp spearheads. Those men about to swear fealty to the Jomsviking brotherhood were in the process of crawling from one end to the other beneath the grassy blanket, their blood mixing with the Trelleborg dirt.

When they had all completed this task, they dropped to their knees, Frode included, grinning with self-satisfaction for having survived, despite blood dripping from their arms and backs, their faces marked with grass and dirt stains. Egill the Fearless, their leader, strode toward them with a stern glower on his bearded face and demanded the oaths of loyalty, not just to him as chieftain but also to their fellow warriors. Each promised to avenge all other Jomsvikings as a brother. None must ever give voice to fear. No man could be absent from Trelleborg for more than three days without permission. No women could be brought into the all-male, monastic-style garrison. Plunder would be shared by all in the warrior community.

The fortress, which could house twelve hundred men, sat on the west coast of Sjaelland, between Kattegat and the Baltic Sea, atop an enormous circular earthworks, with high double-timbered ramparts filled with earth, which were manned at all times. The stronghold was divided into quadrants by two roads that crisscrossed, leading to four openings, with gates that could be dropped in an instant if they were attacked by foemen. Below lay the palisaded harbor town where ale and wenches were available aplenty, for a coin.

Tork picked up a wooden bucket of water and dumped it over his brother's head.

"Hey!" Frode shook his head like a shaggy dog.

They were better able now to examine the boy's extensive injuries, which had been Tork's intention. A deep slice on his shoulder, cutting through the leather tunic and flesh. Several cuts on his legs and a vicious wound on one forearm.

Tork touched the latter and said, "This one might need stitches."

"Nay." Frode gave his wound an admiring glance, then grinned. "Methinks it will make a great scar to attract the maidens."

Laughing, the three of them made for the seaside opening.

The youthling chattered the whole time, even though in most ways he was a man now. That fact was proven when he teased them, "Let us go down to the village and celebrate. Mayhap I can find a wench or two to swive, whilst you two ugly brutes may have my leavings."

Tork reached out to punch his brother, but Frode ducked, and Tork's fist met only air.

'Twas then that Brandr noticed the longship entering the harbor far below. Oh, there were dozens and dozens of longships and knarrs and barges already anchored and some beached for the winter, but none carried this particular flag. A white bear rampant against a black background edged in red. It was Brandr's family crest.

As they got closer, the hairs stood out on the back of his neck with every creak of the oarlocks, and he exchanged a worried look with Tork, both sensing that something must be amiss.

They soon found out.

It was his younger brothers Erland and Arnis, sixteen and twenty years old. *How odd!* And they were in charge of a longship . . . one of the many family longships, but this one manned by a shiphird, or sea army, of a mere thirty men. *Even more odd!* And a scraggly band they were, too. *Beyond odd! Alarming!*

On anchoring, then jumping onto the wharf planking, his brothers hugged him in greeting, then nodded at Tork and Frode, whom they had met as visitors at Bear's Lair on many an occasion.

The first thing Erland did was complain to Brandr, "Frode has become a Jomsviking? You told me I was too young."

"You *are* too young." In Brandr's experience, some males were men at sixteen, whilst others did not mature 'til much later. Erland was of the latter type.

Arnis thumped his brother on the shoulder, causing Erland to stumble. "Lackwit! Dost forget why we are here?" Then he turned to Brandr with a grim expression on his face. "We bring bad news, Jarl Igorsson."

*Jarl?* "What? Me?" he nigh squawked. Those standing hairs on his neck were now waving a warning to him. There could be only one way that the odal right of jarldom would pass to him. Through his father and three older brothers.

Which was impossible.

It had to be.

Arnis put a hand on his arm in sympathy.

*Sympathy?*

"They are all gone."

He closed his eyes for a moment, trying to digest what Arnis was saying. "All?"

Both Erland and Arnis nodded.

"The Sigurdssons came in the night," Erland explained. "Killed and maimed everyone in sight. Father, his wives and concubines, your mother, our brothers Vidar, Bjarn and Sveinn. Our sisters Maeva and Gerda are dead, along with their babes. Housecarls, cotters, everyone slaughtered. Arnora and Kelda survived, no doubt because they were too old to be of any use." Arnora was Vidar's mother, and Kelda was the longtime cook at Bear's Lair. "In truth, hardly anyone was spared by the whoresons, except Liv, who was amongst a handful of women taken captive."

Tork and Frode gasped with horror. A soft cry of pain escaped Brandr's lips, which soon thinned with fury. The Sigurdssons and Igorssons had done each other great scathe over the years, but naught like this.

His sister Liv was only thirteen years old. It broke his heart to think of what horrors the impish girling must be experiencing at this very moment. Last time he heard, she had not even had her first monthly flux.

It hardened his heart to know of the blood that had been spilled and all the more blood he would now be compelled to spill. There would be a virtual flood of sword dew. "And you two . . . how did you escape?"

"We were off to Birka, trading furs for winter goods," Arnis told him.

Bear's Lair was a remote northerly estate, rocky and cold, not conducive to farming. But bears abounded, huge brown creatures, and up near the Arctic region, the prized white bears. "Two days late, we were," Arnis continued, his voice raspy with emotion, his blue eyes glazed in remembrance of the horrors he must have seen. "Not that our presence would have made a difference. We learned from the few survivors that Sigurd came with a hird of two hundred strong."

"How many men are left?" Tork interjected. His good friend would be returning with him, Brandr knew, without his asking for help.

"Three dozen able-bodied, another three dozen injured but will recover, the gods willing, and another dozen crippled for life."

"*Hrafnasueltir!*" he exclaimed and spat on the ground. "Raven starver, that is what Sigurd is. A coward. Less than a nithing."

Tork took Frode by the elbow and led him back toward the fortress. "Looks like you will be blooded in battle sooner than expected, brother. Let us see how many Jomsviking warriors will join us in this good and noble cause."

Brandr would not be surprised if a worthy hird would be at the ready within the hour to travel back with him to his estate, or what was left of it.

How could his life have changed so, in a matter of minutes? This had been a good life for him, a middle son. He had been contented. Well, no more.

Taking out Flesh Biter, his favorite pattern-welded broadsword, tears welling in his eyes for the first time since he was a baby, Brandr stabbed the weapon into the ground with a roar of fury and proclaimed with a loud cry to the high heavens, "This I swear afore Thor and all the gods. We will be avenged!" His throat clogged for a moment before he repeated hoarsely, "We *will* be avenged!"

The howl that followed was like that of a crazed wolf.

That was the day Brandr Igorsson turned berserker.

**You could say they were GI Janes, or more likely, GI Jokes . . .**

"Quack, quack, quack!"

"A-ten-shun!"

"Let's see a little more waddle, duckies."

"A-ten-shun!"

"Move it, move it, move it!"

"If they walk like ducks, and quack like ducks, they must be . . . Navy WEALS."

These were among the taunts hurled at Joy and five other women early that evening by SEALs or SEAL trainees returning to the grinder from the chow hall.

When one of the women muttered something disparaging about their manhoods, Cage burst out laughing. "Now, now, sweet thangs. Doan get yer feathers ruffled. Like my maw maw down the bayou allus sez . . ."

"You are so full of it, LeBlanc," the repulsive Frank Uxley, appropriately nicknamed F.U., said as they walked off. "Screw your maw maw."

"I beg yer pardon, dickhead. How would you like it if I said that about *your* grandmother?"

"I don't have a grandmother, asshole."

"Born under a rock, eh, *cher*?"

The women, all wearing Navy-issue shorts, T-shirts, and boondockers with heavy socks pulled up and folded over, just like the men, were being punished with gig squad in front of the officers' quarters, a Navy method of punishment for infractions too trivial to merit ringing out but too serious to overlook. Mostly, it involved them doing duck squats, a humiliating exercise in which persons squatted down as far as they could go without toppling over, then walked back and forth like a bunch of idiots . . . duck idiots. It wasn't a punishment reserved for the women, though. The SEALs were the ones who made gig squad famous.

Sweat poured off of Joy in rivulets, and it soaked her hair, which had been pulled into a neat, high ponytail this morning but was half-mast by now.

And, really, all the five of them had done was laugh when Instructor JAM . . . aka Lieutenant Jacob Alvarez Mendozo . . . ordered them to do *another* five-mile run on the beach. That following on not only a previous jogging rotation, but a full PT cycle around the various implements of torture on the grinder's obstacle course, like the Cargo Net, the Skyscraper, the Slide for Life, the Wall, the Weaver, and the "Dirty Name" log evolution.

While SEALs were required to build up their endurance to six-mile swims and eighteen-mile runs, the standards were lower for WEALS, but not by much. Unbelievably naive in the beginning, she'd figured that if she could withstand "drownproofing," where trainees were dropped into a pool with their wrists and ankles tied together, the rest was sure to be a breeze. Hah! More like a hurricane. And don't even mention Hell Week.

The day she'd started hand-to-hand combat training had been an eye-opener, as well. But then, she should have been prepared when she'd seen the padded walls of the room and a bald Marine the size of Godzilla waiting for the female trainees with a maniacal gleam in his eyes.

Joy had been in WEALS training for a year now and had earned her preliminary WEALS trident badge, but she felt like a newbie. There was so much to learn, and every bit of it was damn hard. Not just the physical exercise, either.

Commander MacLean walked up and loomed over her.

She continued to duck walk.

"Petty Officer Nelson!" he shouted, about breaking her eardrum. He always shouted. Really, the man didn't have a normal tone of voice. And when he wasn't shouting, he was spouting goofball inspirational sayings, like, "A peacock who sits on his tail is just another turkey," or his favorite, "Join the Navy, travel the world, meet interesting people, kill them."

His shout surprised her, about causing her to fall backwards. She immediately jerked to a standing position, her arms stiffly at her sides, staring straight ahead.

Joy could have opted for officer candidate school when

she'd first enlisted in the Navy's WEALS program, but she'd declined, wanting to get into action ASAP. Not that being an officer would have made her training any easier. And she would still be answerable to Commander MacLean.

"In my office. Oh eight hundred. Tomorrow morning. Don't be late. Resume rotation."

"Uh-oh," she murmured to her fellow duck squatters. "Why me?"

"Never a good idea to be singled out," Dottie Ellison agreed, huffing as she spoke. "Jeesh! My hamstrings are killing me."

"Pain is your friend," April Abramson reminded them of that notorious SEAL motto.

"The commander must be wearing off on you, girlfriend." Dot laughed and spouted another dumb-ass SEAL motto, "The only easy day was yesterday."

"I'll tell you the one I like," said Candy Williams. "If something is hard, it must be good."

"If something is hard, it must be attached to a horn dog Navy SEAL, if you ask me." This from Kathy Billings.

They all laughed then. *A bunch of laughing ducks. Jeesh!*

"Anyone want to go to the Wet and Wild later?" Dot asked. The Wet and Wild was a bar where single Navy personnel hung out, especially SEALs and WEALS. A good place to pick up—uh, meet—guys.

"Yeah, I'm about due to get lucky," Candy responded with a grin. "All work and no play and all that, y'know, is making me a very dull girl."

"Tell me about it. I ain't had some since God was a child," Kendra Black added.

"I'm game," the others joined in.

Except for Joy, who had been celibate for a remarkable two years now after a long line of failed relationships with full-of-themselves, good-looking men. And she wasn't missing *it* at all.

Well, hardly.

Maybe the answer was to find a homely man, or at least one who wasn't in love with himself.

"Give me a break!" Joy was amazed that she could talk and duck walk at the same time . . . an indication of how far she'd come, she supposed. Being a competitive athlete, even a short-term body builder, had in no way prepared her for the rigors of Special Forces training. And all this extreme exercise hadn't reduced the size of her butt one iota. Still, she was in good shape; her deltoids and obliques and quadriceps had been honed to the max. "A warm shower, a five thousand calorie pizza, and ten hours' sleep. That's the closest to an orgasm I want to come . . . and I mean that literally."

They all laughed then.

"I think you're afraid that one of the big bad SEALs will hit on you," Candy said.

"I'm not afraid of those jerks." Joy liked men, even SEALs, but casual sex was not her thing, and she hadn't had an opportunity in like forever to develop a romantic relationship, no matter the kind of man. After Matt's death, she wasn't in the mood for casual anything.

Some psychologist she was! It was obvious that she had serious commitment issues.

"You haven't had a date since we started training a year ago," Kendra pointed out. "Maybe you're afraid of yourself . . . that you're so hot for it that *you* might jump a few male bones."

She grunted her opinion. "Don't be silly."

But then Dot hurled the magic words. "I dare you to come."

### When the Wet and Wild beckons . . .

As it turned out, there were only four of them who ended up at the Wet and Wild that evening, after taking a shower and long nap: Joy, Dot, Kendra, and Candy. April and Kathy had blind dates with a set of twin Navy hot guns, arranged by a mutual friend. Bunk chatter later tonight should be interesting.

Of the four of them who entered the bar, cringing at the

ear-splitting blare of Trace Adkins's "One Hot Mama," only Candy, a self-proclaimed wild child, went through the politically incorrect T-shirt spraying device at the door. Who cared that the rest of them had to pay a cover charge? Joy wasn't about to give a bunch of horny men reason to get hornier. Candy, on the other hand, considered it one of her major goals in life to turn on all of the male species.

The male-female ratio was about three to one, so the four of them were surrounded by testosterone the minute they entered the bar. Luckily, three of the full-fledged WEALS they'd come to know well were sitting at a table on the far side of the bar and waved an invitation, thus allowing them to escape the crowd, a mix of all services but mainly Navy, including some SEALs. There was Terri Evans, a petite redhead with green eyes that always seemed to be dancing with mischief; Donita Leone, tall, black, stunningly gorgeous, a former Olympic swimmer; and Marie Delacroix, a Cajun ex-Marine who'd joined WEALS after her father was killed in the Twin Towers.

"Hey, ladies, how's training going?" Terri asked after they sat down.

The four of them groaned.

The waitress showed up and hitched a hip, not bothering to ask what they wanted, her attitude saying it for her.

"You have to try one of these," Terri suggested, waving her drink in front of them. "It's called a Dark and Stormy."

Joy had never heard of that one before. "What's in it?"

"Good rum, preferably Bacardi Gold, cracked ice, ginger beer, and lime to balance out the sweetness. Yum!"

Joy laughed. "A little too exotic for me, although I do like the name." Turning to the waitress, she said, "I'll have a Sierra Nevada pale ale. And a menu, please." Growing up in a family of men, Joy had learned to appreciate a good beer.

The rest of them ordered drinks, and they all decided to share two everything pizzas and a double order of hot wings, heavy on the celery and blue cheese.

"So they're still working you hard," Donita remarked.

"Like horses," Kendra answered, then laughed as the

band segued into Toby Keith's "Whiskey for My Men, Beer for My Horses."

Donita ignored Kendra pointedly and asked Joy, "Were you able to improve your timed miles with those exercises I recommended?"

Donita had a love/hate relationship going with Sylvester "Sly" Simms, a former *GQ* underwear model, of all things. Kendra loved to goad Donita by flirting with the black SEAL, and Sly flirted right back.

"Actually, I did improve," Joy told Donita, "but still not good enough. I'm not sure God intended women to run so fast."

They all grinned.

"Unfortunately, God failed to tell that to the Marquis de Sade instructors," Terri said.

"When I was back home on the bayou for a little R & R over Christmas las' year, my brother asked me why my thighs were so muscular," Marie said in her deep Southern accent. "After I whacked him upside the noggin, I tol' him it was from doin' a rodeo on so many Navy men. He actually believed me. Talk about!"

"I think special consideration should be given to us short people. Our strides are so much smaller," Terri added. "But Commander MacLean just laughed when I told him so."

"Speaking of sadistic instructors . . ." Donita was staring at the entrance where a group of SEALs had just entered. It was a funny thing, but when out in public, the SEALs tended to stick together and were easily recognizable by their extremely buff physiques. It was like a secret brotherhood kind of thing, she supposed. They'd seen and done things only they could share. Active duty WEALS were the same way.

The SEALS noticed them and immediately headed their way, and they soon had three tables pushed together.

Slick pushed a chair up next to her and gave her a quick, brotherly hug. "How ya doin', toots?"

"Just dandy, if you don't count my sore feet, aching muscles, and lack of sleep."

"In other words, the usual." Slick grinned. Especially

handsome with his dark, brooding good looks, he was in his mid to late thirties, old for a SEAL, but since 9/11, Special Forces of all military branches were in such demand that the rules had been relaxed. He was single and not dating anyone in particular, as far as she knew. Probably commitment phobic, thanks to a bad experience with a divorced wife. Joy's relationship with him was purely platonic.

"Do you ever ache anymore when you exercise?"

"Every day." The SEALs were required to follow complete BUD/S training workouts whenever they weren't on a live op.

"Oh, that's encouraging."

"I hear the commander has a special assignment for you."

That got her attention. "Really?"

He ducked his head. "Oops. Guess I jumped the gun."

"Okay, spill. What's the assignment?"

"He didn't say anything to you?"

"Just that he wanted me in his office tomorrow morning. I figured I was in trouble for something or other."

"You aren't in trouble . . . unless you consider a live op in enemy territory trouble."

"I'm going operational?" she asked excitedly.

"Uh, I can't discuss it with you."

"Will you be part of the operation?"

"Possibly."

"Well, that's good then. You'll watch my back."

He smiled at her confidence in his protection and squeezed her hand. "Whenever I can, babe."

They all plowed into their food, ordered more drinks, then clapped and shouted out their opinions as Cage and Marie, under the direction of Brooks and Dunn's "Boot Scootin' Boogie," did what could only be described as a combination Cajun two-step and dirty dancing. Right after that, half the place seemed to be up and dancing to that old Chuck Berry classic, "Johnny B. Goode," with everyone enthusiastically singing the refrain, "Go, Johnny, go!" Cage and Marie were good, really good.

Slick asked her to dance, halfheartedly, but she told him she wasn't in the mood for tripping the light fantastic. She could tell he was relieved.

Geek, a Mensa-IQ SEAL with a boyish demeanor belied by a wicked grin, asked Candy to dance. Geek liked to give the impression of being a bumbling, inexperienced hayseed, but he'd been the one to help set up a hugely successful site on the Internet called www.penileglove.com. Enough said! A short while ago, when someone asked what his latest project was going to be, he'd answered that he was writing an essay for a book of philosophy about women. His section was going to be on how to determine the kind of sex partner a woman would be by the way she ate her food. At that point, the men said, "Sweet!" and every woman at the table stopped chewing. But, hey, look at him out there on the dance floor. Those hips knew what they were doing. Wild Candy had to work hard to keep up.

JAM, or Jacob Alvarez Mendozo, was once a Jesuit priest or at least studying to be one. She'd bet her one and only pair of Jimmy Choos that there was a story there. JAM led Dottie out to join the others. His dancing was much more sedate.

Terri was yakking away at Scary Larry, who never even batted an eyelash or took part in Terri's one-way conversation. He probably figured Terri would go away if he ignored her. No way! According to the grapevine, Terri had made a vow at one time that she would get laid by Scary Larry, eventually. Different tastes!

Then there was Sly, who stared at Donita for a long moment, then asked Kendra to dance. The jerk! Donita raised her chin haughtily, but Joy could see that she was fighting tears. In fact, Donita quickly rose and made her way to the ladies' room, probably to get herself under control.

"Well, that was pleasant. Not!" she commented to Slick.

"Give the guy some credit. He's crazy mad in love with Donita, but he can't make up her mind whether she wants him or not."

Joy's left eyebrow rose a fraction. It wasn't like Slick to listen to or pass on gossip.

"I'm just sayin'." Slick took a sip of his beer, then exclaimed, "Oh, good Lord!"

Approaching their table was a statuesque thirty-something woman with flowing ebony hair and a creamy complexion. It was Slick's ex-wife Barbara, who had moved to Coronado recently, much to Slick's chagrin, and was working in an aerobics studio owned by one of the SEALs' wives.

"Barb, what the hell are you doing here?" Slick asked right off the bat.

Barb flinched but sat down on Slick's other side. "Just slumming." She reached over and took a sip of his beer.

"That figures. Since when do you drink beer?"

"I learned from the best."

It took him a moment to comprehend that she meant him. "You've got to be kidding. My bank account is empty, thanks to you. What could you possibly want from me now?"

She didn't say anything, just stared at him.

And Joy realized in that moment that all the litigation this woman had filed against Slick over the years was just an attempt to gain his attention. She didn't want his money. She wanted him. A clear case of aggression transferal.

Joy got up to leave them alone. Walking outside to the parking lot and then into an adjoining park, she sat down on a bench. All of a sudden, she felt very lonely.

Sometimes she didn't think she was healed at all. Maybe she was just kidding herself that she'd entered the third phase of her grieving process. Maybe she'd never left step one and was just repressing her outward signs.

Looking up at the starry sky, she wondered, as she often had in the past year and more, if her brother Matt was up there watching her. Laughing at all her efforts to prove herself, once again, in a man's world.

Sometimes it was debatable whether it was her brain or her heart that was splintering apart.

# Chapter 3

**When good men go berserk . . .**

Today was the day. Today the madness would end.

Brandr stood at the top of the rise, staring down into the valley at the last of the Sigurdssons who were camped in tents and hastily erected timber and sod huts. Dawn was just rising, and women were beginning to stir the fires. There would be no stealth required in the fray today.

For three months now, Brandr and his comrades-in-arms had wreaked vengeance on the miscreants in a wave sweeping north of Bear's Lair, through all of Sigurd's holdings. He was most impressed with how his unseasoned brothers, Erland and Arnis, had proven themselves as fighting men. In time, they would make great warriors, mayhap even Jomsvikings, if they chose. Through spring and summer, Brandr's troop had trudged on, awash in sword dew, knowing months-long darkness would soon be biting at their heels. He must be back at Bear's Lair soon to prepare the keep for the bitter cold winter ahead.

Brandr's hird was sixty strong, including thirty Jomsvikings who counted as a hundred when it came to combat skills. Thus far, they had only lost five men, and another three were gravely wounded. But the Sigurdssons and their followers . . . ah, they had fallen like sheaves of wheat afore the scythe. The ravens of death resembled black clouds in the skies over this northernmost Hordaland, feeding on the carrion. So much blood had Brandr shed, so many bodies had he sent to Valhalla!

Joining him today were Jarl Tykir Thorksson of Dragonstead, a neighbor from south of here, along with a full dozen of his hirdsmen. Tykir had been a good friend for many a year, and now he rode at Brandr's side as a good and faithful comrade-in-arms. He was especially grateful since Tykir left behind his wife Alinor and their baby Thork to join him in battle.

But Tykir was not the only one to send soldiers. King Thorvald of Stoneheim had sent men, as well. Although Thorvald had no sons, only five daughters, he spared him a full dozen warriors led by the far-famed Rafn, soon to wed one of Thorvald's daughters once she was of age, so the rumors went.

Forseti, the god of justice, had been at their backs, while Thor, god of war, had guided their sword arms, and now . . . well, now it no longer felt like a hero's mission. Brandr did not regret the carnage. His vengeance was justified. Still . . .

But would he ever be the same?

Did he want to be the same?

Nay, he was a berserker now. The bloodlust was imbedded in him. Rage and fury thrummed through his body with an endless rhythm, especially when in battle. Even when at rest, a blackness shrouded his soul. He knew his own men feared him at times, especially his brothers, who gazed at him betimes in horror at what he had become. Those had been the moments when his arms and chest had dripped with his foemen's blood, spittle foaming at the sides of his mouth like a rabid beast, and still he had roared for more.

Tork, whom he'd appointed as his hersir, came up to him and looped an arm over his shoulders. They were both dressed for battle with padded undertunics, hauberks of flexible chain mail with attached coifs, and tight, thick chausses and cross-gartered leather boots, helmets, and Jomsviking shields with the embossed battle raven. Whetstones had sounded through the night as men sharpened swords, battle-axes, and knives. Archers had prepared their longbows and arrows.

"The men are ready," Tork told him. "Do we strike at dawn?"

Brandr nodded.

"And do we spare the women and children, as before?"

"Yea. In fact, today we spare any who are weaponless."

Tork frowned. "A bear can do great harm even without sharp teeth. Have a caution, my friend."

"We will decide later if they pose any threat. Besides, they will all be sold into thralldom, as before, except for those women and children that our men choose to keep, or those with particular talents. A blacksmith, for example, would not be turned away, nor a leather worker, which we sorely need. Remember, no battlefield rape, or death will be the penalty. And all plunder shall be shared."

"As you wish." Tork recognized, as he did, that some of the men resented being forbidden the slaking of lust on enemy women, but it was a tiny bit of civility in an uncivilized world that Brandr insisted upon before the berserk rage overcame him.

A short time later, Brandr walked with careful silence over the dewy ground toward the men in battle gear who were moving into a tight *svinfylkja* or swine wedge . . . a triangular formation whereby the point faced the enemy. They brandished fierce weapons of all kinds, some in leather helmets but most with cup-shaped metal ones with nose and eye guards, even neck flaps, carrying round wooden and brass shields, only a few in chain armor, like him and Tork. They would be on foot rather than horseback because of the rough terrain. Usually, a chieftain let his men form a shield wall around him, but Brandr insisted on leading the point forward. When they were ready, he raised his right arm high, one of his hirdsmen raised the bear flag, an archer sent up the arrow of war, and Brandr howled like a wolf, then shouted, "To the death!"

Tork joined in, yelling, "Hew them down! Death to the Sigurdssons!"

"Luck in battle!" many of the men hollered to each other, followed by loud war whoops.

And Brandr began the chant that they all picked up, "Vengeance, vengeance, vengeance!"

### The sins of war brought one blessing to him . . .

Many hours later, they had set up camp far from the stench of battle. Corpses and hacked bodies littered the once serene valley. Vultures were already at work.

The last of the Sigurdssons were dead, including Sigurd One Hand, who had taken Brandr's sword through his black heart and wore a blood ring around his thick neck. At the end, Sigurd had taunted him with the way in which he had tortured his family before killing them. "Your mother's thighs were white"—Sigurd had smiled at him through rotted teeth—"and then they were red."

Later, Brandr had put a blood eagle on Sigurd's back, hacking the ribs open from the back along the spine, then reaching in to pull the lungs out, like wings. It was a horrid practice, long put aside by many Vikings. His only excuse was that he had still been in a berserk rage.

Though hours had passed, his ears still rang with the sounds of battle . . . the clanging of swords, the whistling of arrows, the slap of leather, grunts, and death cries. His broadsword had nigh sung with magic today. A killing magic.

Weary beyond imagination, he yearned to sleep the winter through. But there was too much to do.

After a fine meal of fire-roasted boar, ale and mead were being inhaled like air as the men made merry, bragging of their brave feats. 'Twas the way of warriors after battle.

"The captives," Tork reminded him as he drew him toward the tent where four dozen men and women huddled, their hands tied behind their backs. Already tied about their necks with leather thongs were thrall amulets with the runic symbols pronouncing, "I belong to Brandr," never to be removed without permission on pain of death. Toddlers and very young children sat at the thralls' feet, tears staining their mud-streaked faces.

Brandr noted that six of the women sat off to the side, apart from the others, who had been fettered with their hands behind their backs and linked by a thin rope to each other, like beads on a necklace. Two of the six held babes in their arms. He assumed these were ones handpicked by some of his men as prizes of war. Whether they took them home as concubines or thralls, they would not be treated too badly, if they behaved.

He and Tork stepped before each of the captives, one at a time, and decided whether they would go to the slave marts in Hedeby and Birka or be kept as thralls back at Bear's Lair. None would go free.

To one of the young men who could be no more than eleven, he asked, "Your name?"

"Leif."

"Could you swear fealty to me and all the Igorssons at Bear's Lair?"

The boy did not hesitate. "Yea, I could. Sigurd forced me to fight for him, lest he kill me mother."

"And your mother?"

He nodded toward the woman beside him. She could be no more than thirty, but she looked sixty, so harsh were the lines that worried her face.

"These two, back to Bear's Lair," he said.

Soon he was at the end of the line, where a young girl stood, her blonde hair lank, her face gaunt to the point of starvation. A brief glance at him before she swept her lashes downward showed eyes glazed with a dimwittedness that could have come at birth or through vile treatment. One eye was blackened; no doubt she did not follow orders well. What could he do with such a starvling? No one would buy such in the slave markets, and what good would she do them at Bear's Lair, except another mouth to feed?

But then he noticed something. Two things, actually.

The girl was heavy with child. For Thor's sake! Another Sigurdsson snake being bred.

Of a sudden, she stared at him, steady, and his knees nigh buckled.

"Brandr? What is amiss?" Tork inquired from his side.

"Oh, my gods!" Erland said at his back, immediately followed by Arnis's choked out, "Is it . . . ?"

Brandr could not speak over the lump in his throat and his pounding heart.

It was his sister Liv.

She was scarce fourteen now, and she was hugely pregnant.

And she did not recognize him.

Still, with tears misting his eyes, Brandr took her up in a tight hug that surprised both of them.

"Shhh," he kept murmuring. "Everything will be all right now."

But would it be?

### You want me to become a sex *what* . . . ?

"You're going operational at oh six hundred on Thursday . . . to northern Germany," Commander MacLean said.

Joy stood at attention before his desk in the SEALs command center at Coronado, blinking with surprise. She'd come this morning, knowing she might be given an active assignment, thanks to Slick's hints, but she'd never thought it would be so soon or so extensive. "Yes, Commander, sir."

"You'll be part of a team of six SEALs. A black op. Very covert."

"Permission to speak, Commander, sir?"

"Granted. Stand easy."

"Will I be the only woman?"

He nodded.

"Why me?"

"We had someone else. WEALS Ensign Linda Collins, but she discovered she's pregnant and plans to ring out."

Joy knew Linda and that she was going to ring out, but she hadn't known why. "I repeat, why me?"

He gave her a full-body look, head to toe and back up again.

She was wearing Navy requisition shorts, T-shirt, and boots. Her hair was pulled off her face into a tight French braid. She wore no makeup, nothing to attract attention. "You're best suited for this particular mission."

She frowned with confusion. "I'm not nearly as skilled with weapons as some of the others, and there are full-fledged WEALS available."

"You'll be infiltrating a white slave ring."

"Huh?" *Well, that didn't sound very professional. I might as well as have said, "Duh."* "Prostitution isn't the usual SEAL field of interest."

"Not prostitution. White slavery. In fact, it's being run by some fringe Arab terrorist group."

"Arab terrorists in Germany?"

"Pfff! They're everywhere now. Anyhow, in this particular mission, they're providing sex for bombs."

"You're kidding."

"I wish. Apparently some of these nutcase extremists are offering sex slaves to their loyal followers." He tapped a pencil on the desk, then elaborated. "You're mission essential, Nelson. We need *you* to infiltrate. And we need to engage the enemy in the act."

"Ah," she said, beginning to understand why he'd said she would be well-suited. He must be referring to her boobs. They weren't large, but they appeared so because of her thin frame. "There are sexier women than me."

"Sexy isn't the best qualification. That would be too obvious. You're unusual, and it's not just your . . . uh, attributes. Your red hair, for example. You would attract interest right off the bat."

"I beg your pardon. Unusual? Is that supposed to be a compliment?"

"You're tall, for another thing. Some men, especially in foreign countries, like big women."

"*Big?* Now I *am* insulted." She was just waiting for him to say that some men were turned on by big butts. That would be the last straw.

"These aren't regular sex slaves that they're offering. They're . . . um, exotic."

She raised her eyebrows at that. *Me? Exotic?*

"This is a duty billet, like any other," he emphasized, letting her know she had no choice.

*Tell me another one!* "You can't be serious. When was the last time you were sold as a sex slave?" Immediately, she regretted her question, knowing full well it was breaking every military rule in the book to address a superior officer in that way.

His ruddy face flushed with a combination of embarrassment and outrage at her blatant breach of conduct.

She was saved by the bell . . . or rather, by a tap on the door.

"Enter," the commander barked.

In sauntered six of the SEALs she would be working with. She'd met them all previously.

One after another, they greeted her, "Red." "Hey, Red." "How ya doin', Red." "What's up, Red." "Lookin' good, t'day, Red."

Joy hated the nickname they'd given her, but when she protested, they used it all the more.

Omar Jones was half-Arab, half-American, and he would be giving her instructions on the culture she would be entering. The Cajun SEAL, Cage, winked at her. She lifted her chin haughtily, never having forgiven him for paintballing her in the butt. He just laughed.

The Viking Torolf Magnusson, Max, was the only one married among the bunch. His wife Hilda was a real sweetie, even though some of the SEALs referred to her as Hilda the Hun.

F.U. leered at her, as usual. She flashed him her *Drop dead, dipstick!* look.

The mysterious and darkly brooding Italian, Kevin Fortunato, or K-4, could leer at her any time he wanted . . . which

he didn't, darn it. Apparently he was still in mourning, even
after five years, over a wife who had died of cancer.

And the handsome, equally aloof Luke Avenil, or Slick,
who had taken on the role of big brother to her, almost as if
he was reluctantly replacing the brother he had failed to save
for her. And no doubt about it, he considered her a penance
at times. Slick was single and determined to remain that way
forever, due to an ex-wife who was continually raking him
through the courts for more divorce money, or maybe just to
piss him off; that latter being Slick's opinion after the most
recent proceeding.

"Lieutenant Avenil will head this mission," the commander told them, then stood. "I'll leave you to it, Slick."

After he left, Slick told them, "We have five days to put
this together before deployment, and a lot of prep is needed
before that. Are we in this together?"

"Hoo-yah!" they yelled, jacked up with enthusiasm. But
then, they weren't being sold as sex slaves. On the other
hand, they would probably get a kick out of that.

She had an awful feeling that this was going to be another
in a long line of "What was I thinking?" decisions. But she
had six well-trained SEALs to watch her back.

What could go wrong?

### He had a funny feeling . . .

Winter was fast approaching, the fjords would soon be frozen over, and still Erland and Arnis had not returned from
their trading voyage. Eight sennights they had been gone,
and Brandr was worried.

"I've sent men down the fjord toward the sea on the look-
out for *Dragon Wing* and *Wind Biter*," said Tork, who was
now his chief hirdsman, having chosen to join him in giving up Jomsviking. They truly were brothers-in-arms, if not
of blood. "If their longships are in distress, we will know
shortly."

"I daresay those two dolt heads dawdled in Hedeby too
long, when we are in dire need of foodstuffs, cloth for gar-

ments, bed furs, healing herbs, whetstones, cows and goats for milk and butter, and spices, like cloves, mustard, and pepper. Everything." Brandr's jarldom was a huge and goodly estate, but little of it held arable land, except for a side garth where they had planted onions, cabbages, carrots, peas, horseradish, and turnips. Another side garth held fruit and nut trees. Fish and sea birds abounded. But there were no fields of grain, and it was essential that they have barley, wheat, oats, and rye for themselves and the animals to come.

Brandr's family had grown prosperous and complacent, apparently, trading furs for goods. The bears, of course, but also pelts from sable, fox, squirrel, and beaver. Then, too, they traded dried fishes, live and salted seabirds, even feathers for stuffing pillows and mattresses. Occasionally they went far north to join whale hunts; then there would be whale oil, skin, and meat to consume and sell, as well as the precious ambergris used to make perfumes. Still others traveled to the Baltic, bringing back the precious amber, also for trade. Furthermore, the lands of Bear's Lair had a generous outcropping of steatite, or soapstone, which was soft to cut and fireproof, thus good for pots, molds for metal items, and candleholders. It was much in demand in the market towns. All this was supplemented by plunder gained when they went a-Viking to Saxon lands.

It was a harsh land, which by necessity bred strong men. But it held a beauty of sorts for those so inclined toward snow-capped mountains, tumbling waterfalls, and sometimes great barren plateaus, even glaciers in the far north. Its coastline—which in some places dropped steeply to the sea and at others had sweet moors leading to the water—was broken by hundreds, mayhap thousands, of fjords. A unique land, if nothing else.

"Do not forget ale." Tork grinned at him.

Presently, not a drop of ale or mead was to be found, except that taken from the Sigurdssons. An unheard-of condition for Vikings who loved their drink.

"Arnora is nigh driving me barmy with her constant complaints," Brandr added. "I always knew Vidar's mother was waspish, but she is beyond shrewish now. Acts like she is queen of a bloody castle, not just my household. Dost think there is a nunnery that would take her?"

"Kelda is just as bad. I swear, all I wanted was a crust of bread with a bit of honey when I went into the scullery, and she smacked me with her cooking ladle."

"Her cooking cauldron carries naught but meat and unseasoned broth these days. Ne'er did I envision the day I would crave vegetables or some variety in a meal." Brandr gritted his teeth with exasperation. "I will knock my brothers' thick heads together 'til they crack like eggs if I discover they took their own good time on returning."

"Um . . . I hate to tell you this, my friend, but I think I know why they run so late."

Brandr turned to stare direct at Tork, who was squirming uncomfortably in his seat. "Oh?"

"Some of our men may have complained about the lack of bedmates."

"Oh?"

"Erland and Arnis may have mentioned a side trip to go a-Viking to a Jutland village where pretty, blonde-haired maidens are said to abound."

"Oh, good gods! That is all we need. Another war! Over women!"

"You worry overmuch. They promised to use stealth in making raids only in the night. In and out. No one need know who or what hit them."

"Dost jest? I daresay those two lackbrains do not even know what the word *stealth* means. This is a disaster, pure and simple."

"Now, give them credit. They fought good and well for Bear's Lair," Tork reminded him.

"That they did," Brandr admitted. "But that does not relieve my concerns. Misguided as they may be, 'tis not a good time to be on the high seas. Look at the sky. I expect the ground will be snow-covered by morn."

"Come, let me show you the work we have done in rebuilding the ramparts. And, truth to tell, I must accept some blame for your brothers' misdeeds. I might have mentioned I liked my wenches with big bosoms."

"You are a lackbrain, too."

As they walked across the great hall and through the double doors to the bailey, Brandr sighed. "You are right. I cannot waste time gnashing my teeth over what Erland and Arnis might or might not be doing. 'Tis in the hands of the Norns of Fate by now. Besides, there is still so much that must needs be done here."

"I and the other men are here to do your bidding."

"And I do appreciate that."

When they had all—minus a dozen Jomsvikings who returned to their fortress—come back to Bear's Lair, a massive cleaning operation had taken place. The great hall very much looked the way it had under his father's care, and his father afore him. Clean rushes had even been laid down yestermorn, complete with the sweet lavender his mother had gathered last spring. Every time he stepped forth, the scent wafted up, and he thought of her. It took great effort to make that mind picture be of her laughing self, as he'd last seen her, not the horrific image Sigurd had planted in his brain.

Even though the Sigurdssons had burned hither and yon around Bear's Lair, Brandr's main dwelling, of which his mother had been so fond, had survived fairly well. No doubt the villainous Gorm Sigurdsson, head of the clan, had hoped to keep it for one of his sons. More a castle in the Frankish style than a traditional Norse longhouse, it had fireplaces for cooking and warmth with chimneys, rather than the traditional open-hearth fires and smoke holes in the roof down the center of the longhouse. In addition, it had two floors, rather than one, and upper sleep bowers for several of the chieftain's family, unlike most Viking dwellings, which relied on wall benches or closets for night slumber. Some of the wattle-and-daub longhouses with thatched roofs that surrounded the castle, as well as the outbuildings, had succumbed to the fires and were in the process of being rebuilt.

He also thought of his mother when he viewed her empty

looms in the half-framed weaving shed. There was no wool
for the women to spin this winter, because there were no
sheep to provide the wool. They would purchase lambs and
piglets after the spring thaw. Hopefully, his lackwit brothers
would bring finished cloth and salted pork when they finally
showed their fool faces.

The dairy shed was empty, too. Big wooden vats sunk
in the ground should be filled with milk, and the wooden
shelves should hold many rounds of cheese and slabs of
butter.

He would have said that his heart ached for his mother
and all those lost, but in truth he did not think he had a heart
anymore. Mostly, he was just angry. And empty. All the
time.

Much would he have to complain about when he attended
the Althing at Trondheim this summer. King Olaf would not
ignore his grievances this time, despite his call for peace
amongst the Norse families.

Thank the gods that a dozen or so Jomsvikings had
stayed behind to join his hird. Sven the Scowler. Dar Danglebeard. Baldr the Braggart. And other far-famed warriors.
These were battle-keen men, but even they needed a respite
betimes, and the long, dark winter, mostly spent indoors,
was the best time to hone and repair weapons afore going
a-Viking or off to war in the spring.

In addition, women, children, and housecarls who had
somehow escaped before Sigurd's attack returned to the
keep. So the numbers here now approached more than a
hundred . . . more than a hundred hungry mouths to feed.
Nowhere near the three hundred that had called Bear's Lair
home at one time, but a goodly number nonetheless.

Aside from making a funeral pyre of the bodies when
he'd returned from Trelleborg, he and his retinue had left
immediately to pursue the Sigurdssons. On return, they had
to prepare for the icy, indoor-bound months ahead.

As they walked across the bailey toward the timber pali-
sades, they passed men and women busy at work. Some of
them were dragging large deadwood trees toward the wood-

sheds, where they would join the mountains of wood already chopped and stacked to provide not just for the cooking fires but for heat. It got colder than a polar bear's ballocks inside the keep, and toe- and finger-dropping cold outside. In fact, Brandr had seen his breath when he went outside to relieve himself this morn.

No domesticated animals had been left at Bear's Lair, so men had been sent out to hunt for boar, reindeer, elk, and small game, which were plentiful. Nets had been cast here and farther up the fjord to catch fresh- and saltwater fish, even more plentiful than the game. Eels, trout, turbot, lampreys, pike, herring, cod, sturgeon, and the like. Also large seabirds. Across the courtyard, he could see women already setting these out to freeze or dry. Even a giant brown bear, which had attacked one of his cotters, would provide much winter provender with its meat. Taller than two full-grown men, it had taken six hunters to bring the aggressive beast down. Right now, its fur was stretched out on wooden forms to cure and would eventually make its way into the lining of several cloaks or bed coverings.

At one time, bears abounded in this region, thus the name Bear's Lair. Hundreds, mayhap thousands, of them had lived here afore men settled in. Even now, there were a good enough number to pose a threat to those who wandered far afield without weapons. They were mostly brown or black ones, but betimes one of the white ones wandered down from the frigid north.

Children gathered eggs of passing geese and ducks, storing them in straw. The grain needed to make manchet bread was weevily and about to run out. Missing also were spices, even salt, which could make the worst meal savory.

Sleep came hard for Brandr, and so he worked from dawn to well past dark, pushing himself more than any others. If he was too bone-weary to think, then that was well and good.

Liv stayed in her upper-story solar day and night. She spoke to no one. Her pain was Brandr's pain, but he knew not what to do. And so he gave her the solitude she seemed to need.

About to climb the ladder up to the ramparts, Brandr stilled for a moment, staring off into the distance. A strange anticipation filled him, a mixture of apprehension and excitement. Like the blood-pounding sensation he often got afore battle, he sensed that something important was about to happen.

It was probably just the return of the trading longships, which was imminent.

What else could it be?

# Chapter 4

**Take five, and don't you dare look at my butt . . .**

"Don't speak. Keep your face down. Pretend to be übershy," CIA agent Natalie Zekus, a twenty-year, stone-cold-serious operative, advised as she helped Joy dress for her undercover role.

Rather, undress.

Joy nodded and continued to remove her BDUs until she was bare naked, *really* bare naked, standing in the middle of the room, under a bare, hanging lightbulb. Unlike candlelight, it did not enhance the body's features. They were in a safe house somewhere in northern Germany, preparing for her covert role. The SEALs were in the other room, waiting for her. Those six Special Forces operatives, along with a pig load of CIA field agents, would be protecting her back.

Still, Joy was nervous. Of course she was. But it was exciting, too. Her first real assignment.

"Okay, now put these on." Agent Zekus handed her a white bra and panties. They were not Victoria's Secret sexy, nor were they cotton Grandma ones. "We had to come to a balance here. You wouldn't be comfortable exposing your-self to all those men."

*You got that right.*

"But this might be enough to satisfy their curiosity without complete exposure. No worse than a bathing suit, really."

*All those men?*

*Complete exposure?*

*Oh, my God!*

Joy had a feeling this was going to be one of those Murphy's Law moments, as in, if anything could go wrong, it would.

"But if you don't show something, they'll want you to take everything off. They still might."

*They still might.*

*Oh, my God!*

Was this her worst nightmare, or what? Standing naked in a room full of men remarking on all her body imperfections. Like her big butt.

Agent Zekus stared at Joy in a speculative fashion. "Are you up for that possibility?"

Joy threw her shoulders back with determination. "Yes. Yes, I am." It was the job the military had given her. It was for a noble cause, she reminded herself. Matt. She was here to vindicate Matt. And, dammit, she was not going to let a little thing like modesty defeat her now, especially since the CIA had lodged several protests over sending a newbie into this highly volatile situation.

Besides that, when she told her brothers last weekend, while home on liberty, that she was being sent on a covert mission, they had laughed with disbelief. That alone had prodded her to go forward, just to prove them wrong.

Once she'd donned the underwear, along with a pair of sandals, Agent Zekus examined her. "Now, before we cover you, I'm going to call Lieutenant Jones in here. Is that all right with you? He needs to know . . . uh, what he's dealing with."

Lieutenant Omar Jones was the half-Arab SEAL who

would be pretending to offer her for sale to the terrorists. He came in, dressed in Arab attire—a long, white *thobe* with a white cap called a *taqiyah* on his head—and he'd somehow grown a beard since she'd seen him earlier today. He nodded a greeting, surveyed her half-nude body in a clinical manner she couldn't find offensive, then nodded again. "Put the burka and veil on. We'll be walking from here through the marketplace," he told her. "But first, we're going to do a couple of mock rehearsals in the other room to see how you hold up."

Groaning, Joy said, "We rehearsed this scenario dozens of times back at the base."

"This will be a dress rehearsal."

"You mean, undress rehearsal."

"For you, maybe. But wait 'til you see the guys. Sheiks R Us." He grinned. "But listen, there's still time to abort this mission. If you can't handle ogling from a bunch of horny SEALs who are only playing a role, there's no way you'll be able to withstand a bunch of horny terrorists. Okay?"

Joy realized then that she needed to shape up. After all, she'd learned to treat her body as a well-honed instrument during WEALS training, just like the SEALs. No big deal! If Omar was having second thoughts about using her, then she wasn't doing her job. And that was unacceptable.

"Remember," Agent Zekus told her, "speak as little as possible. Keep your face down."

Joy nodded. "The KISS principle. Keep It Simple, Stupid."

"Yep. A blind date poses enough risk," Omar added, referring to a mission with lots of unknowns. "No ad-libbing. Take no chances."

"Whatever you do, don't act angry," Agent Zekus cautioned.

"Well, I've gotta disagree a bit. She can let her eyes show anger or resistance. Some men like the idea of . . . you know . . . taming a woman." Omar blushed as he explained.

Agent Zekus went ahead of them and stood at the back of the room. Joy walked in slowly, Omar propelling her forward to stand in the middle of the room where there were two other heavily veiled women.

"Your chaperones," Omar said, "to protect your virginity."

She arched her eyebrows, not that he could see that through the eyeholes in her veil. She hoped they weren't expecting her to be a virgin or that anyone would ask for proof.

The female chaperones, she soon discovered, were F.U. and Cage, heavily armed and wired. Well, thank God! That must mean that she would have three SEALs in the room with her when the flesh trading took place.

K-4, Slick, and Max, the only light-haired one of the bunch, with his hair and eyebrows dyed black, contact lenses in place, were in flowing white Arab robes like Omar's. K-4 wore a red and white checked turban, à la Yasser Arafat. Slick's turban was all white in the fashion bin Laden made famous. And Max just wore a *ghutra*, a square of cloth held onto his head with an *igal*, or black cord.

Indicating with a motion of the hand that she should stand in the middle of the room with the other two "ladies" behind her, Omar, hands gesticulating expressively, began to speak Arabic to Slick, K-4, and Max, all of whom were relatively fluent, as well. Joy was impressed with their language skills. The men's eyes kept shifting to Joy, who watched surreptitiously, even though her face was downcast.

"He's extolling your virtues," Cage whispered from behind her, then laughed.

"What?" Joy whispered.

"He's *really* extolling your virtues, darlin'."

"If he mentions my big butt, he is in big trouble."

Cage chuckled, but it was F.U. who whispered, "That's not the big things he's praising. Whoa, do you really have nipples the size of marbles?"

"Silence!" Omar said, turning on her. "Take it off."

Her head shot up. She'd been expecting this, but not so soon.

"Help her," he ordered the two other "women," who took

off her veil and gown. When F.U. went to unsnap her bra, she turned on him and, with her foot, gave him a karate chop to his private parts, which caused him to yelp and moan in a bent-over position, "Holy crap! I was just teasing."

"Oh, yeah? Well, I was just teasing, too, then."

"Uh . . . I think we need to start over," Omar said.

"Tell slime-o to keep his paws off of me."

"What're you gonna do if one of the tangos touches you?" Omar asked.

"I'll close my eyes and think of Krispy Kreme donuts."

"You're supposed to say Uncle Sam, *chère*." Cage laughed.

"You think of Uncle Sam. I'll think of something sweet, thank you very much."

K-4 winked at her.

She was in such a state that the wink didn't even turn her on as it might have done otherwise. One good-looking hunk, he more than earned the Italian Stallion pejorative the SEALs sometimes hurled at him. Oops! She forgot. She'd given up good-looking hunks, having decided a few years back that they were too high-maintenance.

*Yikes! My brain is splintering away here.*

But then Slick, leader of this mission, turned on her. "Listen up, Nelson. F.U. can be Dickhead of the Month—

"Hey!" the dickhead protested.

"—but he's also a damned good SEAL."

"Damn straight I am," F.U. huffed.

"If this mission goes FUBAR," Slick continued, "do you want a training operative like F.U. at your back or a namby-pamby may-I man?" She was about to say something, but Slick held up a halting hand. "Make up your mind right now. No more jump kicks to a man's goodies, whether they be SEALs or tangos. We're a team here. Either you're serious about being a lady SEAL, or you can get a desk job with the Navy back in Coronado."

"I'll do it, dammit."

However, she lost her cool halfway through the second rehearsal when one of the Arab terrorists, i.e., Max, walked up and circled her underwear-clad body, stroking his fake mustache as he remarked on various parts of her anatomy in Arabic. She didn't need to know the language to tell that one of his comments related to her behind because the word J.Lo was mixed in. Turning on him, she snapped, "What are you gawking at?"

That led to rehearsal number three where Omar did in fact flick the hooks on her bra, exposing her boobs. Everyone in the room went silent. Her breasts were always a surprise to men the first time she went full monty. Because she was so tall and slim and athletic, they probably expected pancakes.

Fortunately, no one said anything. But they thought it.

It took them a half dozen rehearsals before they got it even remotely right. Agent Zekus was railing over the impossibility of Joy pulling this off. F.U. was still complaining about his pain. Slick was giving everyone last-minute instructions.

"I can do it," she promised the agent. "Really, I can do it. I promise." And she would, too, or die trying. She hoped that wouldn't be literal.

"If it looks as if she can't handle it, I'll tie her hands and put a gag in her mouth," Omar told the agent. "A resisting sex slave wouldn't be a stretch."

Oooh, Joy didn't like the sound of that.

The plan was to get inside the tango hideout. CIA and SEALs would be stationed outside. She had a high-tech device implanted just under the skin behind her ear. It could listen to what was being said within ten feet, give her messages, and in case of emergency, allow her to signal for help. It also had a GPS locator in it. Despite all the technology, it still needed people to make this work. *People*, meaning her.

"Okay, folks," Slick said then. "Everyone good to go?"

"Hoo-yah!" they all answered, even Joy.

As they walked toward the designated location, Omar swaggering in front, with her and the two other "women" following meekly behind, Joy got her first flash of intuition that something was going to go wrong. Loud and clear, a message was beginning to pound in her brain, and it wasn't saying "Hoo-yah."

Nope, it was that same old *What was I thinking?*

### You could say *Snafu* was her middle name . . .

It was worse than Joy ever could have imagined.

But if ever Joy had any doubts about taking part in this mission, she had none how. How could she, when she saw the three young girls, in purdah, already purchased by the terrorists? Huddled in one corner, they wept copiously but silently, after being slapped across the face a few times by the guard at the door.

The girls, two from Spain and one from South Africa, could be no more than thirteen. Children, really. But not for long if the leering glances of one of their purchasers was any indication. He was a particularly evil-looking man, bone-thin, eyes like ice, but lips thick over yellowing teeth. A livid scar ran from his left eye to his chin, drawing his mouth up on one side in a perpetual sneer.

Omar had told the men that Joy was from America, thus explaining his occasional use of English with her.

Her group had not arrived here yet when the girls had been brought forth for examination by the half dozen Arab men in the room, but she suspected it had been more than humiliating. Especially when she noted a morbidly obese woman in a burka but no face veil, wearing disposable rubber gloves. If the bitch dared to put those rubber gloves near her, Joy was afraid she would not be able to hold up her pretense, and it was dangerously important that she do so now that they were in the midst of these snakes.

Drawing her to the center of the room, Omar flipped her face veil off. Immediately, she bent forward, using her long hair to hide her face. She'd been advised to leave her hair loose, another selling point, she supposed. They must have gotten a bit of a peek anyhow, because one of them said something in a snide tone to Omar.

Omar argued back in Arabic, then repeated it in English for her benefit. "Yes, she is older . . . almost twenty-one . . ."

Joy almost snorted at that. She was closer to thirty . . . well, twenty-seven . . . and hadn't been carded in ages.

". . . but her assets more than make up for being long in the tooth." Omar motioned to the two chaperones, F.U. and Cage, to disrobe her, which they did immediately and without fanfare.

"Aaaahhh," the Arab terrorists said as one.

Scar-face made an arrogant slash of his hand to Omar that could only be interpreted as *Take the rest of her clothes off*.

Omar shook his head vehemently, rattling off a bunch of Arabic. Back and forth they argued. Only then did he repeat some of it in English. "You have seen enough. If you want to see more, put an offer on the table. Let us say, fifty thousand dollars."

Several of the terrorists laughed at that, obviously thinking she wasn't worth that much.

"I have more like this one," Omar inserted slyly.

Scar-face stood and walked toward her. Omar stepped in front of her, and she could feel F.U. and Cage stiffen behind her. Then everything went haywire at once. Scar-face grabbed her by the arm, pulling her to the side with a headlock, his chest pressed to her back, a sharp knife to her neck. Omar and the two chaperone SEALs were screeching something in Arabic. The girl captives were screaming. The Arab woman was running around like a chicken with its head cut off.

And in her ear a message was being shouted, "Mayday! Abort mission! Tangos approaching! Stand down, stand down! Mayday!" Omar and the other SEALs were getting the same message and trying to assess how to get out of this place with her and not alert the Arabs to their true identities. The fact that she was now half-naked didn't seem important in view of these other calamities.

Just then, a bomb went off outside, diverting everyone's attention. She was able to escape Scar-face's hold on her, and everyone was rushing for the back door. "Wait here 'til we see if the coast is clear," Omar told her, then muttered under his breath, "This is a freakin' cluster fuck." For just a moment she was left alone in the room.

But then there was another boom. Closer. The building shook. Ceiling plaster fell.

And everything went black.

**Yep, she was barmy, all right . . .**

The first time Joy awakened after the explosion, she noticed the goose egg that felt as if it was splitting her skull open. And she noticed that she was wearing a drab brown gown with a rope belt over the plain white underwear she'd donned that morning. She was lying on a wide bench attached to the wall of a strange, primitive room. Like a hut of some kind, with woven twig sides and a thatched roof.

She must be dreaming.

So she succumbed to unconsciousness again.

The second time she awakened, she registered that she was not alone. There were others. Men, women, even children, similarly attired. Some of them were weeping. Others were murmuring amongst themselves. In some foreign language. It wasn't Arabic. Or German. No, it was something else that almost sounded like English. And, oddly, she could understand what they were saying. Like she had some translator in her brain.

"What language are they speaking?" she asked the old woman next to her.

"Norse."

"You mean Norwegian?"

"No, lackwit. Norse."

*Okaaay.* "Where are we?"

The woman frowned at her as if she was crazy. "Hedeby."

"Ah." They had passed the quaint model village on the way here yesterday, Joy recalled. Apparently, it was a reproduction of a Viking market town from a thousand years ago when this part of northern Germany was actually part of

Denmark. The Danes had lost the territory to the Austrians and Prussians during some seventeenth-century war. She would have liked to visit it if she'd had time.

But why would the Arab terrorists bring her here?

These people hardly qualified as sex slaves. Only one of the women was even passably pretty.

And where were the SEALs who had been with her?

She pressed the implant behind her ear three times, paused, then pressed three times again. Code for distress. Nothing. And she wasn't hearing anything, either. Well, hopefully, someone would follow the GPS locator and would be arriving shortly to rescue her. No sweat.

As she moved her hand away from her ear, she touched something odd on her neck. It was a leather cord with a metal disk in the center. She tried to look down at it, but it fit too tightly. "Huh?" She tried in vain to undo it.

"Now what?" her not-so-friendly bench companion asked.

Joy realized that everyone in the room seemed to have similar metal "necklaces" around their necks. "What is this?" she asked, pointing to her neck.

"Thrall collar. You really are barmy, methinks." The woman shifted away from her.

Thrall collar? What the hell was that?

She must have spoken aloud because the woman snapped, "Slave collar. Once you are purchased, your new master will replace your amulet with one of his own."

This must be related to the terrorists' sex for bombs business. "How do we get them off?"

"Bloody hell, wench! Best ye be holding yer tongue lest one of the slavers hear," a scruffy man across from her said. "They be quick to use their whips."

*Whips? Oh, good Lord! What have I gotten myself into this time?*

"If ye must know, the collar can only be taken off by yer master once he releases you. *If* he ever releases you. Best ye be hopin' ye get bought by one of the Northmen. They be kinder to their thralls and willin' to free 'em if they serve well fer ten years."

Whoa! Hadn't they heard of the Emancipation Proclamation? Slavery was illegal.

But wait a minute. Northmen? Did she mean men from Northern Iraq or Northern Afghanistan? Or somewhere else?

There was something else strange here. She touched her head. Everyone, man and woman alike, had their hair chopped off, except her.

The man, sensing her thoughts, explained, "All slaves must have their hair chopped off at first, fer the lice. Later, the women can let their hair grow, as long as it's tucked under a kerchief, but the men's scalps mus' be bald. The kerchief and the shaved heads are signs of thralldom. But they think yer red hair will bring more coin."

It was too much for her aching head to comprehend, so she let herself fall "asleep" again.

Next time she awakened, it wasn't of her own volition. Someone was shaking her. A rough-looking man who reeked of bad breath and BO. "Get up, wench. No more dawdling. Everyone is waiting."

She grumbled as she sat up, fuzzy from sleep and the knock on her head.

"Make haste! Hurry, hurry! Here," he said, handing her a filthy thing that might have been a comb. It appeared to be made of bone and had several teeth missing. "Run this through yer hair and take off that gunna."

"Gun? I don't have a gun."

His eyes about bugged out. "Gunna, wench. I said *gunna*. *Gunna* is a robe."

"Well, why didn't you say so? But, no! Not the undressing business again." She backed away from him, hitting the stick wall. "Nudity is overrated, y'know? It would be better to keep them guessing. Yep, that's my philosophy. So, what do you say?"

"Thor's teeth! Ye really are demented, jist like Gird said. Well, keep yer teeth shut when ye get outside. And make haste."

"Why? What's the rush?"

"It be yer turn now."

"Turn for what?"

He glowered before pulling a whip from his belt.

"Now, now, no need for violence."

Only then did he answer. "Yer auction."

# Chapter 5

**She wasn't gift wrapped, but she was going to be a present . . .**

Erland and Arnis were strolling away from the plank wharf at Hedeby, which was located at the junction of several major trade routes. A horn blew, announcing the arrival of yet another seafaring vessel.

They entered the town through one of the three gateway tunnels of the fortified ramparts that were higher than six tall men atop each other. Behind them, fifty or so longships of various sizes were anchored, not counting the new arrival, which carried the flag of a far-famed Rus merchant.

Hedeby was an exciting town they had visited on numerous occasions in the past. But there was always something new to see. Animals of any size or shape, not to mention their skins. Even the prized seal and walrus rope noted for its strength and durability; it was made by cutting the skin in a single spiral strip from shoulder to tail. The tusks were also an important trading item. Many of the market stalls featured jewelry . . . silver, gold, amber, ivory, and crystallite. Samite from Byzantium, fine wool from Northumbria, sable-lined cloaks. Craftsmen could be seen blowing glass, hammering precious metals, carving wood and tusks, firing clay pots, making candles.

"Brandr is going to tan our hides for taking so long," Erland said to his older brother.

"Well, we had good reason for our delay. The spices he wanted from the eastern lands did not arrive 'til yestereve. And there were those repairs needed for *Wind Biter*'s hull. And those women we captured in the Saxon lands were not so willing to travel with us to the Norselands. Twice they escaped us here in the market town. Good thing I am an expert tracker." Arnis grinned at him.

Erland grinned back. "Truly, the men at Bear's Lair will be gladdened at our foresight in providing for their pleasure. Despite the delay."

"Yea, there is that," Arnis agreed. "And leastways, both of our dragonships are nigh groaning with all the goods we have purchased, most importantly the grains, but also the Frisian wine on top of barrels of mead and ale. That litter of pups will surely prove helpful for hunting when full grown."

"I but wish there was something we could get especially for Brandr to lighten his heart," Arnis remarked. "He has become so dour of late."

"With good cause," Erland pointed out. "But I wonder . . . dost think that once a berserker it can ever leave a man?"

"Only the gods know." Arnis sighed. "What kind of life must it be to have that rage inside all the time?"

They were both grim as they pondered that unpalatable prospect. Walking along the plank walkways that traversed the mud of the busy market town in an orderly fashion, they bypassed the area where permanent residents lived in neat wattle-and-daub homes with front-fenced courtyards. Instead they made for the merchant and craft section where tents and stalls had been set up facing the wooden sidewalks. They stopped here and there to examine the wares, even as they conversed.

"Look there. That would make a fine gift for Liv," Arnis said.

They both went silent then, recalling how Liv had looked when they'd left Bear's Lair more than eight sennights ago. Eyes sad and vacant, body thin as a pole, except for her huge belly. The baby must have been born by now. Had Brandr put the infant out on the cliff to die, or let it live, unwanted by one and all, including its mother? He could not imagine Liv ever softening toward the child. How could she want a reminder of her captivity and brutal rape? Sad it was, because Liv, now almost fifteen, had been long promised to and found favor with Einar Egillsson from Iceland, but that was before her being so despoiled. Would Einar still want her? Probably not.

Arnis purchased the polished brass mirror nonetheless. Mayhap Liv would be more her old self by now. And Erland, like-thinking, bought her an amber pendant on a thin gold chain. They bought themselves new silver-etched arm rings. Bone combs for the household. Shoulder brooches for some of the men to fasten their cloaks. A box of matched spoons with carved wood handles to be used at the high table on special occasions.

"Let us go back to the harbor," Arnis said then. "Make certain all is ready for our departure at first light tomorrow."

Erland agreed.

They were approaching the slave auction mart where they had taken their Saxon captives to be sold just two days past and purchased some others as well, including a much-needed blacksmith. They were about to pass by when something caught their eyes.

It was a woman, but she was unlike any either of them had seen before. And it wasn't just her wild, flame red hair. Or that she was nigh naked, except for scraps of white cloth over her breasts and nether parts. No, her uniqueness lay in the odd, jerky movements she made around the auction platform. Raising a leg high. Kicking out sharply at the men who tried to subdue her. Hitting some of them, painfully, it would seem by their yelps. And she was making chopping motions toward them with the raised heels of her hands, as if they were weapons. The whole time she was making guttural noises that sounded like "Kee-yup!" or "Hie!" when she was not spouting coarse Saxon curses.

And then, no longer distracted by the thin garments she wore, they homed in on her breasts. And a well-rounded rump that would scarce fit in a big man's hands.

Erland's mouth was gaping open.

Arnis was momentarily speechless.

Then they both looked at each other and grinned.

"Brandr," Erland said.

And Arnis nodded.

Both of them chuckled.

They had found the perfect gift for Brandr.

### Heigh-ho, heigh-ho, it's off to the Black Sea we go . . .

"Okay, joke's over. Ha, ha, ha! Untie these freakin' ropes."

Ever since a man had shouted, "Cast off!" immediately followed by "Out oars!" and they'd begun this ludicrous voyage, Joy had experienced one amazing debacle after another. In fact, her life had become one bleeping debacle.

Joy was sick of complaining to her "captors," if that's what these bozos were. And they were sick of hearing her complaints, more than one of them had said.

They weren't Arab terrorists, that was for sure. Mostly tall and blond, the men more resembled ancient Vikings. That idea was reinforced by the dragonship they were riding across icy Black Sea waters.

"This is no jest, wench," one of them, obviously a captain or something, said.

"Call me wench one more time, and you'll have black and blue balls when I'm free."

"Milady then, though I know few ladies who would discuss manparts in public." The jerk grinned at her. "Brandr is going to enjoy taming you."

"Who is Brandy?"

"Brandr," he corrected her. "Our brother. That is my brother Erland." He pointed to another blond-haired male on the other ship, which rode low in the water beside them.

Erland was supervising the sixty-plus rowers sitting on sea chests that lined both sides of an immense longship, just like theirs. Their creaking oars hit the water with wet, rhythmic slaps, for hours on end.

She had to admit the vessels were impressive with their carved prows and red and black checked sails and flags showing white bears rampant against black backgrounds edged in red. Colorful shields were arranged over the sides. "Are you with that model village at Hedeby? Is this some kind of half-baked reenactment? If so, you better release me right away, or you are going to be in big trouble with Uncle Sam."

"Huh? Uncle who?"

"Read my lips, bozo. Un—"

"My name is Arnis, not Bozo."

"Aaarrgh!" she said and would have pulled at her own hair if her arms weren't tied behind her back and around a mast pole. "Read my lips, *Arnis*. Untie. Me. *Now!*"

Arnis just smiled. "Read *my* lips. Nay!"

"Tell me again why you've captured me."

"We did not capture you. We purchased you at the thrall auction to take back to Bear's Lair."

"Oh, that's just great. You're taking me to a bear's cave."

"What? Oh. You missay me. Bear's Lair is the name of our family estates in the Norselands."

"Well, that's explains everything. Not!"

"You were purchased and will be a bond slave to Brandr. Those thralls over there," he pointed to a group of young women huddled together, "now they are captives. We captured them, and some others that we already sold, on a raid of Saxon lands. Once free, they will now be thralls."

"Why?"

"Why what?"

"Why did you capt . . . purchase me?"

"For Brandr. I already told you that."

"Why?"

"Why, why, why! Brandr has been sour of mood since he turned berserker. He needs a love slave to sweeten him up."

"You can't possibly think I'm going to have sex with some berserk Viking stranger."

"Yea, I can. Willing or not, you will be sharing my brother's bed furs within a sennight, or I will toss you in the fjord myself."

"Violence accomplishes nothing. I'm a psychologist, you know. And anger management is one of my specialties. I could help you learn more diplomatic methods of handling your problems."

Arnis blinked at her. "My grandsire always said diplomacy is like saying 'Nice doggy' until you can find a spear."

"That makes no sense at all."

"By the by, are you perchance a virgin?"

She gave him a look that told him exactly what she thought of that question. "Are you?"

"Nay, but I am a man."

"And that matters . . . how?"

"Men are not prized for their virginity. Women are."

"What a bunch of sexist crap!"

"From the beginning of time, Norsemen have been bred to go a-Viking and drink good ale, whilst Norsewomen have been bred to spread their thighs for their heroes when they come home."

"Are you kidding? What is that? The mission statement for Male Chauvinist Vikings?"

"You talk a lot. What country are you from?"

"America."

"Is that near Iceland?"

*This guy is a flaming idiot.* "Let's start over. My name is Joy Nelson."

"A fine Viking name is Nelsson."

"Stop interrupting. My name is Joy Nelson. I am an ensign in the U.S. Navy. I am training for the WEALS."

"You are training to be a wheel? Mayhap I should train to be a flagpole. Are you sure you are not barmy?"

"WEALS is a female SEAL program," she informed him through gritted teeth. "We are an elite female special forces unit. Soldiers."

"Warriors?" he asked incredulously. "A band of female warriors?"

"Yes. Exactly." Finally, he was beginning to understand.

"That is some story! You almost caught me with your jest." He slapped a knee with appreciation. "Methinks you should be a skald for us on the long winter nights."

"Skald?"

"Poet. You could tell us sagas about your country and your, ha, ha, ha, fierce fighting women. Our old skald Alviss is a terrible storyteller. Anyone could do better."

"Elvis? You have a storyteller named Elvis? That is too cute. Does he like peanut butter and banana sandwiches?"

Arnis stared at her for a long moment, then snapped his gaping mouth shut. "Yea, you will be our new skald. When you are not tupping with Brandr, that is."

"Forget this sex with Brandr business. It is not going to happen. And I'm not going to be your damn poet laureate either."

Just then a wave hit the ship, causing the boat to list a bit before righting itself, but in the process she and Arnis were soaked. Arnis didn't seem to mind being wet from neck to toe, but she was beginning to shiver, being now not only cold to the bone but wet as well.

Did Arnis notice her discomfort?

No. He was staring at her shabby gown, which was molded to her breasts and hips and legs. Glancing downward, she saw that her cold nipples were standing out prominently.

"Yea, Brandr is going to be very pleased," Arnis said just before walking off.

"Pervert!" she muttered, then shouted to his back, "Hey, I'm freezing here. Unless you want to deliver a frozen corpse to this berserk brother of yours, you better untie me and let me huddle under a blanket somewhere.

Instead of doing as she asked, he stomped back a short time later with a huge white fur, which he wrapped around her twice. The thing still had a head on it.

"What is this fur?"

"Polar bear."

"Are you crazy? Polar bears are an endangered species."

"Wouldst rather freeze to death?" When she just glared at him, he said, "I thought not."

And so it went for the next five days. Although her rope restraints had been removed, she continually argued with anyone within hearing, mostly the thickheaded Arnis but also with his brother Erland, who was equally thickheaded.

At one point when both of them stomped over to say that their sailors were complaining about her constant "blathering," she said, "I wouldn't need to 'blather' if you two idiots would listen to me. This is a huge mistake. I am not intended to be here. Whether you are reenactors or part of a primitive tribe that managed to escape civilization, I'm supposed to be on a live op to capture some Arab terrorists. And if you don't let me go, all hell is going to break loose."

Instead of heeding her words, Arnis remarked to Erland, loud enough for her to overhear, "Dost recall what Ivan did to his wife Signe when she nagged overmuch?"

"Yea. He sliced off her tongue and fed it to the hounds in his great hall."

"Yeech!" she contributed, even though they were probably kidding.

"A sad case indeed," Arnis said on a fake sigh. "But the blessed peace that abounded after that was well worth the bloody mess."

They were traveling down some narrow fjord now. Well, narrow compared to the open sea they'd been on before. Igorssfjord was actually as wide as a football field. It had begun to snow this morning and was so darn cold the waterway was beginning to ice up on the sides and on the oars, which had to be continually banged against the sides of the ships to free the buildup. That's all she would need . . . to be ice-locked in some godforsaken country. They were so far north it could be the North Pole, for all she knew. All anyone would tell her was that it was the Norselands. Like that made anything clear.

*Where am I?*
*And why?*

"Bear's Lair!" someone shouted from high up on the mast pole. "Home at last!"

"Home," Joy murmured to herself. Landfall, at last. After this past grueling week, she wondered if she would ever see home again. Or would this be her new home?

**What every good Viking needs is Joy . . .**

At the end of another long, hard day, made harder by the snow, which was coming down steadily, and his worry over his brothers' return, which could be forestalled for the winter once the fjords froze over, Brandr decided to relax in the steam house. It was empty this late in the day, a blessing when he needed quiet to contemplate his choices.

Should he sail out and search for his brothers? After all, they might be in trouble.

Or should he wait and trust in their dubious abilities?

With the loud blare of a horn, immediately followed by another, the choice was taken out of his hands. These were the signals of two ships approaching. It had to be Erland and Arnis. *Please, gods!*

Almost immediately following the horn blaring, a smiling Tork opened the door. "They're home."

"Thank the gods. Tell Kelda to prepare a feast and order all the housemaids to help. Send everyone else down to the wharf to help the ships unload. We will be snow-buried afore morn. The animals must be stabled immediately, assuming the wooly-wits purchased milch cows and goats. And chickens. The coops are ready, are they not?"

Tork nodded, a huge smile on his face. He was no doubt thinking of the women who might be aboard. Hopefully a comely lass to warm his bed furs this night.

Brandr would not turn away a good swiving himself.

Alone again, Brandr took his time scrubbing the dirt off his body and donning a clean tunic and braies. It would take at least an hour before the two ships were secured and anyone would be able to come ashore.

Erland and Arnis were grinning from ear to ear when he

walked carefully in the deepening snow down the roadway
to the fjord. Despite all his grievances against his brothers'
delays and all the questions he had for them, he took one,
then the other, into a tight hug of welcome. They were the
only blood family he had left, except for Liv, who was more
dead than alive these days.

"Greetings, lackwits," he said, looping an arm over each
of their shoulders as they walked away from the longships.
There were men and women aplenty to bring the animals
and supplies up to the keep. The longships could be beached
on the morrow, joining his other six vessels. "Didst have a
successful journey?"

"Yea, we did," they both said at the same time.

"We got everything on your list, Brandr," Arnis told him,
"and more. Including some winsome women to please your
men on the long winter nights."

"Is that why it took you so long?" He tried his best to keep
the annoyance from his voice. Now was the time for rejoic-
ing. The recriminations would come later.

"Yea. That and the present we bought for you." The mischievous gleam in Erland's eyes boded ill for Brandr; he was
sure of it.

He made his face deliberately blank.

Arnis motioned with a jerk of his head toward the huge
white furry mound that one of his men, Gorm the Giant, was
carrying up the hill from the fjord. Arnis also had a mischievous gleam in his eyes.

What deviltry were these two up to?

"You bought me a polar bear fur for a gift? How . . . nice!"

"'Tis not the fur that is the gift but what is inside," Erland
told him.

Gorm was just passing them when Brandr noticed that
the fur was moving, and he could swear he heard a voice
inside say something that sounded like, "Damn stupid idiot
Vikings!"

"Please let that be a parrot." Years ago, when he was a
youthling, his father brought him a talking parrot from the
eastern lands after one of his trading voyages. What a noise-

some pest! And it had no respect for Vikings, continually chanting that famous ditty Saxon soldiers prayed as they pissed their pants in fear, "Oh, Lord—squawk—from the fury of the Northmen—squawk—please protect us. Squawk, squawk!"

"Uh, not quite," Erland hedged.

"Let us go up to the keep and warm our bones afore opening any gifts," Arnis added a mite nervously.

Erland and Arnis exchanged meaningful anxious looks.

Well, Brandr was not going to worry about it now. This was a day for celebration. Nothing could mar that joy.

Little did he know that the Joy about to enter his life was going to change him forever.

# Chapter 6

**Joy to the (Viking's) world . . .**

Hours later, Brandr leaned back in his chair at the high table, watching everyone feast with great joy. Three roasted reindeer, leftover boar, a brace of hares in a new stew, dozens of fresh fishes, pickled eels, sweetbreads in a gelatinous mold, honey, even some of that horrid Scottish fare, haggis (another *yeech!* dish for him, but others—doltheads, to be sure—liked it), hard and soft cheeses, apples, pears, long-absent vegetables, and manchet bread were consumed in large quantities. That and the ale, of course.

But even in the midst of this gaiety, Brandr felt alone. He tried to hide it from his brothers, his friends, and his comrades-in-arms. He raised his horn of ale. Many times. He clapped his brothers on their fool backs. He even sang along with Tork in a ribald song about the gods' gift to men: maids of easy virtue. But he was different since he'd gone berserk. He knew it, and they knew it.

More than anything, he wished he could entice his sister Liv to come down the stairs and join them, but she was fearful of men and preferred the solitude of her own bedchamber. How could he force her to change, when he could not do so himself? Leastways, he'd sent her a tray of the various dishes along with her favorite honey oatcakes.

Ah, well! He turned to Arnis and said, "So, where is this great gift you have brought for me?" He recalled the large white fur one of the shiphirds had been carrying from the boat hours ago.

Erland, overhearing, hit himself aside the head. "Holy Thor! I forgot."

"You lackwit! Where did you put her?" Arnis asked Erland, whacking him on the other side of his head.

*Her? He refers to a fur as "her"? Oh. Must be it is a she-bear.*

"In the storage room," Erland replied with a cringe of embarrassment.

"You did unwrap her, did you not?" Arnis had his hands on his hips, standing now, scowling at his younger brother.

"Um," was all Erland could utter.

"Good gods! She's probably dead of suffocation by now."

As the two idiots rushed off, Brandr had a bad feeling about this "gift."

"What now?" Tork asked, sinking down into the chair next to him, pulling one of the new thralls down onto his lap. Ebba, her name was, he recalled now. Though no longer a young wench—she was twenty-five, if she was a day—Ebba had impressive bosoms and lips that could no doubt suck the skin off a turnip. She claimed to have a talent for weaving, but Brandr suspected it would be her other talents utilized the most.

"I know not what the two lackwits are up to now, but methinks it bodes ill for—*what*? For the love of Frigg! Look at that!" Brandr's eyes widened as he saw Arnis and Erland walking back into the hall, carrying the rolled-up fur, one end over each of their shoulders. A *squirming* fur.

"Uh-oh!" Tork said.

"That is precisely what I was about to say."

The music and chatter began to die down as everyone

began to follow the progress of the bundle being carried, then dropped to the rushes at the bottom of the steps leading to the dais.

"Come down and see your gift, brother," Arnis urged him.

"And she is not even a little bit dead," Erland the Idiot said. *Yea, that is going to be my new name for him. Erland the Idiot. And a new name for Arnis will be Arnis the Addlebrained.*

Brandr exhaled loudly and proceeded across the dais and down the steps. "Well?"

With a flourish, his brother unrolled the fur, and out jumped a body. A body that was tall and slim with wild red hair and . . . breasts. It was a woman but unlike any woman he'd ever seen before. *A Valkyrie?* She wore odd white under-raiment. Scraps of white fabric barely covered her woman's fleece and buttocks and cupped her breasts— very nice breasts, he observed, by the by—held up by thin straps. But the most amazing thing was the stance the woman took, legs braced apart as if for battle, in her hands a poker she'd grabbed from the nearby fireplace, and shimmering fury in her green eyes. *Yea, she must be a Valkyrie come to earth.*

"I am going to kill you two idiots," she warned Arnis and Erland.

Brandr's temper rose at the insult to his kin, but only a notch. After all, he considered them idiots himself. "This is your gift to me?" he questioned said idiots.

"Yea, your new bed thrall," Arnis said proudly.

"She might need a mite of taming," Erland added.

"Why not just give me a mangy she-cat to bed?" he sniffed, then added, "a mangy, smelly she-cat."

The two dimwits seemed to consider his remark, the sarcasm passing over their thick heads.

Not so the woman, who growled. She actually growled. "I am no man's slave. Any taming to be done will be at my hands and no one else's. Furthermore, if I smell, it's because I've spent three days wrapped in a stinking endangered species fur. Believe me, the Alaskan Wildlife Preservation Society is going to hear about you . . . you criminal poachers."

A ripple of laughter ran through the hall at her words . . . words that were in a strange dialect. English, but a strange English, he was thinking. Old Norse and Saxon English were very similar, and each could understand the other. The same was true of this wild wench.

"Dost think to tame me then, wench?" he inquired, stepping closer, then stopping when she raised the poker in her right hand and drew forth a sharp knife in her left hand. She must have grabbed the blade off one of his brothers when they'd unrolled her from the furs. This was not a meek housemaid. She knew how to use a weapon, of that he was certain. But not a Valkyrie, he concluded. This was no dead goddess. Not even a live goddess.

"She says that she was a warrior in her land," Arnis told him, reading her action the same way he had.

"And what land is that?" he asked her.

"None of your business," she snapped.

"Have a caution, wench. You are in my land now."

"Big deal!"

" 'Tis a big deal, for a certainty, when I am master and you are slave."

"Blah, blah, blah."

He was not sure what that meant, but it was not a compliment, he concluded, especially when accompanied by that unattractive sneer on her grimy face.

"She has red hair," someone in the crowd behind him pointed out. "Mayhap she is one of the Sigurdssons still prowling about. Mayhap we did not wipe them all off the face of the earth."

'Twas true. Most of the Sigurdsson clan had varying shades of red hair. "Are you a Sigurdsson, wench?"

"No, I'm not a cigar-whatever. I don't smoke and certainly not cigars. But here's a news flash, mister—"

"Not mister. Master."

"That is so not funny. Earth to alien Viking: If you want to carry on a civil conversation, you better stop calling me wench. And here's another news flash: I'll call you master the day hell freezes over."

"Unwise speech for a slave."

"Slavery went out with the Civil War, buster."

"What war?"

"Never mind." She waved the knife in the air to indicate her indifference.

"I know not this land of women warriors. Are your men so weak?"

"Talk about gender bias! You talk funny, by the way. What country is this?"

"'Tis not I who talk funny. This is the Norselands."

"Yeah, yeah, that's what your brothers said, but quit the joking. Where am I really, and when does this nightmare joke end?"

He did not understand half of what she said, but not because he did not glean the meaning of her brand of English. 'Twas more the words themselves. Why would she think her being here was a jest? Because she'd spent a sennight in his fool brother's company, that was why, he answered himself.

"What is your name?"

"Joy."

"Well, I wish you joy, too, but what is your name?"

She rolled her eyes, as if he was the idiot in this room. "My name is Joy. Joy Nelson, and don't be telling me it's a fine Viking name. I'm not a Viking. Or a wench. Or a slave. And you better let me go, or my SEAL team will be after you like gangbusters."

He looked at his brothers, then at Tork, who'd come down to stand beside him, and they looked back at him with equal confusion.

"Seals?"

"Yes. I'm in WEALS. That's like a female SEAL."

"You are a seal?"

"Yep. Now, are you ready to release me? More than that, you better take me back to that village in Hedeby. That's where my men are no doubt searching for me."

"Your men? You have more than one?"

"Six on this trip."

"And you bed them all?" *Hmmm. Mayhap she has talents that are worth exploring.*

"At one time?" Erland wanted to know.

*Definitely worth exploring.* He shoved Erland aside with an elbow.

She stared at them for a long moment before making a clucking sound of disgust. "Men! Why does it always come down to sex? No, I don't have sex with the men on my team, and definitely no ménages. We are operatives on this duty billet. That's all."

"Are you saying that you are comrades-in-arms with them?"

"Exactly."

"Are you barmy?"

"If that means crazy, the answer is no, but I'm beginning to think I've landed in a nuthouse."

Nuthouse? What could she possibly mean? Does she mean a tree? Well, it mattered not. Enough of this nonsense!

He dumped the fruit from a large wooden platter and held it in front of his chest as a shield, moving toward her. Before he could anticipate her next move, she yelled out something that sounded like "Hee-yup!" She feinted to the left, then right, twirled around, and aimed a kick at his groin area. It was only his ducking at the last minute that saved his manparts. Instead, she hit the edge of his "shield," knocking it out of his hands. Since she was barefooted, it had to hurt, but she betrayed none of her injury, holding her knife and poker at the ready.

"We can surround her," Tork told him from his side.

"Nay." He motioned for everyone to step back. "I will handle this myself."

"Big mistake, Mr. Dark and Dangerous," she said.

"Dark and Dangerous?" He was standing still, assessing the situation, even as she did likewise. A formidable opponent, for a woman.

"Yeah, I have big brothers who think it's cool to play the dark and dangerous role to charm women. Believe me, I am not charmed by you."

For some reason, her words annoyed him. *Can I possibly want her to be attracted to me?* "Dost think I would try to charm such as you? Believe me, I could if I wanted."

"Hah! Better men than you have tried, and frankly, I suspect you are charm-challenged."

"Dost claim to be a virgin?"

"Jeesh! You're as bad as your brothers. No, I'm not a virgin. No, I'm not a slave. No, I'm not from your country. No, no, no. And, by the way, I could charm you if I wanted."

"You could try," he offered.

"You'd like that, wouldn't you?"

"Mayhap."

"Well, forget about it. I wouldn't let you screw me if you were the last man on earth."

"Screw? Is that what I think it is?"

"Probably."

"Milady Wench Warrior, you are going to be tupped, whether by me or some other man in this hall. That I can guarantee."

He saw the fear flash on her face, then be quickly masked with some icy resolve. Before he could guess what she would do next, she grabbed for the woman sitting on the nearest bench. Ebba, it was. Dropping the poker, she held Ebba with one arm tight around her waist. In the other hand, she held the knife up to the white throat, already drawing a thin line of blood. "Move any closer, and she is dead," she warned him.

Would she really kill someone? he wondered. Most women were loath to look at sword dew, let alone spill it themselves. But then, she was obviously like no other woman. "Do what you will." He shrugged, pretending indifference. "Think carefully. I am Brandr Igorsson. This is my estate. If you do not obey me, in the end, you will be the one to suffer. Hurt this woman, and your suffering will be far worse."

"Not if I kill myself, too."

"You could not manage two kills in the time I would reach you."

"Think again, Igor."

"Why do you call me Igor? That was my father's name. My name is Brandr."

"Igor is the name of Frankenstein's assistant. You know, the hunchback, deaf, mute monster. It's sort of a cliché name for an ugly, beastly man."

His eyes about popped out. She dared to compare him to a beast . . . an ugly beast. He was not ugly. Was he? He would have to check Liv's looking brass. No, he would not! He did not care if he was ugly or not. Damn the woman for her impertinence! "I repeat, wench. You cannot manage two kills at once. I will have my hands about your stubborn neck in a trice."

"I know exactly where to slice and dice for the most effective, quick kill." She pointed the knife at the large vein in Ebba's neck.

She was right. She might just be able to do it. "My name is not Igor," he gritted out, as if that mattered a bit. " 'Tis Brandr."

"Same thing."

He fisted his hands to keep from leaping on her like the beast she'd named him. "What is it you want?"

"Freedom. Safe passage back to Hedeby."

*You have lost your senses if you think I will let you go now.* "That is all?"

"A glass of water to wet my parched throat. Your brothers are asses. They forgot to feed me or give me a drink since yesterday."

He glanced over at Erland and Arnis with reproach.

"I thought he did it," each said of the other.

They *were* asses, just as she'd said. Not that he would tell her that.

"Put down the knife, and I'll give you a horn of mead. And a platter of food."

"What about the other demands? Freedom and safe passage?"

*Not in this lifetime! Thralls do not make demands of their master.* "I will ponder those later."

Her shoulders dropped, but not her knife. She whispered

something in Ebba's ear, which caused the woman to relax. Then the wench—Joy—began to back up toward the stairs. She must have asked Ebba what was up there, because he heard Ebba say, "The master's bedchamber, a solar, and several other bedchambers, including Liv's at the far end."

"Who is Liv?"

"Don't answer her, Ebba."

Ebba looked at him helplessly. "She'll kill me," she moaned, then told Joy, "The master's sister. I hear she never leaves her room."

He said a rude word, a famous Anglo-Saxon one.

"Does he care about her?"

"Yea, he does. Very much, I am told. But what do I know? I arrived on the same ship you did."

Once again taking him by surprise, she shoved Ebba at him, causing them to both topple over to the floor. When he righted himself, she was already racing up the stairs, taking the steps two at a time. By the time he caught up with her, she was on the other side of the door in Liv's bedchamber. He could hear the bolt being slid into place.

Liv was crying.

But then she was not.

"Wench, if you hurt her, I will kill you slowly. First I will skin you. Then I will feed your eyeballs to the vultures. Then—"

"Yeah, yeah, yeah. I told you before, my name is Joy. Not wench."

He pounded against the door with both fists, but it held fast. Having helped his father build it years ago, he knew how sturdy it was.

"I have no intention of harming your sister," she said. "We will talk later. Now I want you to bring us some food and water, lots of water. By the stench in here, your sister needs a bath, and this room needs a good cleaning."

"Of course . . . Joy," he agreed. Readily. Once that lock was undone, he would be in there in a trice with sword a-ready.

"Not through the door," Joy added. "I'll draw the basket of food and buckets of water up through that arrow slit window."

"How am I supposed to get a rope up that high? My aim is not that good, Joy." He hated using that ridiculous name for her, but using it made him appear amenable to her demands, even if he was not.

"I bet one of your archers could do it. Barring that, I'll make a rope myself."

"I'll bloody hell do it myself. Are you all right in there, Liv?"

He was not surprised when he heard nothing from Liv. She hadn't spoken since they'd brought her home. Even during the birthing process, when she'd dropped the Sigurdsson whelp, not one sound did she utter.

"Liv is fine. She and I are going to become best buds by morning," the wench told him.

"You can be all the flowers you want, but Liv better not be changed in any way."

"You are an idiot," the wench said. "A bud is a friend. A buddy. Liv and I are going to become friends."

He would like to see that. Liv hadn't responded to one single person in almost four months. Not even him, and he had always been her favored brother.

"By the way, I noticed you have a vein sticking out in your forehead. Anger-related, I'm sure," the wench said from the other side of the door.

*"What?"* he blurted out before he had a chance to check himself.

"Anger does that to a person. It's called anger psychosis. If you're not careful, you'll have a stroke one of these days. But not to fear, I'm a doctor—well, almost a doctor—of psychology. You know, emotions, mental illness, that kind of thing. I can help you with some anger management tools."

First she claimed to be a warrior, now a healer. What next? A wizard?

He was incensed that she would dare to say he had a problem with anger and that she would attempt to cure him. What kind of bloody warrior would he be without anger? He sputtered, then expressed his opinion in the only way he could without offending Liv's sensibilities with foul curses. He kicked the door. So hard he had to limp away, biting his lip at the pain. He had probably broken a few toes.

Even then, the wench yelled out loud enough for him to hear down the corridor. "See! Anger psychosis."

### Another "What was I thinking?" situation . . .

Joy had landed in the middle of some Monty Python nightmare.

She had no idea if it was someone's idea of a joke, a warped reenactment event, a primitive society that had escaped detection like those tribes in the Amazon rain forest, or a big, bad nightmare. Or could it possibly have something to do with the Arab terrorist threat and slave trading?

With a deep sigh, she resolved that she would somehow get herself out of this mess, like all the others in her past. But for now, she was hungry and thirsty, she had to pee, and she was in a locked room with a girl who was gaping at her like she was Elvira the witch just come through the arrow hole window on her trusty broom.

She explored the room and found a pot with a lid behind a folding screen. Once she relieved herself, she washed her hands in a brass bowl of water and dried them on a piece of linen cloth. Coming out, she extended a hand to the girl on the bed, "Hi! I'm Joy Nelson."

The girl flinched and edged away to the other side of the bed, refusing the handshake.

"I'm not going to hurt you, Liv. That is what your name is, isn't it?"

The girl nodded.

"Honest. I would never hurt you. I do fight, but only in self-defense or to eliminate bad men."

Liv's blue eyes brightened. She could be pretty if cleaned up with that long, blonde, almost white hair. She had pretty facial features and a tall, slim body.

Reflecting on what she'd said that would cause the girl to brighten, she concluded, "You don't like bad men?"

Liv nodded hesitantly.

"I heard that you won't leave your bedroom. Is it because of all the men downstairs?"

She nodded harder now.

"Has some man hurt you?"

Liv held up one finger and shook her head in the negative. Then she held up the fingers of both hands and nodded.

Joy's skin went cold. "Many men?"

She nodded again.

*Oh, my God, no!* "Rape?"

The girl groaned and nodded.

"Oh, sweetie!" Despite her resistance, Joy crawled up onto the bed with the girl and held her in her arms. At first, she squirmed and shoved at her, trying to get away, but then she relaxed in Joy's embrace and began to weep softly.

Joy had studied about and actually worked with rape victims, both as a psychologist and a crisis center volunteer. Liv's retreat into herself, refusing to speak, was not unusual. The scars of such an experience, especially if multiple rapes were involved, stayed with a woman forever, but there were ways of getting past the trauma. Joy could help the girl; she was sure of it.

"Liv, honey, you are not to be afraid of me. I'm not going to force you to do anything you don't want, but I can help you. That's my job, what I'm trained to do. Do you understand?"

Liv nodded against her chest, then glanced up, a hopeful expression on her face, which clouded over as she looked toward the door.

"No, you don't have to go downstairs until you're ready."

She eased herself off the bed and took Liv with her, still holding her at her side with an arm over her shoulder, intermittently stroking her back in a soothing manner. Liv pulled against her hold, unsuccessfully, when Joy unlocked the door, but stepped only as far as the open doorway. With a yell that jolted Liv, she called out, "Igor! Get your butt up here!"

Almost instantly, Brandr was up the steps and rushing toward her, a crowd of other men behind him.

She held Liv tightly at her side. "Don't be afraid. No one is going to touch you. I promise."

Brandr came to a screeching halt, his eyes going wide at the sight of his sister standing next to the wench from Hel.

"Your first mistake, wench, was opening the door for me."

She used her free hand to wave dismissively. "Don't come any closer, or you'll scare Liv."

"Liv is *my* sister," he roared.

"Right now Liv is a rape victim who needs my help."

"*Your* help? You overstep your bounds, thrall."

"Thrall shmall," she chirped. "Do you want your sister to get better?"

He straightened his shoulders with affront. Was she hinting that he did not care about Liv? He would kill any person who said such, even a woman. "Of course I want Liv to get better." He looked at Liv, who for the first time in such a long time met his gaze, but immediately she looked to the wench for help.

"I need your help," Joy said.

He would like to pick up the wench, toss her over his shoulder, and either take her down to the fjord and feed her to the fishes or take her to his bed furs and swive her silly. But he restrained his baser urges, both kinds. "What help?"

"A maid or two to help clean Liv's room. Frankly, it stinks. All that hay on the floor should be swept up, the floor scrubbed, and a carpet laid down, if you have one. The chamber pot should be emptied *and* cleaned. There are cobwebs in the corners a year old. The bed linens are so old and worn they'll probably rot in the wash water. A tub—no, two tubs of hot water for bathing. And don't forget the soap, washcloths, and towels. Also, bring clean clothing for me and Liv."

"Is that all?" He folded his arms over his chest, his ankles crossed as he leaned against the opposite wall.

"For now, Igor," she said, putting in that name just to

annoy him and remind herself that he was the enemy, not a six foot four, dark-haired hunk of a Viking. The belted tunic and slim pants with cross-gartered half boots couldn't hide a buff body that would put some SEALs to shame. Not that any of that mattered.

"You and I have a score to settle, *wench*," he said, emphasizing without words that if she continued to call him Igor, he would call her wench, "but I am willing to put my grievances aside for the moment if it will help Liv. Just know that you will not escape my punishment."

There was a gleam in the brooding man's eyes that told her what form that punishment might take. She didn't need to peer downward to see that her nipples reacted to his promise, and not with fear. Brandr saw, too, and he nodded at her with satisfaction. "Methinks you need no fine garments. Those you wear are sufficient."

Only then did it register that she wore only the bra and panties. "You would think so!"

"What manner of dress is that?"

"Underwear."

"I cannot help but wonder about what is beneath."

"You'll never know."

"You think not?" Then, without further word, he turned to the astounded crowd behind him, motioning for them to leave with him. Already he was barking out orders to fulfill Joy's requests . . . uh, demands.

She took Liv back into the bedchamber.

And the most amazing thing happened. Liv grinned at her.

"You like the way I held my own with your brother?"

Liv gave her a full-fledged smile, then nodded.

"I have a big brother, too. Two, in fact. I used to have three, but that's another story. Bottom line: I know what big brothers are like."

Liv patted her bottom.

Joy laughed, understanding completely. "Yep. They're a pain in the ass."

# Chapter 7

**He was becoming en-thrall-ed . . .**

Brandr sat before the fire at a far fireplace, nursing a silver goblet filled with a fine red wine from the Franklands. His brothers had bought several barrels of the wine as a special treat.

He'd checked outdoors last time he used the garderobe, and the snow was already knee-high. 'Twas a blessing that his brothers had returned when they had. Not that a good longboat couldn't travel in snow. Nay, it was the freeze that would close up the fjord in a short time. Still, there would be much work to do on the morn, and it would be hindered by the snowfall.

Most everyone was asleep, or leastways abed. He could hear snoring, loud and soft, from all around. Not sleeping were those lucky enough to have someone to share their bed furs. Those sounds, too, he could hear.

He was ashamed of himself and embarrassed that a stranger—a thrall, no less—had pointed out the condition of his sister's bedchamber. Because Liv hadn't wanted any men coming into her presence, including him, he hadn't made the effort to determine how his household was treating her. A mistake, one that would not occur again, considering the tongue-lashing he'd given to the lazy lot of them. Then he'd made them work for hours putting the bedchamber in a state befitting the sister of a high chieftain.

If that was not bad enough, the woman—a thrall, no matter what she claimed—had made more inroads with Liv than anyone since she'd been taken from Bear's Lair. For that, he had to be thankful, but it was hard being thankful to a person who challenged him at every step, and more than that, gave insult. Igor, indeed!

Joy, she called herself. What a misnomer! More like Pain, her name should be. Pain in the arse. And, yea, one of the maids had reported that as being the selfsame way that the wench had described him to Liv.

Tossing back the remaining wine, he stood and walked across the hall and up the stairs. Sleep did not come easily for him. Too many night images haunted him. Usually he had to drink 'til he nigh fell over, but tonight the ale and wine had failed to numb him.

He passed the solar, the small room occupied by Arnora, his aunt by marriage, the three large sleep closets assigned to Tork, Arnis, and Erland, and started to go into his own bedchamber, then hesitated. Instead, he treaded softly down the rest of the corridor to Liv's room. Easing the door open—thank the gods it had not been locked again—he peeked inside.

The air smelled fresh in here now. Floral. Ah, must be it was the lavender-scented soap his mother had favored. It was one of the few things the Sigurdssons had missed on their brutal raid.

Liv was sleeping peacefully, more like her old self with clean, plaited hair and a soft white night rail. She was cuddled up against the thrall, who wore similar night attire . . . Liv's, no doubt. But, unlike Liv's slim, almost boyish frame, Joy's breasts and hips were clearly those of a woman grown. Her clean, red hair was no longer a wild, tangled bush, but sleek, flame-colored silk left loose to spread about the pillow. She snored softly through lips that were rose-hued and moist.

An immediate shock of a reaction hit below his belt, which surprised him. Erotic pulls this fierce had been rare in his life for years. Oh, he liked copulating good and well, but for the most part any reasonably attractive female would do, and when under the influence of the alehead and a darkened bedchamber, appearance mattered not a whit to even the most finicky Norseman. This was different. And he did not like it. Not one bit.

Liv made a snuffling sound in her sleep and rolled over and away from Joy, leaving the thrall practically hugging the edge of the mattress with space enough for another body betwixt them. Without thinking, he walked over, picked Joy up, and put a hand over her mouth, quickly moving out of the bedchamber, closing the door behind him. Pulling her tight against his chest, he inhaled her scent—lavender and sweet woman skin—then whispered against her ear, "Stop struggling. I am not going to hurt you. I just want to talk."

She kicked up with her knee and almost clipped him in the chin.

He chuckled. The wench was e'er a combatant. Edging the door of his bedchamber open, then edging it closed, he noted that a candle had been lit, and there was a thin stream of moonlight coming into the chamber from the arrow slit window.

Quickly, he tossed her onto his bed furs, following after and over her, pinning her to the mattress. He put a hand once more over her mouth just as she'd been about to scream. As if that would gain her aught! The only one who would heed her call would be Liv, and Liv did not leave her room.

She struggled wildly, trying to shove him off. When she bucked up, actually moving him, his raging "enthusiasm" caught her attention, and she stilled.

"I will remove my hand if you promise not to scream. Otherwise, I will put a gag between your teeth and tie you to the bed. Then you will have no choice but to listen. Agreed?"

She hesitated, her green eyes flashing murder, but then she nodded.

"Wise wench!"

She growled.

"You promised."

"I promised not to scream. That does not mean I have to like it. Get off me, you big gorilla."

"Say please."

She said something else.

"Tsk, tsk. That is a word ladies rarely use, but then I forgot. You are not a lady. You are a wench . . . a thrall."

"Read my lips. I. Am. Not. A. Thrall."

He lifted the amulet from her neck. "Dost know what these rune letters say?"

"N . . . no."

"I belong to Brandr. That is what it says."

"No way!" She yanked the amulet out of his hand and tried to undo the thong, to no avail.

After watching her struggle in vain, he took both her hands and placed them above her head and out of the way. To keep them there, he laced his fingers with hers.

"If this is your idea of talking, spare me. And if you don't stop prodding me with that . . . thing, I'm going to bite it off first chance I get."

He froze. His cock *was* indeed poking at her, but most females would ne'er mention the fact, lest they be whores or of a wanton nature. *I can only hope.*

*Nay, I do not hope that she is wanton,* he argued with himself.

*Liar!*

*Well, mayhap I am a mite tempted.*

The mental voice just laughed.

He shook his head to rid his bemused brain of such unwelcome musings. "You would bite off my manpart? That should be interesting, since you would have to put it in your mouth first."

"So?"

The wench shocked him. Continually. In truth, he had not

heard such wicked speech from other than a strumpet. "Are you saying you have done such?"

"Are you saying you haven't?"

"This is a ridiculous conversation."

"Isn't that the truth? Let me up. You said you wouldn't hurt me, that you wanted to talk."

"'Tis true," he said, "but first I deserve a forfeit."

"For what?"

"For denying your thralldom. For fighting me in front of one and all. For calling me a beast. For causing me to break a toe kicking your door. For saying you would ne'er be attracted to such as me. Is that still true . . . that you are not attracted to me?" *What an idiot I am! Begging a thrall for crumbs of affection.*

"Well," she said, licking her lips in a most seductive manner as she stared at his hair and face and mouth.

He'd shaved earlier today when in the hot spring bathing house, and he wore war braids on either side of his face, not for preparation to battle but to keep errant strands out of his eyes.

"In different circumstances, I might find you attractive," she admitted.

His foolish heart swelled at the gleam of interest in her sparkling green eyes. "What different circumstances?" He could not help himself. He leaned down and nuzzled her clean hair. How long had it been since he'd savored a woman for her scent alone?

"If I hadn't been kidnapped by your idiot brothers and you hadn't behaved like an overconfident male chauvinist pig when you first saw me, and—"

"I've decided what my forfeit will be afore I let you up."

"Goody, goody! I can't wait to hear."

"A kiss," he said, and before she could protest, he placed his lips on hers. To his amazement, she did not resist or slap him aside the head or try to shove him off. In fact, she moaned softly and opened to him.

Brandr had kissed many a maid, though not so much of late. But this kiss . . . this he could do forever.

As far as kisses went, it was a mere shaping and learning, coaxing. It should have been nothing spectacular. But it was.

So sweet and tempting was her kiss, and, yea, she was kissing him back, that he wished he could burrow inside her, to be soothed by her softness and light. In that moment, he realized that the darkness had left him, if only for an instant, and was replaced with the most untenable thing: hope.

He tore his mouth off hers and stared at her with a mixture of wonderment and horror. With senses inflamed, ribbons of lust unfurled throughout his stunned body. Their hands were still linked above her head. "You are a danger to me, wench. I swear you are."

She furrowed her brow in question. 'Twas hard to miss the slumberous haze of arousal in her eyes. She did not attempt to escape his hands holding hers.

He could not be tempted. He could not!

"That was some kiss," she observed.

"Yea, it was, and, truth to tell, I am not all that fond of the lip-locking nonsense as foresport. Best to get on to the tupping."

"Like dumb men everywhere! Think kisses are just a pit stop on the way to intercourse." Then she seemed to think of something. "Now you feel differently?"

"As you say, it was *some kiss*."

She studied him. "Why am I a danger?"

"You are a thrall; I am a high jarl. Methinks you would disdain being a bed slave to me or my men, not that your opinion will matter in the end. You are a stranger with odd ways, mayhap even one of our enemy."

"Bull!" she declared.

He rolled off of her and arranged some pillows behind him so that he half sat. She did the same . . . and glared at him.

Even when she was glaring, she tempted him mightily. Apparently she did not realize that her night rail was thin and well worn, displaying her charms to his already lustsome survey. The hem had ridden up to expose long, well-formed legs, despite the bristles. They must have been shaved at one time, if he did not miss his guess, like a harem houri. He even imagined he could see the dark red of her fleece. And her breasts—praise the gods and pass the mead—but she had fine, plump breasts that would fit—

"Stop staring at my breasts."

His lips twitched with a barely suppressed grin. "Your nipples are pointing at me like little arrows. Must be you find me 'charming' after all."

"Hah! File that under the Department of Wishful Thinking." Her face bloomed red.

'Twas a good sign when a lustsome man could make a woman blush in bed.

"You're easy on the eyes in a Genghis Khan kind of way," she admitted, "but it's just that the rough fabric of your shirt abraded them. Don't for one minute be thinking that you turned me on."

He could guess what "turned on" meant. Aroused. When they had kissed, she had been "turned on" all right, or he was not a Norsemen with an eye for good sex. Just as he had been "turned on" and still was.

He took one of her hands and ran the palm over the fine, *soft* wool of his tunic, giving lie to her words. When she didn't protest, he remained braced on one elbow and opted for another liberty. He ran the backs of the fingers of his free hand over one of said nipples, then quickly pulled his hand back lest she bite it off. But she was not biting. Nay, she stared at him, overwhelmed as he was by the shock of pleasure that hit them both. He had meant to taunt her, but instead the mock caress had come back to taunt him. The sap was rising in him at such a rapid rate it was surprising it did not ooze from his ears and nose and, yea, even his eyeballs.

"Are you a witch?" he asked in a sex-husky voice.

She shook her head slowly, still dazed.

"Who are you?"

"I told you already. I'm Petty Officer Joy Nelson in the Navy WEALS training program at Coronado, California."

"I do not understand what you say by half."

"You could say I'm a soldier. But I'm also a psychologist."

"Sigh-call-jest?"

"Psychologist," she corrected. "An expert on the human mind and behavior. A person who helps people heal from different mental maladies, like intellectual disabilities . . ."

"Dumbness?"

She clucked her tongue at him. ". . . behavior or mood disorders . . ."

"Grumpiness?"

"Stop interrupting me. Also, personality disorders."

"Ah! Like me, I suppose."

"Exactly."

"What were you doing in Hedeby?"

"I wish I knew. Well, actually, I was on a mission there. I got hit on the head, and before I knew it, I was in this old Hedeby reenactment village, and you know the rest."

Either the woman lied or she was demented. "Can you help my sister?"

"Maybe. Probably."

It would be insanity to trust the witch. Still, no one else had succeeded. Why not give her a chance? "I will give you four sennights . . . a full month to try."

"Gee whiz! Thanks. And if I don't succeed?"

"I will chop off your head."

He was jesting, but she regarded him as if he were a barbarian. Which he was, of course, but he did not lop off heads at will.

"Let's make a deal."

"Thralls do not make deals."

"Aaarrgh!"

"My mother used to make that sound when I did something she deemed particularly lackwitted."

"I think I'm going to like your mother."

"She is dead. And do not ask how or when, or I will indeed lop off body parts, starting with your running tongue."

"Okay, not that I accept that I'm a thrall or slave or whatever, but here's my offer. I work with your sister for a month, and if I help her, you take this damn necklace off of me, then take me back to Hedeby to find my team."

"You do not ask for coin?"

"No. I have plenty to live on back home. Why would I want your money?"

"All women want gold or silver or jewelry."

"You've been hanging with the wrong crowd, buddy."

"Buddy? That is a word you used about my sister. Friend, you said it means. Know this, I have no desire for you as a friend."

"Whatever!"

"I do not accept your offer."

"You don't?" His denial of her deal clearly shocked her.

"Nay. Instead, here is my offer. You work with my sister for one month *as a thrall*. At the end of that time, we will discuss whether you merit freedom. Or not."

"That's no deal at all."

"One more thing. You will share my bed furs during that time."

## The trick got tricked . . .

Joy stared at the brute, not believing what he'd just said. Then she glanced down at the furs on which they lay. A bubble of hysteria rose in her already befuddled mind. "If you mean what I think you mean, forget about it."

"You have no choice."

"Rape . . . that's what it would be."

"I have ne'er raped a woman in all my thirty years. I am not about to start with you. Nay, when we engage in bed-sport, you will beg for it."

"What an egotistical—"

"In any case, I did not say I would swive you, just that you would sleep at my side. For now."

"What a crock! That's the biggest line in the book. Right up there with, 'Slip into the backseat with me, honey. I'm not going to touch you. We'll just check out the stars.' Listen up, bozo, I am not some cheap trick you can bamboozle into a one-night stand or two."

"Huh?"

"What kind of deal is it where you get me as a bed partner, sex or no sex, and a free therapist for your sister, and I get sucky face nothing?"

"Huh?"

"I don't know where I am or why I'm here. I suspect you're connected with the Arab terrorists. But know this: the way to get a woman to have sex with you is not to give out ludicrous orders. In fact, my brothers would be the first to tell you that is tantamount to a dare in my book. 'I dare you to deny me sex.' Oh, yeah! We'll see about that sharing the furs business."

"What was it you said so eloquently earlier this evening? Ah, now I remember. Blah, blah, blah."

She almost smiled. The oaf had a sense of humor, after all.

"Keep rattling on. I find your constant chatter tires me. I am a man for whom sleep comes hard these days, and I did not soak my brain with ale tonight, as I usually do."

"Why can't you sleep?"

"Demons."

"What? I've heard the expression, 'I see dead people,' but never 'I see demons.' Wow! Real demons? You see real demons?"

"Of course not! I mean demons of the mind."

"Ah! The berserker stuff."

"Who told you that?"

"Your brothers."

"Lackwits!"

"I was wondering . . . um, when you go berserk in battle, are you naked? Do you bite your shield? Do you howl like a wolf?"

"Holy Thor! I am a berserker. Not a dunderhead. What warrior would bare himself to the enemy?"

"I just remember reading—"

"The only time I am naked is when I am in the bathing house or in the bed furs. Wouldst like to know what I am biting then? Nay? I thought not. As for roaring . . . the only roar coming from me would be one of triumph at the peaking."

"Jeesh! Don't overreact. You know, I could help you, as well as Liv. With the dark demon business, I mean."

"Please! Spare me your help. You would enjoy making me into a milksop, would you not?" He yawned widely, then rose, beginning to take off his clothes. First he undid his silver chain-link belt, then lifted his tunic up over his shoulders and off, leaving bare wide shoulders and a chest covered with black hair and a number of battle scars, old and new. Even while she gaped at him, he toed off one boot, then the other, then began unlacing his slim pants.

"What do you think you're doing?" she squealed.

"Preparing for bed." He yawned again, then dropped the pants and stepped out of them. "I am surprised that Liv sleeps in a bed rail, or that she gave you one. 'Tis a waste of good cloth."

"She's afraid of nudity."

"Oh. I should have realized that."

Joy couldn't seem to look away, and so she got an up-close and personal view of the big man . . . six foot four and well-muscled . . . who stood before her, buck naked, except for two glittering etched silver bands on his upper arms. *What a fashion statement!* His erection stood out like a blinking neon sign warning her. *What a sexual statement!*

When he caught her gawking at him, he said, "Do not be fearful. I am too tired to dip my wick tonight."

*Dip his what?* "And that?" She waved a hand toward the offending member.

He glanced downward and seemed surprised at his arousal. "I will either pleasure myself, or it will go limp on its own. Have I not said I would disdain bedsport tonight? I am a man of my word."

"Hah! A hard-on has no conscience."

His eyes went wide, and that was another thing. His midnight blue eyes were framed by black lashes so thick they would do Heidi Klum proud. With a dismissing gesture as if it was futile talking to her, he crawled back onto the bed, with a huge bed fur under them, fur side up, then drew another bed fur over the top, fur side down. Impossible as it was to conceive, he closed his eyes and was about to go to sleep.

"You can't possibly think I'm going to lie here with a naked man . . . a naked man with a woody. Even you can't be that much of a dunce."

He opened one eye a fraction. "Keep squirming around, and my woodcock will not go away, and *you* will have to do something about it."

"Not woodcock. Woody. Jeesh!"

He wiggled his butt as if to get comfortable. "Go on. Talk. Bore me to sleep."

Joy should have been insulted, but she found herself charmed by the jerk.

"Talk," he repeated, closing his eyes. "I am so tired. If I could sleep for an hour or two . . ." He yawned. "Just keep talking, and, for the gods' sake, stop hugging the other side of the mattress afore you fall off." With that, he reached over and yanked her to his side. There was still a good six inches between them, but Joy could scarcely breathe at his closeness. The heat thrown off by his body was searing. "I can feel the rise and fall of your body; even the rhythm of your heartbeat makes me drowsy."

"You could get a cat."

He chuckled. "Cats cannot speak, and I do not relish the prospect of claw wounds in my tender parts by morn."

"What makes you think I wouldn't claw you?"

"Blah, blah, blah." There was amusement in his voice.

Nice to think he considered her a comedian! Not!

To hide her nervousness, she began to talk. "Tomorrow is the anniversary of my brother's death. Matt died two years ago in combat. I don't know why I'm telling you that. I don't talk about Matt much, and usually only with my other two brothers."

She breathed in and out several times to calm herself.

She thought he was already asleep, but he said softly, "Go on, dearling."

*Dearling? He called me dearling. What an odd, wonderful endearment! But why use it with regard to me? Oh, hell! I'm probably misreading his intentions, and, really, why should I care?*

"I know how hard it is to lose a loved one," he went on. "All in one day, the Sigurdssons took my mother, my father, two of his other wives, four concubines, three older brothers, two sisters, and dozens and dozens more of our people. Liv is one of the few survivors, and she is half-dead."

Joy went stiff with horror. He spoke of that carnage with dispassion, but she knew that for the defense mechanism it was. She did the same sometimes. "I am so sorry."

"Why should you be? You did not know them. Nor do you know me."

"Oaf! Can't even take a speck of sympathy without insulting me." Even so, she began to ramble in a clumsy effort to give comfort, "After Matt's death, I went kind of berserk. Oh, shit! I can't believe I used the word *berserk*. Sorry. I'm not usually so insensitive. What I meant was that I behaved like a maniac, and after that I became a zombie. That's why I joined the military. Seemed like the only thing that had meaning at the time. Probably one of the biggest mistakes of my life. I'm always making mistakes, though. Usually because my brothers egg me on, but I'm getting too old to fall for their challenges. They would laugh themselves silly if they could see me now. Lying in bed with a bare-naked ancient Viking warlord who's probably some kind of throwback to a primitive culture. It would be just my luck that we're being filmed by National Geographic . . .or Candid Camera."

He remained silent, and she thought he might be asleep. But giving him a sideways glance, she saw his chest was moving. "Are you laughing at me?"

"Why would I do that? 'Tis a commonplace occurrence for my thralls to call me a 'bare-arsed ancient Viking warlord.' "

"You mentioned your father's other wives? Are you people Mormons or something?"

"Well, yea, we Vikings are more man than most, but, nay, my father followed the old ways of *more danico*. Multiple wives."

"And you believe in that practice, too?"

"Nay! I follow both the Christian and Norse religions. In fact, I have been baptized, for expediency when traveling in the Papist lands. But, truth to tell, I do not have even one wife. Nor do I want any, although my brothers and I will have to wed eventually to provide heirs."

For some reason, that bothered her. "And concubines? Are they the same as thralls?"

"Nay. Concubines are free women. Thralls, when they share the bed furs, are mere love slaves."

"That is so sexist and downright crude. Unfair!"

He shrugged. " 'Tis our way."

An uncomfortable thought occurred to her. "Do you have concubines?"

"Not at the present time."

"Not at the present time," she mimicked him. "Someone ought to castrate the whole bunch of you."

"Come here, wench." He tugged her closer and wrapped a thick swath of her hair around his fingers, which he closed into a fist, then raised it to his nose to smell with apparent pleasure. "Go to sleep. Mayhap if you snore like you were doing afore, that will put me to sleep, just as your blather does."

And with that, he was out like a light.

And he expected her to sleep? *I don't think so! Not with Mister Nude Hunk lying next to me.*

But then, amazingly, she did.

When she awoke the next morning, alone, she realized that she'd slept like a baby. Fully refreshed and ready to start a new day. Time to employ some of her WEALS training, to remember all the rules of engagement when taken prisoner. Holy cow! She was a prisoner of war. Sort of. How about that? Hopefully, she would not share Matt's fate. Somehow, she knew that she would not. On the other hand, maybe that was wishful thinking.

She lay still for a few moments, relishing the warmth of the furs on her back and front. It was a sparsely furnished room with only the massive bed, a chest at its foot, a table holding the now-extinguished candle, a pottery pitcher, and bowl of water, with wooden pegs on the wall for clothing. The hazy light coming from the arrow slit window did not enhance the room's drabness. It appeared to be an overcast day outside.

She stretched, got out of bed, and walked across the room. It was then she got her first shock of the day.

The big, thick door was locked.

# Chapter 8

**She was better than Ambien . . .**

Brandr felt wonderful.

He sat at a table in the great hall, eating a bowl of porridge with milk and honey drizzled over the top. Who could have guessed that he would have craved such plain fare after these long months of deprivation?

Dawn had barely covered the hills, and for the first time in what seemed like forever, he had slept through the night. His body abounding with renewed energy, he could not wait to begin a new workday. Mayhap even a new life.

And all because a bothersome thrall had slept beside him, unconsciously sharing her warmth and softness. He could not help but wonder how he would feel after sinking into her depths. And they would make love, eventually, of that there was no doubt.

Tork slipped into the seat beside him, carrying his own bowl of porridge. Apparently they shared the same tastes in food. Others stumbling groggily into the hall were reaching for horns of watered ale with cold meat or fish and manchet bread left over from last evening's meal.

"Well, well, well! You are looking like a self-satisfied rooster who has had his tail feathers stroked. She was that good, was she?"

"Who?"

"You know precisely who."

"I would not know how she was."

"Really?"

"Really."

"She was that bad, then?"

He elbowed his friend for his foolery. "We shared bed furs, and that is all."

"Why?"

"She bored me to sleep with her incessant talking."

"You could have stopped her prattle in the age-old way."

"I was too tired."

"A man is ne'er too tired for fucking."

"Do you question my manhood?"

"I am not that much of an idiot. Besides, I understand your indifference. She is not much to look at."

He recalled the wench's appearance in the thin bed rail with her silky clean hair. "She is not so bad."

"Mayhap I should give her a try."

"Not if you value your life."

Tork's lips turned up with amusement.

Brandr had no idea where that possessiveness had come from, but he did not like what it implied, so he added, "Not 'til I have had my fill. Then you may have her."

Tork nodded. "I wonder what the wench would say if she knew you intend to pass her on once you've had your fill of her."

"She has already mentioned castrating me. With her teeth."

Tork grinned. "But first she'd have to take your cock in her mouth."

"I told her the selfsame thing."

"It was strange last night . . . how she protested so strongly that she is not a thrall."

"They all do, at first."

"Well, yea, but this seemed different. So she now accepts her bondage?"

"Hah!"

"She does not accept, then?"

"We shall soon find out. I have locked her in my bedchamber, and she will not be permitted to leave 'til she dons a thrall gunna."

"Uh-oh!" Tork said, then, "Why do you get to have all the fun?"

It was such a ludicrous statement, knowing how dour his life had been for ever so long. But, in truth, Brandr realized that he was enjoying himself . . . and all because of a witless thrall who thought she was a woman soldier.

Just then, there was a scream of outrage coming from above stairs, *"Igor, you rat!"* followed by pounding, no doubt on the bedchamber door. Then there was a crashing noise, followed by another and another. Probably the pottery pitcher and bowl and the soapstone candle holder.

Tork grinned. "Your thrall calls."

### Then the war games began . . .

Joy was fuming.

For the past hour—or two, who knew with no clock—she'd screamed, pounded on the door, thrown everything in sight, to no avail. Tugging a heavy chest over to the wall, she now stood and gazed out of the arrow slit window—an opening about two feet wide by three feet tall, with a shutter to keep out the cold—and saw mostly snow, and more snow. It must be twenty inches deep, at least, and it was still coming down. People in furs and tanned hide clothing bustled about some thatch-roofed outbuildings. Down by the fjord, the two big dragonships were being beached for the winter. They joined another ten or so of various sizes already on the shore.

*How the hell am I going to get home?*

*Better yet, where am I?*

*Who are these people?*

*Are they terrorists . . . or working with terrorists?*

They appeared to be Scandinavians, but since when had Norway or Denmark or Sweden been the hub of terrorism? In fact, Sweden was supposed to be a pacifist country, wasn't it?

Hearing a key turn in the lock, she stepped off the chest and waited. Her hands fisted to keep from flying at the person dumb enough to enter with her in her present mood.

It was Brandr . . . or Igor, as she liked to call him. He didn't smile at her, which would have been the last straw. Instead, and it was equally irritating, he was fully dressed in a dark blue wool tunic over suedelike pants tucked into knee-high leather boots. A writhing dragon brooch on one shoulder held together a short black cape lined with fox fur. The same impressive silver link belt he'd worn yesterday tucked in his tunic at the waist.

And here she was shivering in a thin nightgown. She grabbed for the poker leaning against the small fireplace, which was stone cold, the embers having died out hours ago.

He eyed the "weapon" in her hand as if it were a lollipop, nothing to fear, then scanned the room. "You've been busy, I see."

Bed furs and feather-stuffed pillows were scattered about, broken pottery was on the floor, and she'd stomped on a drinking horn, a bone comb, and a wooden chair.

"You had no business locking me in."

"My sister is in distress. I suspect she is wanting you."

"Well, let me go to her then."

"Dress first. Then clean up this mess." He tossed a garment at her with a piece of rope and a pair of leather slippers. When she declined to catch, they landed on the bed. With a snort of disgust, he went down on his haunches to restart the fire.

"What the hell is this?" She was staring at the fabric on the bed. "It looks like a burlap sack."

"A gunna."

"A gunna, huh? I'm *gunna* kill you, first chance I get."

He was blowing on the embers, tossing little sticks onto the sparks. "A gunna is a gown. That is a thrall gown. Put the damn thing on."

"Now I get it. I put on the gown and the rope belt, and that denotes my accepting that I'm a slave."

His silence said everything as he continued to build up the fire.

"Will you chop off my hair, too?"

He didn't even smile at what she'd meant as sarcasm.

"Not today. Mayhap later."

"Exactly what would my duties be?" She folded her arms over her chest, as much to stop shivering with cold as to protect her modesty.

"Help my sister. Serve meals. Work in the scullery. Wherever you are needed."

"And as a soldier?"

"Absolutely not! You are a wench . . . a thrall. Possibly the enemy. Ne'er would I allow you near a weapon." He eyed the poker in her hand. "Try to strike me with that thing, and you will find yourself stripped and whipped down in the great hall afore one and all."

"You despicable, lousy, slimy, sonofabitch! No."

"Insults ill suit you, milady slave." He stood, dusting off his hands. "No?"

"No, I won't put on that stinking gown. No, I am not a slave. No, I won't help your sister if I'm regarded as a slave. And, by the way, where are my bra and panties?"

"If I knew what a bra and panties were, I could tell you."

"Never mind." She quivered, despite her best efforts.

"You are cold. Step over to the fire, and put on the gown. There is food and drink down in the scullery for you, and, nay, you do not eat in the great hall with free men and women."

"Why not just place a dish on the floor, and I can eat and drink like a dog?"

His jaw clenched with consternation. "We do not ill-treat our slaves."

She rolled her eyes at his ignorance.

He picked up the gown and rope, handing them to her. She slapped them away, letting them fall to the floor.

"I could make you."

"Then it would miss the point. My acceptance."

"When you are ready to comply, knock on the door. A guard will be posted outside. Otherwise, no food or drink will be brought for you. And clean up this filthy mess."

He opened the door and paused. "I would treat you well."

"No, you wouldn't. Slavery in itself is ill-treatment at its highest level."

"You will have to give in eventually."

"We shall see." She perceived in that moment that she had not been taking her captivity seriously enough. Despite the unreality of her situation, she was a POW as much as one taken in Iraq or Afghanistan. Like other military, especially Special Forces, she'd gone through weeks of SERE training . . . Survival, Evasion, Resistance and Escape, designed specifically for survival during captivity.

Every captivity was different, and she'd not been tortured . . . yet. Brandr had already hinted at other captive techniques that would be used on her, such as prolonged isolation, forced nakedness, sexual humiliation, subjection to extreme cold, deprivation of food and water. She had to treat this as the threat it was.

"The Geneva Convention demands you to abide by certain rules when treating me as a prisoner of war."

"Huh? What war? And what is a Geneva Convention?"

"Playing dumb again, huh?" She began to recite the military Code of Conduct: "I am an American, fighting forces which guard my country and our way of life . . . I will never surrender of my own free will . . . When questioned, should I become a prisoner of war, I am required to give only name, rank, service number, and date of birth. I will evade answering further questions to the best of my ability—"

"Oh, good gods!" Brandr slammed and locked the door after him, but even through the thick wood, Joy heard him grumble, "Bloody barmy bullheaded lackwit!"

**She was a brick wall . . .**

Brandr was fuming.

But he could not let anyone know, or they would regard him as a weak-willed, sorry excuse for a man. No true Norsemen allowed a woman to lead him in a merry chase. Leastways they did not admit such in public.

Two whole days the wench had stayed in his bedchamber. His men probably thought he tired her out with swiving all night long. Hah! He should be so lucky!

No food or drink had been given her, though he suspected she ate snow and morning dew off the windowsill. She slept nude beside him at night, but only because he'd ripped the night rail to shreds. He had to admit that he was sleeping like a baby with a mead teat, despite his cock standing at attention night and day. He was frustrated and should seek out some woman on his estate, but he did not want anyone else, untenable as that was to him.

During the day she sat before the fire wrapped in a bed fur, her nose raised haughtily to the ceiling. She would not speak to him, except when spouting some nonsense about military codes of conduct and giving him, over and over, her name, rank, and some long number of identification. Apparently her army gave its warriors numbers instead of names. How odd!

And then there was his sister Liv, who wept incessantly, for want of the wench's company. You would think they had been lifelong friends instead of new acquaintances. He was finding it hard to deny his sister anything. Still, Joy had to be taught her proper place.

All this chaos over a simple matter. A garment, no less.

Meanwhile, he worked dawn to late at night, mostly with Tork by his side. They assigned winter duties to every living body, male and female, freeman and thrall: spinning and weaving, sewing, cobbling, animal care, blacksmithing, carpentry, cooking, cleaning, and serving.

And a part of every day was spent on the exercise fields, honing battle skills. There was always the chance of attack, if not by any remaining Sigurdssons, then other villains who abounded in the north.

He also inventoried the storerooms and treasure chests. Bear's Lair was slowly coming back to its old state, nowhere near as prosperous, of course, but still a far cry from what he'd seen when he'd first come back from Trelleborg. The walls were bare of tapestries or fancy weaponry. Most of the foodstuffs were basic, not fancy imported delicacies. But they would be warm and well-fed during the long winter. That was something.

A hird of men had been sent to the far north wearing snowshoes to hunt for seals. Their meat would feed plenty, and the skins could be traded for goods in the spring, especially those skins made into rope. Seabirds, both live and dead, also made for good food and trade. Animal skins of any beast—fox, bear, even rabbit—would be put to good use.

And of course they could go a-Viking once the snow thawed. Plunder was an honorable way for Norseman to make a living.

Still, the wench and her stubbornness nagged at him.

Late that afternoon, he stomped up the steps and opened the door abruptly. She was sitting in the broken chair, wrapped in furs. It was damn cold in here, even with the small fire. She glanced up at him guiltily.

What would she have to be guilty of?

Hmmm. Best he should be wary.

He hitched one hip, then the other, not sure how to proceed. "Have you heard Liv crying?"

Her body stiffened with caution. "I have."

"Methinks she wants your company, though I cannot see why. She only met you that once." *Nice, Brandr. Tempt her to your urgings with insults!*

"She recognized someone who could help her."

"Mayhap," he conceded, then swore under his breath when she did not take his concession for the compromise it was. "Come down to the hall and join us for dinner. There is roast chicken and smoked eel," he coaxed.

"You told me I would have to eat in the scullery."

"I could make an exception."

She stared at him warily, and his heart softened a bit. Her face was gaunt with hunger, even after only two days, but who knows what and when she'd eaten afore that? "Bring me a gown . . . a gown like a Viking woman would wear, and take this amulet off my neck. Then I'll come down."

"You will wear the gunna I have given you, or not at all."

She shrugged her answer. It was not a positive one.

"Why make things so hard on yourself? You will have to give in, in the end."

"We shall see."

He slammed and locked the door on his way out. He was getting very good at slamming doors.

# Chapter 9

**You can't hold a good woman down . . .**

Joy had a plan.

Once she had accepted her POW status, she'd begun to recall all her SERE training. The most essential component was escape. She'd had survival training. She could cope once outside this strange fortress, or whatever it was. Cold and snow were going to be her biggest problems.

She'd picked the lock on the chest, a talent learned not in SERE but from her brothers, and closed it in a way that no one would suspect it had been opened. Already, she'd begun making a rope of clothing and bed linens she'd found in the chest. At the last minute, hopefully later today, she would also use the ropes that held up the mattress on the bed.

She should be able to fit through the arrow slit window, going sideways, at first. The rope could be anchored to almost anything, probably the bed. After that, rappelling down two stories should be a breeze.

She would wear Brandr's clothing laid out in the chest. Too big for her, of course, but she could manage, and the most important thing was to stay warm.

The window was on the side of the fortress, and Brandr rarely came to his bedchamber until late at night, so she hoped to be able to gather some food, gloves, and snowshoes from one of the outbuildings, especially if she waited until nightfall.

She would follow the fjord out to the sea, then walk the shoreline in the general direction of Germany. Hopefully, she would find friendlies way before then or at least be able to phone in to the command center.

And, by the way, wasn't it odd that the implanted microphone behind her ear hadn't worked since before the explosion? So much for high-tech engineering!

Another thing was that Joy would miss Brandr. Crazy, that's what it was, but Joy felt some odd connection with the brute. In another time and place, they might even have become lovers.

She laughed out loud at that ridiculous notion.

### The best laid plans of mice and foolish wo-men . . .

"You have got to see this," Tork said, coming up to Brandr in the bathing house where he was trying to soak out the aches and stresses of another full day.

"I am busy," Brandr said, sinking down in the hot spring-water until it covered him completely.

"Hurry. I mean it, Brandr. It is the wench. You would not believe what she is doing."

Brandr went instantly alert. "What wench?" But he already knew before Tork grinned and said, "Your bed wench."

A short time later, they had trudged through the deep snow in snowshoes to the other side of the keep where Joy was hanging out of the upper floor window. Nay, she was not hanging. She was expertly maneuvering a makeshift rope, which included, if he was not mistaken, his second best leather braies, torn into strips. With her feet braced against the wall, she was walking downward like a trained monkey he had once seen in the eastern lands.

"What are those garments she is wearing?" Tork asked

him in all innocence, even though he knew very well they were his, rolled up and belted to fit her much smaller frame. Her red hair had been balled up into a wool cap.

The wench hadn't yet registered that she was drawing a crowd. Brandr motioned for everyone to step back and remain silent. Only he moved forward.

Once she hit the ground, she reached for the fur-lined cape she'd thrown out the window before descending. Only then did he speak.

"Fancy meeting you here, wench. Are you going somewhere?"

She almost jumped out of her skin, so surprised was she. Her shoulders drooped for a second, then she straightened and stared at him before boldly asserting, "I was practicing my WEALS training. It's called rappelling. Would you like me to teach your men how to do it? It might come in handy in scaling walls next time you go raping and pillaging."

He laughed. He could not help himself.

But then he picked up the willful wench, tossed her over his shoulder, and carried her back inside the keep. But not before whacking her across her upraised bottom.

### Beware of rogues with dimples . . .

Joy had never felt so humiliated and defeated in all her life. Tomorrow she would get her act together, again, but for now she just wanted to crawl into a corner and lick her wounds.

The jerk carried her like a sack of flour—a sack of flour with its big butt up in the air—through the crowd of laughing Viking men and women. Up the steps to the wood-and-stone fortress and then, instead of taking her back to his bedroom, he went into a huge hall with massive fireplaces at either end and several open hearths arranged across the middle. More steps, and they were on a raised dais where he sank down into an armed chair and arranged her on his lap.

"Let me go. I can sit myself." She tried to struggle out of his arms, but he wouldn't let her go.

"Be still, or I will be forced to punish you in a way you will not like. My people will demand it."

She stilled, then turned. At least a hundred people, mostly men but a couple dozen women, were streaming into the lower level of the hall and sitting on benches around the entire room before food-laden tables. She suspected that the low benches, at least a yard wide, turned into beds at night. Some of them—the brothers Arnis and Erland and an attractive blond man whom she thought Brandr had referred to as Tork on the walk back—sat down on either side of them on the dais.

A twenty-something woman with breasts the size of melons leaned over Tork's shoulder. By her attire, i.e., burlap sack, Joy assumed she was a thrall. By her ingratiating demeanor—running back and forth to bring him the best morsels of food and practically wagging her tail when he smiled at her—she knew she was a thrall.

And this is what Brandr wanted her to be!

She couldn't think about that now. She must observe her surroundings, plan her next escape.

This was the same hall where the Brothers Dim, as in dimwit, had brought her the first day, but she hadn't had a chance to get a good look then. It was a scene out of some crazy B movie. Primitively dressed people in a primitive castle. Monty Python with a twist. The men wore belted tunics over slim pants with leather boots, some ankle height and cross-gartered up the calves, others knee-high.

It appeared that only thralls had short hair. Most other men and all the women wore their hair at least collar-length. Some had mustaches or beards, and the latter were braided or laced with colored crystal beads. Many wore thin braids on the sides of their faces, like Brandr.

The women wore collarless, ankle- and wrist-length linen or wool gowns, over which hung open-sided, pinafore-style aprons of a finer quality cloth, usually wool. Some wore their hair in a knot at their napes, younger women a long braid down the back, and still others sported either little white caps, similar to a baby's, rounded on the top and tied under the chin, or hood-type caps that fit over the head and tied behind the neck with the hair or braids hanging loose down the back. Everyone sported ornate brooches, usually writhing animals of some type. On the women, they fastened the straps of the apron, sometimes holding sets of keys. On the men, they held together short and long capes. The fabrics, mostly wools and leathers, ranged from drab to fancy, depending on status, she supposed. But the colors were bright—blue, red, purple, yellow, and copper—aside from the thralls, that is.

This was really taking reenactment to the extreme, in her opinion. And, whoo-boy, if it wasn't reenactment, she was going to have enough material to write a book when she got back. She'd be on *Oprah* and *Larry King* and be such a hotshot celebrity, her brothers would have to grovel at her feet.

It was a sign of her mental state that she was making jokes with herself, she decided.

"Oh, good Lord!" she said. Now she knew what had happened to her bra and panties. One flat-chested lady was wearing her bra, *on the outside* of her gown. And a young boy was wearing her panties on his head like a sort of beret. She stifled a giggle at the absurdity and went back to studying the crowd.

Mostly silent, except for shuffling sounds and murmurs, everyone seemed to be waiting expectantly before eating.

Brandr raised a hand, and a waitress or serving maid or whatever poured beer into a cup and shoved a large platter of food in front of him: slabs of red meat, vegetables, sliced apples, flat bread.

"Drink," he said, raising the wooden cup to her lips.

"I can drink myself." She reached for the cup, but he held it beyond her reach.

"You will drink from my cup or not at all."

She stared at him and the implacable expression on his face. "Does it symbolize some crazy notion or other?"

"Drink the damn mead!"

*Time to choose your battles, girl,* she told herself. She was very thirsty. So she opened her mouth and drank the potent honeyed brew. *Whoa!* She knew her beers, having grown up with three beer connoisseurs and being in the military where beer was almost a sacred beverage, but this mead stuff was sweet and strong. Good, but strong.

Then he drank from the same cup.

The crowd took that as a signal to begin their meal, and the voice and chatter of a communal dinner began. She was not being ignored, but she was no longer the center of attention.

It was clear by his place on the dais and by the way many of the servants referred to him as "master" that Brandr was something special in this society. "What are you? Some kind of Lord of the Fjord or something?"

"Or something," Old Dour Face snapped.

Jeesh! The guy had no sense of humor.

The brothers made rude remarks about what kind of lord he was. Tork made an especially snide comment about the lord's low taste in bed thralls.

Joy leaned forward and told Tork, "You should talk! You and Miss Brain-dead Udder of the Month!"

The rest of them laughed, except the dumb bimbo, who didn't get the insult. Fearing that she would come after Joy when she finally understood, Brandr shoved the cup at her mouth again, forcing her to drink the rest down to the dregs. She licked her upper lip, then turned her nose up and away from her captor. Just because she'd accepted the mead didn't mean she was turning into a docile dishrag, she told herself. She refused to be put in the same category as Boobs R Us.

He yanked the cap off so that Joy's hair flew out, onto her shoulders and around her face. "That was some feat you accomplished out there, climbing down the wall like a monkey."

"I *was* good, wasn't I? You should have seen me climb trees when I was a kid. A regular Tarzanette."

Again, not even a grin from Scrooge. "Didst consider the danger? Bears abound in these parts, and they are especially fond of nubile wenches on a snowy day. Even the hardiest man would not venture forth alone in this icy region. You could freeze to death in a heartbeat if stranded, even if only overnight."

"Needs must, babe."

His eyes went wide at her calling him babe.

"Just for the record, I haven't been nubile a day in my life."

"Dost ever stop talking?" He rubbed a strand of her hair between thumb and fingers, as if to test its texture.

"I talk when I'm nervous."

"Do I make you nervous?"

"No, but being in a room with about a hundred big swords does."

"In any case, your attempted escape today was foolish, but I must needs commend your skill." And then he smiled. Which was a shocker. She turned on his lap to get a better look at him. She couldn't recall even a grin breaking on his grim face before.

She gasped then. "Oh, that is just great! Life is so not fair!"

He cocked his head to the side, still smiling. "What? You are insulted by a compliment now?"

"Not that! You have dimples. Good grief! Bad enough that you are sex in a longboat, but dimples are too much for any girl to handle."

"I do not have dimples," he said, even as he dimpled at her. "Do I have dimples?" he asked Tork at his other side.

Tork said, "Now that you mention it." Then Tork grinned at Joy and gave a little wave.

"Pfff!" Brandr turned back to her. Then some idea seemed to occur to him. "Are you saying you are attracted to me?"

"You already know that I am."

"I do?" Obviously pleased, he picked an apple slice off the plate and put it to her mouth.

"You are not feeding me," she asserted, even as he shoved the fruit into her mouth, then clapped a hand over her lips so she couldn't spit it out.

She chewed, despite her resolve not to, and after more than two days of fasting, it tasted like ambrosia. Crisp and

juicy sweet. A piece of unidentifiable meat, possibly venison, then turnip, carrot, and a scrap of bread followed. She
tried to turn her face away from the offerings, but he forced
her to eat. Besides that, her mind was getting fuzzy from the
mead and the shock of her ordeal.

She wasn't so sloshed, though, that she couldn't balk at a
strange meat swimming in a white liquid. "What is that?"

"Eel in dill sauce."

"I don't eat snake."

"Eel is not snake. Eel is fish."

"According to whom?"

"You might like it. Have you ever eaten snake, by the
by?"

"Yes, in survival training, and it doesn't taste a bit like
chicken. And before you ask, I've also eaten slugs and spi-
ders and roaches, too. Not to mention roots and leaves and
even dirt. Yeech!"

His mouth dropped open in surprise, then clicked shut.
"The soldier business again?"

"Yes."

"Is that where you learned how to scramble down a building wall? You could have crashed to your death."

"It's called rappelling. No sweat."

He was lost for speech. Then, "I do not understand you."

"Welcome to the club."

Bypassing the eel, he said, "Try this. It's honey cake.
You'll like it."

"Why are you doing this?" she asked, chewing with delight. It *was* good. "I mean, letting me eat here in your hal-
lowed hall?"

"I am bending the rules a bit." When she just stared at
him, not understanding, he went on, "Thralls are not permitted to eat in the hall with free men and women, but if you are
being fed, that is different."

"There's a leap of logic in there somewhere," she said.
Then, "Being fed? Like a dog?"

"Just so."

She tried in earnest to squirm off his lap.

He wouldn't let her go. "Keep wiggling your arse on my cock like that, and you will get more than you bargained for . . . and I do not mean food and drink."

"In your dreams!"

"Why do you continue to fight your fate?"

"Wouldn't you?" Tears welled in her eyes.

Troubled, he wiped the tears from under her eyes with a thumb. "Eat and drink, sweetling. That is all, for now. Then we are going to come to an understanding." At her glower, he added, "A compromise."

"Don't try to soft-soap me with endearments. I don't like your compromises. I end up naked in your bed at night, behind a locked door all day, and starved to death."

Tork and the brothers snickered on both sides of them.

Brandr ignored them. "Hardly starved to death," he murmured, but she saw the flush of guilt on his very handsome face.

Dimples and a handsome face and now a smidgen of sensitivity! She was doomed.

"This will be different," he promised.

"Famous words! Right up there with, 'You can't get pregnant if you just let me put it in a little bit, honey.'"

Brandr gawked at her for a moment before letting out a hoot of laughter.

After that, the folks—those not playing dice or some kind of board game—were entertained by a lady playing an instrument that resembled a mandolin. Then some young boys did amateur acrobatics in front of the dais. Finally, an old man stood and began reciting the Yngling Saga, his monotone voice droning on about the fantastical origins of the Viking race.

"That is the skald I was telling you about," Erland reminded her. "Remember. The horrible skald."

"Shhh. Do not let Alviss hear you," Brandr cautioned.

"Right. Don't be cruel," Joy crooned.

No one laughed. *Jeesh!*

"On the journey here from Hedeby, I was telling Joy that she would make a wonderful skald with all her tales of her country," Arnis told a clearly skeptical Brandr. "Leastways, she would be better than Alviss."

"Brandr says my talk bores him to sleep," Joy told Arnis.

"You talk in the bed furs?" Arnis asked. "And Brandr allows such? Really? Methought my brother was a better lover than that. Unless you mean bawdy talk. *That* he would abide."

Brandr reached over and swatted his brother on the shoulder. "Behave, halfbrain."

"I'm not a poet, and I'm not going to be your free entertainment," Joy asserted.

"We shall see," Brandr said, repeating her favorite phrase back at her. Then, for her ears only, he whispered, "Besides, I much prefer to be entertained in private."

When people started to clear and dismantle the tables, Brandr stood, putting her on her feet. "Come. 'Tis time for our reckoning."

"Reckoning? I thought you said compromise."

"Reckoning, compromise, same thing."

She didn't think so! Still, she let him take her hand in his and lead her through the hall and up the stair. Twice she had to stop and pull up her pants, which fell to her ankles. Brandr seemed to enjoy watching her tug his *braies*—that's what they called men's pants in this country—up her bare legs.

Instead of going to his bedroom, as she'd expected, he took her to a small room that smelled to high heaven, where he lit a wall torch with a flint he carried in a side flap of his pants.

Holding her nose, she asked, "What is this?"

"The garderobe. Have you ne'er used such? 'Tis an indoor privy."

Joy examined the room more closely, still holding her nose. There were three toilet seats, like an outhouse, but it appeared as if this room hung on the outside of the fortress. On the floor was a basket of moss and another of large green leaves. Surely not replacements for toilet paper? Eeew!

Glancing inside one of the holes, she saw nothing way down below. "Where does it all go?"

"The fjord."

"You dump your waste in the river outside your home. Do you comprehend how much disease that could breed, not to mention contaminate drinking water?"

"I misdoubt that. My grandsire was far ahead of his time. He studied the ancient Romans' methods of waste removal. There are underground trenches with thin currents of water that lead to a point in the fjord downstream from us."

"Oh, that's just great. Pass the problem on to your neighbor."

"Our nearest *neighbor* lives almost a half-day's ship ride from here," he replied with consternation at her verbal attack. "Besides, the Thorssons deserve to be contaminated. They are a vile bunch. In any case, I did not bring you in here to discuss shit and such." He was reaching up to the ceiling, where there appeared to be an iron ring hidden in the wood. Pulling hard, a sort of ladder came down. Holding the torch in one hand, he indicated with the other that she should climb up in front of him.

"Is this some sort of upper dungeon you're going to put me in? Stink me to death as torture?"

He chuckled. "Just go. I'm about to show you my compromise."

Once she was up there, and Brandr had followed after her, she twirled around with amazement. It was a sort of treasure room, low-ceilinged and packed with chests of coins and jewels and piles of fabrics.

"Here," he said, shoving several garments her way. They were ladies' attire in the Viking style, except the materials were of finer quality than most. "They belonged to my deceased mother and sisters."

"You store all this precious stuff in a privy?"

"Not in a privy, above a privy. And really, they do not smell much. Leastways, they can be washed or aired out, if they do. Some say it makes the cloth resistant to moths. The most important thing is that they survived the raid by the Sigurdssons because of this very stinksome hiding place."

"And you trust me with that information?"

"What good would it do you? You will not be leaving here. Now, don't go raising your chin at me again. I am here to make compromises." He pushed her down to sit on a big chest, and he sat on another facing her. "I will allow you to wear these garments. You will help Liv; that will be your duty here. You may be asked to help with work around the keep where needed, but your main chore will be as companion to Liv . . . or healer, if you will. The bedchamber doors will not be locked. You may move about above and below stairs, within reason."

"Those are all concessions on your part. What do you expect in return?"

"Loyalty. You will continue to wear the amulet under the garb. I find that I like the idea of something, if not you, saying that you belong to me. You will sleep in my bedchamber at night."

"Naked?"

"Of course. Odin's breath! Everyone sleeps naked, for the most part."

"Would I be expected to have sex with you?"

"Only if you want to."

"And that's all?"

"You must promise not to try to escape again."

"I can't promise that. It's my duty as a soldier to escape the enemy."

"I am not the enemy."

"Yes, you are. Making me a slave is not the act of a friendly nation."

"Then you will be forbidden to go outside the keep."

She shrugged. They could try to keep her inside. Didn't mean they'd succeed. "Sounds as if we have a Catch-22 here. I lose either way."

"Or you could say you win either way."

She sighed and glanced around the small storage room. "Where did you get all this stuff? Is it stolen?"

"Nay. Some was bought in the markets of Birka and Hedeby and Kaupang, or even in the Arab lands. Still others were prizes of war, like this." He held up a magnificent tapestry, almost like the Bayeux Tapestry, but much smaller, about two by three feet. "This once belonged to the British King Athelstan. I was a Jomsviking for many years afore coming back to defend my estates when the Sigurdssons . . . well, you know all that. I was a Jomsviking, and as such, paid warriors, we rode with Eric Bloodaxe again King Eadred, Athelstan's nephew. This tapestry was amongst the spoils of war. If I were not so preoccupied in getting Bear's Lair back to its former self, I might have joined an army against the current King Eadred, Athelstan's nephew several times removed, who is rumored to be ill and close to death. No doubt his young brother, Edwy, will take over as king of Britain, but I must say, a more sorry, immoral man there ne'er was." He stopped speaking when he realized he was rambling and that Joy was staring at him with disbelief.

"There is no king of England now. The ruling monarch is Queen Elizabeth."

Brandr frowned. "I have ne'er heard of any Elizabeth in the House of Wessex. You are mistaken."

"Tell me again what you said about the various kings."

He looked at her as if she was crazy, and that's just how she was feeling. "Back some years, there was Alfred the Great, a good and wise ruler in Britain, though not a lover of anything Viking, followed by his son Edward and then his grandson Athelstan, who was a collector of books and precious objects. But that was during my father's time. After Edward came Edmund, then Eadred, who now holds the throne."

"Elizabeth is the queen of England. The sole ruler. There hasn't been a king in Britain for more than fifty years, since her father George died."

He shook his head and repeated, "You are mistaken."

Joy began to feel lightheaded as an impossible thought entered her mind. "Brandr, what year is this?"

"Nine hundred fifty-five, as you well know."

Joy made a gurgling sound, then stood, as did Brandr. "No, you idiot. It's two thousand and nine."

They gaped at each other, equally stunned, but it was Joy who fainted.

# Chapter 10

**Sex was sex, even with a thousand-year-old woman . . .**

What a mess! The jester god Loki must be having a grand time laughing at him, or mayhap the Christian Satan was wielding his usual deviltry.

Brandr had caught the demented wench when she fell into a dead faint . . . and, yea, he was now sure she was demented. First a soldier, then a mind healer, and now a time traveler. For the love of Frigg!

With great care, he managed to pick her up in his arms and still carry the torch as he climbed back down the ladder and staggered back to his bedchamber. Along the way, he met up with Tork and his latest bedmate, the one Joy had mocked. "Do not ask!" he replied to Tork's raised eyebrows.

Tossing her on the bed did not make the wench even stir, so he went back to the garderobe and closed the hidden ladder door, after first gathering the garments he had offered.

She was still "asleep" when he returned, so he called out to one of the house thralls to bring a pitcher of ale and cups to his bedchamber. After building up the fire, he turned back to the bed.

Joy was splatted out on her back, arms and legs spread, like some bloody sacrifice. He'd like to sacrifice her, all right. To think he had been considering bedsport with the wench a short time ago . . . a thousand-year-old woman! Not that she was really a thousand years old or a time traveler. More like an escapee from a hospitium for barmies. That was just as bad. In the midst of satisfying his "enthusiasm," she might just go into a raging fit.

The warped side of his manhood said, *Hmmm! There might be some pleasure in that shivering and convulsing.*

But then he corrected himself, *Nay! That would make me as barmy as she is.*

Well, he was in a tight spot, for the moment. Mayhap it would be best if she slept off this fainting spell. Afterward, she might be saner. He downed half the pitcher of ale, which a male house thrall brought in, trying his best not to gawk at Brandr's "captive." He probably thought Brandr had done something to knock her out.

Setting down his empty cup, he began to remove her clothing. As he took off the boots, then the man's braies, tunic, and rope belt, he felt an odd pleasure in seeing her in his clothing. It made him feel as if she actually did belong to him, willingly.

Now there was a joke! Joy coming to him willingly.

On the other hand, he was a liar if he denied wanting such, even though he did not want to want her to want him. Truly, he did not. Because that would make him weak. There would be a hole in his defenses, one she could use to her advantage.

*I am bloody hell thinking too much.*

With the last of her garments tossed aside, Brandr stared down at her. Usually, he did not like red hair. Too brassy. But he liked *her* red hair, both above and below. Unlike many redheads, she had only a few freckles . . . on her nose and shoulders. Her nipples and areolas were a pale rose color, matching her lips, which were pouty when closed, as they were now. Pale, cream-colored skin covered her tall frame. He even liked her long toes and high-arched feet.

You would think that he would be painfully hard with arousal, looking at her naked form. He *was* hard, but the greater pain was in the region of his heart. For some strange reason, he was breathless. His dumb heart ached.

Her eyelashes began to flutter, and he quickly pulled the bed fur over her, not wanting to be caught ogling her body. He could only imagine the sharp words she would hurl his way.

When her eyes opened, he shoved a cup of ale into her hands, which she drank thirstily and handed the cup back. Then she stared at him, and he could tell that she was slowly becoming aware of the words they had exchanged in the treasure room. Then, like before, she surprised him, this time by opening her arms to him. In a low, whispery voice, a bit slurred by the alehead, she pleaded, "Come. Hold me. I am so scared."

If ever a man made a new record time for undressing, it was he. He'd always had woman luck in the old days before he became a berserker. He must have his old charm back. No doubt Joy had been stifling her lustful urges for some time, but now she had crumbled under an overwhelming desire for the mating with him. It happened like that betimes.

She had scarce lifted his side of the furs before he was in his bed, holding her, skin to skin. The pleasure was so great that he was the one who almost fainted.

With a sigh of pleasure—from him or her, he was not sure—he rolled onto his back, taking her with him to his side, where she nestled up against him, her face buried in the curve of his neck, an arm thrown over his chest, one of her nipples caressing one of his nipples, and a knee raised and covering his standing manpart. He kissed the top of her sweet-smelling hair.

Then came surprise fifty or so, by his estimation.

She fell asleep.

So much for her lustful urges!

### God's gift to women: a fine male tush . . .

Joy awakened in the middle of the night to the most delicious sensation of fur upon her naked breasts.

Really, when she got back home, she was going to buy herself a fur coverlet for her bed. Fake fur, of course. And she was going to sleep naked. No more Snoopy PJs.

But then the fur moved, and she heard, "Why are you smiling, wench?"

Her eyes shot open. It wasn't fur. It was a man . . . a man with a furry chest. And he was leaning over her, nibbling at her neck and shoulders, his calloused palms moving over her arms and waist and thighs, everywhere but where she really wanted them.

But wait. The events of the past day rolled over her like dominoes. Her thwarted escape, being fed like a puppy in the dining hall, the treasure room above the outhouse, and then . . . and then, the recognition that she had traveled back in time a thousand years. No, no, no! That wasn't true. Time travel was impossible. Still . . .

"What are you doing?"

He had just licked one of her nipples.

"Engaging in a bit of foresport. Methinks I would like to try more of those kisses, then mayhap some tasting of other parts of your body, then—"

"Whoa, whoa, whoa! Somebody's got the wrong idea here."

"I have an idea, all right, and it is a very good one." He rubbed his knee against the juncture of her thighs to demonstrate, and she just about swooned . . . again.

But she had to be strong. "No. I can't do this. All the rules of engagement in the military forbid a prisoner having sex with a captor."

"Aaarrgh! I did not capture you."

"Semantics! Your brothers did, and they did it for you."

His eyes knifing her with consternation, he gritted out, "You invited me to couple. You opened your arms to me. We were skin to skin."

"Earth to alien Viking. I was forced to be naked."

"You invited me to hold you, whilst you were naked."

"I did. That was probably a mistake." *Definitely a mistake, but it felt so good at the time. Still does.* "I was weak after that shocker about time travel, and, no, I don't want to discuss it."

"Are you saying that you do not want to tup with me?"

"Tup? Now there's a nice word. Not!" She inhaled and exhaled for patience . . . and to tamp down her raging attraction to the lout. "Brandr, I do want to make love with you. I don't know why, because you are not the most sophisticated man in the world, babe, more like rough around the edges. There's probably some subconscious psychological reason for it. Sexual regression or something. Maybe I have a genetic memory of making love with a caveman."

She could tell he didn't understand most of what she said. "Did anyone ever tell you that you talk too much?" He leaned down and gave her a quick kiss.

"All the time, babe. All the time." She had to clench her fists at her sides to keep from yanking him back for another, deeper kiss.

And he could tell. Darn it! "I know how to be smooth when it is warranted."

She smiled at his wounded pride. "Oh, babe, did I hurt your itty-bitty ego?"

"Why do you keep calling me babe? I am not a babe."

"I beg to differ. You are definitely a babe."

"You cross the line with your insults."

"Babe means a hot, sexy individual who exudes sex appeal."

He grinned. "So you are attracted to me, after all."

"There is this strange attraction, but I am part of the U.S. Navy and—"

In that instant she heard a whimpering noise and realized that was what had awakened her, not her fur lover. "Get off me," she demanded. And because he wasn't expecting it, when she shoved against his chest, he fell off her and onto his back. Before he could grab for her, and he did try, she was off the bed and pulling on one of the new under-gowns . . . soft, unbleached linen, which was long-sleeved, ankle length, and collarless.

"Where in bloody hell do you think you are going?" Brandr was half sitting, with his body propped up on his elbows.

"Can't you hear that?" She pointed to the wall.

A whimper resounded in the still air.

"Liv!" he said, jumping out of the bed. He was bending over to put on a pair of the slim leather pants he usually wore. Despite her hurry, she had to pause and admire the fine, fine body of this man from the past . . . if that's what he was. She shook her head to clear it. "No, let me go to her. This might be the breakthrough we've been waiting for."

He paused, glancing at her over his shoulder, one leg in and one leg out of the pants. "Mayhap you are right." He waved her toward the door.

She went out, closing the door after her, but then she opened the door again, and peeked in, "Just one thing."

He cocked his head in question.

"That is the finest male tush I have ever seen." She pretended to ogle his behind.

He was still puzzled until she patted her own bottom while staring at his.

"I would much rather have you admire my other side," he said with a laugh.

And out came those damn dimples.

Thousand years old or not, this man was going to be her downfall. She just knew it.

### She was a light in a dark place . . .

Brandr allowed himself an hour before going to check on Liv and his bed thrall. Some bed thrall! More like bad thrall!

He almost ran into Tork in the hall. By the light of the sputtering torch he carried, he could see Tork tying the laces of his braies. He must be coming from the garderobe.

"You are grinning!" Tork accused him.

"And so?"

"You have not grinned in the past year that I know of."

"Is that such a sin?"

"Not a sin, but a shame."

"You would have me become a grinning lackwit." He made a clucking sound of disgust.

"Where are you going?"

"To check on Liv . . . and my bed thrall." He chuckled, knowing how Joy appreciated that designation.

"Grins and chuckles. What next?"

He elbowed Tork with his free arm. "Didst know that I am a babe?"

"Whaat? You and I are of the same age, and I am definitely not a babe."

"Too bad! Because *babe* is a person with massive amounts of sex charm. Women attain pleasure-peaks just looking at a man-babe. The gods envy men so endowed. In fact—"

"You arc so full of—"

"Shhh! Liv was having a nightmare. I do not want to disturb her if she has fallen asleep again."

Carefully, he opened the door, and the two of them peered inside. Joy had lit a candle near the bed where she had pulled up a chair. Propped against the pillows, Liv was allowing her to hold both of her hands in hers. And Joy was talking, as usual.

But the important thing was that Liv was listening.

There was little light in the room, except for the candle, but it cast a weird glow around Joy, turning her red hair into a flame about her head, like a halo of fire. Mayhap she was an angel, not a time traveler, and she had been sent to save them all.

Nay, nay, nay! He did not want an angel in his bed. Just the opposite.

"I know how real the nightmares can be," Joy was saying. "You're reliving the horrors all over again. In my case, it's my brother Matt's death. I can see in my mind, and in my dreams, how he must have looked when they were torturing him before he died. The terrorists can be vicious.

"The nightmares are going to stop eventually, Liv, that I promise. I also promise that you don't have to speak or leave this room, ever, if that's what you want. But I have to tell you that you would heal better if you could talk about your ordeal.

"The men who did this to you are pigs, but they're at fault, not you. It was not your fault. I repeat, it was not your fault. Be hurt over the physical assaults. Get angry if you want. But don't ever feel you are to blame for something that was beyond your control."

Liv glanced up at Joy with hope in her eyes, and Brandr realized that Liv must have been feeling just that. Without a doubt, the people at Bear's Lair had stared at her, some even with recriminations, especially when her pregnancy had shown.

Liv's mouth moved as if she wanted to say something, and then she smiled.

"You're welcome, sweetie. How about I crawl into bed with you 'til you fall asleep again?"

*What? She is supposed to crawl in bed with me.* Immediately, he chastised himself. Liv's needs superseded his. For now.

He closed the door carefully. Luckily he'd oiled the hinges last month. His heart was beating so fast he could scarce breathe, and his eyes burned.

Tork looked at him. "The wench is helping Liv?"

"It would appear so." He blinked away the tears.

"She is helping you, too, my friend." Tork looped an arm over his shoulders and squeezed.

"Huh? I have no need of help."

But he did. Deep down, he knew that he did. There was such a darkness in his soul. Could she bring some light? And what if she brought light, then went away, and the darkness enveloped him again? Would he be able to withstand the pain?

Such maudlin thoughts!

He decided to do what most Viking men did when troubled. "Let us go find a horn of ale, or five."

# Chapter 11

**Where's the FDA when you need it . . . ?**

Joy had the world's biggest headache and not an aspirin to be found.

She should be happy. Since last night, she'd already made progress with Liv. No speaking yet, but she *was* using hand signals and facial expressions. Speech couldn't be far behind. The first step toward any breakthrough in therapy was personal initiative. A victim had to want to heal before the process could begin.

Niggling at Joy, though, was the most incredible, ludicrous, impossible suspicion. Could she possibly have traveled through time a thousand years?

The logical side of her brain said absolutely not.

But the other side kept niggling at her with oddities that just did not make sense unless they took place in another time.

Brandr contended it was the year nine hundred fifty-five. Ludicrous, of course, but he described in detail things that had happened to his family.

This keep, or fortress, was too authentic to be a reproduction. It was no Williamsburg, of course, but even the smallest reproduction would have a few modern facilities hidden somewhere, like toilets or a vending machine.

Language was an issue, too. Yes, she could understand this bastardized version of English, but there were odd words, like *braies* and *manpart* and *bedsport* and *skald*. And Brandr didn't understand many specific words of hers, either.

And what was it with all this Viking nonsense? Vikings, per se, didn't even exist today.

How about the food? Joy wasn't even sure that boars roamed wild in the last few centuries. When was the last time she'd seen boar burger on the menu? Never.

Then there was Liv, who had clearly been gang-raped. She was not pretending.

There was another thing bothering her. She'd dodged a bullet sex-wise with he-who-oozed-sex-appeal. She was falling for a brutal, morose, stubborn, chauvinist Viking who considered her his slave. It was only a matter of time before they made love; she'd be a fool to deny that.

The possibility of Stockholm syndrome occurred to her, but only for a blip of a second. Despite everything, she had a hard time viewing Brandr as an enemy.

And, darn it, he wasn't even her type, physically. Oh, she liked tall, dark, and handsome well enough, and those deliciously thick lashes over wicked blue eyes were hard to resist, but he wasn't the lean, muscle-toned type she was usually attracted to. No, he was big all over, like a male tank. And he was hairy, unlike the bare-chested, cover model type of men she usually favored. *And look where that got me.* The only explanation she could come up with was that there was a sadness deep in his eyes that pulled at her. That, and his touching affection for his emotionally wounded sister.

*Who am I kidding? Forget all the convoluted explanations. Sexual chemistry sizzles between us, pure and simple.*

Right now Liv was taking a nap, so Joy plaited her hair into one long braid and donned her new garments . . . over

the blasted thrall amulet. Quite nice, actually, in a Viking
sort of way. A jade green undergown of linen, pleated in the
back and on the sleeves, covered by a lighter green, full-
length, open-sided, wool apron. The gown was belted but
not the apron. The only thing was . . . no underwear. What
did women do when it was that time of the month in a sans
paper society? Probably the same thing they did for toilet
paper.

She decided to take a tour of the place, especially since
she'd seen through the arrow slit window that most of the
men were outside engaged in some primitive war games, using swords, broadaxes, maces, spears, and bows and arrows.
Maybe a walk would ease her headache.

Upstairs were three bedrooms, Brandr's, Liv's and an el-
derly relative she had yet to meet, plus three smaller cham-
bers that could only be described as bed closets, with fold-out
pallets. There was also a larger room that would have been a
solar in another time. Five women worked there.

"Hi! Can I come in?" Since no one objected, she walked
in, but they weren't welcoming her either. They probably
didn't know how to treat her, whether she was a thrall or
not.

Of those free women, judging by their hair and attire,
the oldest, wearing an outfit similar to hers but with a white
apron over a red gown and gray hair tucked under a trim cap,
was weaving cloth on a tall loom; it appeared to be a blanket
with varying shades of blue.

"Forget the animal furs. That should keep some Viking
stud warm on a cold winter night," she joked.

The woman just stared at her.

Okay. No sense of humor.

Another used a handle spindle to card rough wool.

"You could get a job at Williamsburg doing that. Probably better pay."

Still no response.

Another was embroidering metallic gold and silver patterns on strips of red silk, which would no doubt edge some
male or female clothing of the upper classes.

"That's really pretty. What do you call that kind of embroidery?"

Reluctantly, the young woman who had a bad case of acne, replied, "Osenstich."

And that was that. Conversationalists they were not. At least not with her.

Of the two thralls, one was cutting rough fabric on a long table to make the hated thrall gowns. The cloth was cut into a T-shape, then a circle made in the center for the neck. After that, it was folded over, and seams were sewn by another thrall from under the wrist, underarm, and down to the hem. Very basic.

The thralls kept their heads down, meekly, but the three free women kept glancing her way.

"Nice meeting you." She exited and closed the door behind her.

Next, she went down the stairs to the massive hall. Here people worked diligently, as well. Some were doing a haphazard job of cleaning off the greasy trestle tables with dirty, wet cloths. At one end, a woodworker was carving a bowl out of a block of wood, using a pole lathe. As he pressed his foot down on a treadle, the wood spun on the lathe at the same time he pressed a chisel in the appropriate space.

"Hi! My name is Joy Nelson."

The man stared at her for a long second, "Are you a thrall?"

Joy hesitated. She could say no and get the cold treatment again, in reverse, but that was no way to case enemy territory. "Brandr says I am. I say I'm not."

He nodded, "My name is Osmund. I was taken on a Viking raid in Wessex."

"What are you doing with all of those?" There were blocks of wood all around him.

"Bowls, cups, plates. When the carpentry shed is rebuilt, I will make furniture, as well. Not enough room to do it in here, I daresay. The only one of the outbuildings restored so far is the smithy's. His work cannot be done indoors, and there is more of a necessity for swords and knives and tools."

Whoa! Finally someone who can put more than two words together.

"Do you have family?"

"I have a wife."

"And she was left behind? I am so sorry!"

"She was taken, too." Osmund motioned toward Tork's bimbo who was shoveling ashes out of one of the fireplaces at a pace so slow it would take her a full day to fill a wooden bucket. But then, Ebba probably wouldn't be reprimanded if her primary duty were on her back in some vile Viking's bed.

"You must be so angry." She patted his hand.

"'Tis the way of the world. She spreads her thighs willingly ta save us both."

"What do you mean?"

"The heathens woulda lopped off me head if Ebba had not tol' them of me carpentry skills."

"Don't you resent them using her like this? Or your bondage, for that matter?"

"What good would that do? And our lot is not so bad. In five years, if I do good work, I have been promised freedom. Then I can earn enough coin ta buy back Ebba's."

"That's horrible!"

"Nay, it is not. I was a bondservant to an English thane afore. My treatment there was no better than this, and I had ten years ta go."

Joy barely paid attention to the nearby man carving combs and knife handles out of deer antlers, as she walked away, so upset was she by the Viking class system, if that's what it was.

She wandered through a corridor and into a huge kitchen. The dozen or so people in there, free servants as well as thralls, stopped talking when she entered. She weighed her options, then lied, "I'm a thrall, sort of. A free thrall."

Her words were met with a bunch of frowns, and then they resumed their work, ignoring her. Some of them also resumed talking amongst themselves. Everyday things: menus for the day, chores to be done, gossip, and men.

But Joy was more interested in her amazing surroundings, for the moment. The cooking fireplace was big enough for five full-grown men to stand in it, side by side, two deep. Some animal, possibly a cow . . . no, a deer . . . was being roasted on a spit, being turned by a little boy, no more than eight, who picked his nose with boredom at the tedious job. An enormous cauldron bubbled with some kind of stew.

Nearby, a barrel of water was filled almost to overflowing with live eels, one of which had already met its fate and was being skinned by yet another servant. For the evening meal, no doubt. Yeech! Several baskets held fresh and salted fishes.

Another small boy, possibly twin to the one at the spit, schlepped two buckets of milk into the kitchen. One he handed to an old man working a butter churn, and the other he took down some steps, which she presumed led to a cold cellar.

A girl of about twelve was grinding grain into flour with a stone quern, a primitive device that involved two round stones, one on top of the other, with a hole on top through which the grain was poured. When a handle was turned, the grain was squashed into flour.

With dull efficiency, a free woman in drab clothing—a servant, she guessed—was kneading bread dough, which she rolled out into large circles with holes in the middle. When baked in the hearthside stone ovens, the flat wheels were slipped onto a tall pole for storage. It was unleavened bread, except that Joy knew from a cooking class she once took that there was a small amount of yeast in fresh-ground grains. The girl was a one-woman mass production machine. Even as Joy stood there, twelve breads were taken out of the oven and stacked on the pole and twelve more put in the oven.

"That must take forever," she remarked.

The girl shrugged and pointed to a huge bowl where she was dumping the flour, what amounted to about what would fill the ten-pound bags Joy had seen in supermarkets. "That took me 'bout an hour."

"How can you tell time?"

The girl waved a floury hand toward a tall, thick candle sitting on a wall shelf. It had black lines marked at even intervals on the sides. "That be a timekeeping candle."

Amazing what humans could accomplish without all their electric gadgets, she thought.

"I could do better, but me arms get sore," the girl added.

"Maybe I could help you later."

The girl looked appalled, as if Joy was trying to take her job away from her.

An old lady with dried apple skin and gnarled hands was defeathering several headless chickens, which still dripped blood onto the hard-packed dirt floor. And bony old chickens they were, too. No force-fed, fatty poultry here, but the meat would probably be tough as old leather. The old lady dipped the birds into scalding water to aid the removal of the feathers, all of which were being dropped into a burlap type sack for some future use. Pillow, maybe? Awaiting the defeathering process were also a bunch of plump pigeons and a dead duck.

In another corner a litter of puppies lay in a pile of straw, which hadn't been changed in days, by the smell of it.

Peering through an open door, Joy could see a large pantry or storage room with numerous shelves where two men continued to unpack the boxes of supplies that had been brought on the two longships from Hedeby. Barrels and sacks of flour and grains. Dozens of eggs. No sugar, but honey still in the combs. And vegetables, like turnips, peas, leeks, onions, beans, carrots, cabbages, and mushrooms. Fruits and berries, some still fresh but most dried. Various kinds of nuts. And vats and vats of ale and mead, and smaller amounts of wine.

Considering how many people had to be fed two or three times a day here, she supposed all these people and all these food supplies were a necessity.

Going back to the huge butcher block–style table in the center of the kitchen, she approached the woman cutting up the eel and placing it in a clear amber liquid that smelled like vinegar with slices of onion floating on top. To Joy's disgust, she noticed that there was a rim of old grime under the woman's broken fingernails, and the table was so dirty it must not have been cleaned in weeks, if ever. Even the worst restaurants knew that kitchens needed to be "broken down" each evening and all work surfaces scrubbed and disinfected. This was bacteria heaven. "Are you the head cook?"

"Huh?" said eel lady. "Nay. Kelda be the cook here since the master were a bratling."

Since the bratling she referred to was probably Brandr, and he must be in his early thirties, she figured the cook's work history spanned more than three decades. "Where is she?"

"Kelda? Ah, she has a bad case of the roiling bowels t'day. Ta the privy she went."

"Fer the fifth time since morn," the bread maker added. The two women grinned at each other. Obviously, Kelda was not a favorite of theirs.

"She be breaking wind like a cow in clover," the boy at the rotisserie added with a giggle.

*TMI,* she told herself.

"Beans will do it ever' time," opined the old lady plucking feathers. "I tol' her ta take the strings off the beans. That removes the farts. Hee, hee, hee." She cackled at her own words.

Everyone laughed, and the bread lady said, "Oh, Gran Olssen, you be sayin' that ferever. Ya know 'tis not true."

"What is not true?" a short, heavyset woman asked, bustling into the kitchen from outdoors. Before anyone could answer, assuming they would answer, the woman looked at Joy and demanded, "Who are ye, and what are ye doin' in my kitchen?"

If there was any doubt that the woman stomping into the room was Kelda, it was dispensed when she let loose a loud fart and didn't even break stride. Although there was stifled humor throughout the room, no one dared laugh outright. Except Joy, who couldn't help herself.

"Sorry," she said to the unamused woman, whose hands were placed firmly on her wide hips. "I'm Joy Nelson."

Eying her up and down, taking in her attire, the cook asked rudely, "Be ya thrall or lady?"

"Both."

"Whaaat?"

"I don't believe in slavery."

All the jaws in the room dropped.

"Well, ain't that jist wonderful? Ye come here ta free all the thralls?" the cook ridiculed her. "Blessed Frigg! Wait 'til Master Igorsson hears 'bout this."

"I never said . . ." Joy stopped, watching with incredulity as the cook took one of the plucked chickens over to the butcher block table and slit it from neck to bottom on the underside, then began pulling out the guts, some of which she dropped into a bucket sitting next to the table and the rest going onto a separate pile, which included the liver, gizzard, and heart. One of the puppies scampered over and grabbed a string of guts from the bucket before the cook could manage to kick it away. The puppy ran off with the slimy gore to share with his yipping brothers and sisters.

She noticed a number of things in succession. The cook had not washed her hands after coming back from the privy and was now handling food . . . chicken of all things, which everyone knew was a breeding house for germs. Plus, she was working on a table that needed a scouring with a wire brush and bleach.

"Stop! You can't do that," Joy said, approaching the table. "You need to go wash your hands with soap and water. Everyone should . . . before handling food, but definitely after leaving the bathroom . . . I mean, privy. And look," she said, taking another knife in hand and scraping it across the top of the table. At least an inch of caked-on grime came away, revealing a whitened board beneath. "This is disgusting. Bacteria heaven."

The cook's mouth worked like a puffer fish. "Back-tear-ya? I will give ya back-tear-ya, like me tearin' up yer back with me cleaver." She raised the huge knife up high and came after Joy with a menacing snarl.

Everyone in the kitchen stopped what they were doing and stepped back to leave room for the combatants.

This was not the kind of combat Joy envisioned when she began WEALS training. But she had the good sense to circle around the other side of the table, grabbing her favorite weapon, a poker, along the way. "I said bacteria . . . tiny bugs. Thousands of them. You know, germs."

"Ger-mans? Now yer sayin' I got Ger-man bugs. Are ye barmy? Or mebbe yer tryin' ta take me job."

"Me? A cook? No way! Really. I'm sure you're the best cook in the world." *Okay, that's a stretch.* "But it's true what I said about bacteria. The little buggers are all over the place, contaminating the food, causing illness. They're bred by lack of proper cleaning." *Oops, I didn't mean to go that far.*

"I am gonna kill ya."

"Now, no need for violence. Let's start over. My name is Joy Nelson."

"When I am done with ya, they will be callin' ya Boy, not Joy, 'cause I'm gonna cut off yer tongue and stick it up yer sheath. Folks will come from far and wide ta view the talkin' cock."

"That kind of crudity is uncalled for."

Every time Kelda moved, Joy moved in the opposite direction, the table separating them. Joy considered a rush for the door leading into the hall and up the stairs, but she didn't think she'd be able to make it, even with Kelda's much shorter legs coming after her.

Paying no heed to Joy's plea for nonviolence, Kelda said, "Ya ain't heard crude yet, girlie. I am gonna slit yer gullet from yer bloody mouth ta yer nether parts. Then I am gonna toss yer innards in the stewpot."

"Yeech! Well, it won't be any worse than the crap you're putting in there now."

Kelda's eyes about bulged out. Then she made a rush for her, slipped in the slime on the dirt floor, and went flailing down on her big butt.

Joy reached down to pick up the cleaver and put it out of harm's way when the outside door crashed open, and Brandr, in battle gear covered with a dusting of snow, rushed in, taking in a scene that must have appeared amazing to him, especially since she held a poker in one hand and a cleaver in the other and was standing over the cook, who was moaning, "Oh, me arse! Me sore arse!"

"What in bloody hell is going on in here? We could hear the screaming all the way to the exercise fields." Other men were crowding the doorway behind him, most of them grinning.

Joy stood with as much dignity as she could, considering her now-filthy apron, her hair half in and half out of its braid, and the "weapons" in her hands.

"Kelda and I were just having a little friendly chat." *If you believe that, I have a fjord to sell you in Brooklyn.*

Brandr, arms folded over his chest, arched a brow at her, then turned to the old lady still plucking the dead birds. "Gran Olssen?"

"The wench says there be thousands of bugs all over the kitchen."

Turning back to Joy, Brandr remarked. "I do not see any bugs."

"That's not exactly what I said."

"Gran Olssen does not lie."

The old lady, who ought to be in a senior citizen facility or upstairs knitting, not plucking chickens, flashed her a toothless grin.

"They're too small to see with the naked eye, but, believe me, they're there. Especially when you consider that Kelda just came back from the privy and didn't wash her hands before touching raw food."

Brandr's gaze shot from Kelda's hands, which were indeed dirty, to the cooking pot, then back again.

From her prone position, Kelda said, "I am going to kill the red-haired bitch and feed her heart ta the wolves. She dares ta tell me what ta do in my kitchen."

Brandr's dark blue eyes scanned the room, then went wide, as if he seemed to notice the lack of cleanliness for the first time.

Joy jumped on what was probably her only window of opportunity. "I bet Kelda's not the only one with a bowel problem. Forget the cabbage. It's probably salmonella or gastroenteritis."

Then, proving Joy's point, the cook did what she did so well. She farted. Again. Really loud.

# Chapter 12

**Who cut whom the deepest . . . ?**

Brandr did not know whether he wanted to roar with outrage or with laughter.

Dragging her into the storage room, the closest private place, he motioned for the maid working there to leave. Then he kicked the door shut behind him.

"What in the name of all the gods were you doing in the kitchen?"

"Liv is napping, and you said I could go anywhere indoors."

"I did not give you permission to create a disturbance. My people are already troubled by my favored treatment of you." He flicked a finger to indicate her garments, which, he had to admit, looked very fine on her. The green of the apron brought out the green of her eyes. And even with the apron, he could see how the belt accentuated her waist and outlined her breasts. Her fiery hair was coming loose from its braid, giving the appearance of bed-mussed activity. *I wish!*

He was wagging his forefinger at her. For each step forward he made, she took one back, 'til she landed against a table along one wall, which was used for sorting goods.

"Don't threaten me."

"How am I threatening you? With a finger?"

"It's the tone of your voice."

He rolled his eyes. "You are presumably a female warrior, and you fear an angry voice?"

"I didn't say that. I just said—"

"What *are* you afraid of?" He lifted her by the waist to set her on the table, then stepped between her legs. Before she could object, he put his hands under her rump and yanked her forward. He closed his eyes for a second as his legs went weak as dragon piss. Stars danced behind his eyelids at the sheer, tortuous pleasure of his cock resting against her cleft.

He would have been embarrassed. In truth, he feared he might disgrace himself, so rapid was his rise to raging enthusiasm. But then he opened his eyes and saw that she was equally affected. Her soft whimper was an aphrodisiac to his already heightened senses.

He kissed the inside of her elbow, then the inside of her wrist, then her palm.

She sighed.

He took that as a good sign. "Well?" he asked.

"I forget the question."

He laughed.

"I love your laugh."

He smiled

"And your smile. It brings out your big dimples."

"Dimples, dimples, dimples. I care not a jot about dimples. I would much rather you admire my big—"

She put a hand over his mouth to prevent what would have probably been a crude word.

"We fit well together, wench," he rasped out.

"I don't know what you mean," she said, even as she wriggled her arse forward for a better fit.

They both moaned together. Then they both grinned at each other.

"Seriously, Brandr, I need to talk to you about the kitchen and the way—"

"Kiss me."

"What?"

"Kiss me like you did that other time. With your mouth open. And perchance you could tongue-tickle my teeth."

"Why?"

"Because I say so."

"I shouldn't," she said, even as she began to trace the seam of his lips with the tip of her tongue, wetting his, then her own lips. After that, she pressed moistness to moistness and moved her mouth back and forth 'til she got the fit she wanted. "Like this?" she teased against his parted lips.

He nipped her bottom lip with his teeth. "More."

She put both hands on his head to hold him in place. *As if I am going anywhere!* Then she kissed him and kissed him, darting her tongue in and out, testing the waters, so to speak, sending ripples of desire coursing through his blood.

Enough! He took over the kiss, forcing her mouth wide, plunging his tongue deep, then slowly abrading out. Advance, retreat, advance, retreat . . . Really, when he thought about it—and, nay, he was not thinking much now—kissing was a form of war exercise. Who would have thought a mere woman could teach him, the lord of swordplay, aught about battle moves?

With all his musing, he was scarce aware that her hips were undulating against him in a matching rhythm. Yea, she could teach him much, and he was a fast learner.

Even as they kissed, he undid the brooches holding her apron shoulder straps together, and was already unlacing her gunna.

"Wha . . . what are you doing?" she asked, the lust-hazy green pools of her eyes blinking at him.

"A good soldier needs to see what he is doing," he replied, and tugged the gown down 'til it trapped her arms at her elbows. He stared at her exposed breasts. Pale rose circles in the center with darker rose nipples. "I have wanted to do this for so long." Without any preliminary caresses, he took one breast, nipple and areola together, into his mouth and began to suckle hard.

She jerked with surprise, muttering, "This is so not a good

idea," but then she wrapped her legs around his hips, pressing herself tighter against him. Her immobile hands tightly grasped the table under her, but she thrust her breasts forward in invitation. By the time he moved to the other breast, licking, then sucking, she was keening out the start of what promised to be a fierce peaking. He reclaimed her lips then, taking her cries into his open mouth.

But things were happening too fast . . . and in the wrong place.

Dragging his lips away from hers, he whispered in her ear, "Slow down, dearling. The voyage is sweeter when the longboat takes the slower route to harbor."

She laughed shakily. "And sometimes fast and furious makes a better ride."

He nipped her earlobe for her sauciness, but then he paused. "What is that?"

"What?" She tried to turn her head, but he would not let her.

Pushing strands of loosened hair off her face, he examined the skin behind her ear. "A buzzing noise. Is it possible a bee got in your ear? But, nay, there are no bees this far north this time of year."

"Oh, my God! It's my mike." She moved back slightly from him, giving her enough room to pull her gown back up. Quickly, she traced the area he had been examining with her forefinger, then began to tap in a strange rhythm. Like a code.

"It is not a bee?"

She shook her head, dazed, and he was not fool enough to think the daze was left over from their almost-lovemaking. "Before I left, I had a mike implanted behind my ear so that I could communicate with my team, especially in case of an emergency."

"Being sold into thralldom . . . would that be considered an emergency?"

She nodded.

"Are you saying there is a device under your skin which will allow your fellow fighters to locate you?"

She nodded again.

"Impossible!"

The buzzing resumed.

"They want my coordinates so that rescuers can be deployed. Normally, we can communicate by voice with this mike. It's highly sophisticated, but the voice component isn't working, just the Morse code section."

"I do not understand what you say by half." He stepped back and closed her knees. "But I am not such a dullard that I do not recognize danger. After all the special treatment you have received at my hands, you would lead the enemy to my gates?"

"They're not the enemy."

"Will they carry weapons?"

"Of course."

"Enemies, then," he declared, and without giving her warning, he forced her to lie facedown on the table. With one hand pressing her face immobile, he used the other to pull out a knife from his belt sheath, ignoring her shrieks of outrage and pleas to wait and let her explain. The time for talking was over, as far as he was concerned. Without hesitation, he slit the skin behind her ear and pulled out a little metal circle the size of a pea.

Stepping away, he let her rise to a sitting position and place a hand behind her ear to stanch the flow of blood. Tears welled in her eyes as she gazed at the piece of metal sitting in the palm of his hand. "You cut me."

"You betrayed me."

"I did not, you big baboon."

He looked down at the tiny bit of metal, then at her.

"Give it to me."

"Nay! I know not whether this . . . this thing can actually work, but that does not really matter. What matters is that you have shown where your loyalties lie. I protect those under my shield, and you are a danger to me and mine, *thrall.*"

With those words, he dropped the metal on the floor and stomped on it 'til it was flat, and the buzzing stopped.

"It is done," he said with icy flatness in his voice. "We are done."


## Who wants to be Julia Child today . . . ?

It was a scene out of any man's worst nightmare.

When Brandr reentered the kitchen, he almost turned on his heel and went back to his other nightmare. Instead, he girded his loins and went forth.

Kelda was lying facedown on the kitchen table, gunna thrown up to her shoulders, and her big bare arse exposed. A big, bare arse that was turning black and blue. It was not a pretty sight. Examining said arse was Folki, the closest they had to a healer at Bear's Lair. Folki, over seventy years if he was a day, had not been this close to a female arse in many a year, and was no doubt getting great pleasure from his prodding and poking.

Once Kelda saw Brandr, she began to wail. "Oh, Master, I hurt so bad. I must take to me pallet, mayhap with a cup or two of ale fer the pain. But who will do the cookin'?"

"Do not be worrying about that, Kelda. I will find someone to take your place." At worry on her old face, he added, "Just 'til you are better."

He watched grimly as Folki and one of the housecarls, both of them grinning, helped her to her feet and out into the hall where her bed closet was located. She would be deeply into the alehead afore noon.

Once they were gone, he surveyed the kitchen. "What a mess!" Then he looked at the bloody pieces of chicken still on the table and at the cauldron that Kelda had filled using her unwashed hands. The boiling would probably kill any "bugs" she might have transmitted, as it would any bug he had ever seen. But he, having no taste for insects, dead or alive, would not bepartaking of it tonight.

Something needed to be done to correct this mess. He glanced around the kitchen at all the expectant faces. "Who wants to be the cook?"

"Not me, not me, not me," one and all said.

"Where is Arnora?" he asked. Arnora was the mother of his oldest brother Vidar, who had died during the Sigurdsson assault. Although having seen more than fifty winters, she handled household matters at Bear's Lair. Poorly, but who was he to complain?

When Arnora arrived—reluctantly, he noted—he asked, "Can you take over the cooking duties for a while?"

"I heard what the thrall said about the kitchen . . . *and* about the way I keep the great hall so unclean. Let her do it." With that, Arnora swanned out.

Grunting his disgust, he turned to the closed door of the storage room. Could his life get any worse than this?

**It was an offer she couldn't refuse . . .**

Joy tried to hide it from him, but he could see that she had been crying when he stomped back into the storage room in the same angry manner in which he had left.

"Are you hurt?" he asked gruffly. "Not that you don't deserve it."

"Thanks a bunch for your sympathy. I'm hurt, all right, but most of the pain isn't physical."

Huh? That sounded like the usual woman trap of words, and he wasn't about to be caught that way. "What are you blubbering about, thrall? My life is the one going down the privy."

"One bright light in my dismal day."

"Sarcasm ill-suits you, wench, and does not to help your thrall status."

"Thrall, thrall, thrall! We're back to that nonsense, are we?"

"We never left."

"Then you're a liar, because . . ."

"You dare . . . you *dare* to give insult when I hold your life in my hands!"

"You hold more than my life in your hands, if you only knew."

"What?"

"Never mind."

"First you will apologize to Kelda. She has taken to her bed, so great is her pain."

"Apologize to that lazy slug? Hah! She was just looking for an excuse to get out of work."

"Kelda has worked for me for many a year. She has proven her trustworthiness. Unlike some—"

"What a pity! I could mark those years in the grime built up on your tables, like rings on a tree."

*It is not really that bad. Is it?* "You will apologize."

"Will you have her apologize to me, too? After all, she threatened to cut out my tongue and stick it in my vagina and make me a boy."

At first Brandr was startled. *Can she possibly mean . . . ?* He put a hand over his mouth so that she could not see his grin.

But she saw. "It's not funny. I don't want to be the first sex change operation in history performed without an anesthetic. In fact, I'm happy with my present gender, thank you very much."

"Sex change? What is that? Oh, please! Do not tell me that people change their sexes where you come from."

"It's called transgender surgery."

*The woman is a bloody font of wisdom on every subject in the world! She has a word for everything!* Even though she had to be jesting, he would have liked to ask her more. Later. For now, he had more important issues to resolve. "You and Kelda will both apologize."

"Only if she goes first."

He rolled his eyes. *'Tis like talking to a stone wall.*

"I'm going to need stitches for this cut."

"Let me see." He stepped forward, and even though she flinched at his closeness, she let him look.

"You smell."

"Of course, I am aromatic. I have been sweating like a warhorse."

"In that freezing cold?"

He shrugged. *Next she will say that her soldiers only*

*work on sunny days.* "I must needs work myself and my men beyond their limits, lest we be unprepared next time there is an attack."

"You expect another attack? I thought the Sigurdssons were wiped out."

"There is always another enemy." He looked her in the eye pointedly.

"Me?" she squawked. "If you'd let me explain—"

He put up a halting hand. "The time for words is long gone." He shoved her face to the side, roughly, and lifted her hair. "The cut is not so bad, but it is deep. Yea, a few stitches would not go amiss. I will call for one of the seamstresses."

"Oh, no! You're the one who did it. You're the one who will sew it up."

"My hands are too big."

"Lots of surgeons have big hands."

"You would trust me with a knife near you again?"

"Yes, I trust you."

"Why do you not say that about other things?" *Like swiving.*

"Dream on, big boy. It's not going to happen now."

"*It* will happen if I want it to." *And I do.*

"You lost your big chance when you attacked me with a knife."

"I did not attack you. I merely removed your . . . weaponry."

It was her turn to roll her eyes.

A short time later she was lying belly down on the table again, and Brandr was sewing up the wound, cursing under his breath, just as he had been cursing aloud at her demand that he wash his hands and the thread, and purify the needle over a candle flame.

"Have I told you that you have new duties?" he asked as casually as he was able.

"What duties?" Her body went rigid with apprehension, as it well should.

"You will be the new cook."

"What?" She jerked, causing his hands to falter and the

needle to jab her hard. Once she calmed down and he explained that she must take over until the cook was back on her feet, she asked, "What about Liv? I thought helping her was my job."

"You will do both." He finished stitching her cut and smacked her on the arse to indicate he was done.

"Brute!" she said, rubbing her bottom as she sat upright. "How do you figure I can do both?"

"I do not know. Bring her down to the kitchen with you. Work without sleep. Just do as I say."

Instead of being affronted at that idea, Joy tapped her fingertips on the tabletop, deep in thought. "It would do Liv good to be among other people, friendly people, even if she doesn't talk. Okay."

"O-kay?"

"That means yes. I'll do it."

"Gods help me," Brandr muttered as he left the storage room and made for the outdoors once again. In the mood he was in, he would soon be knocking a few Viking heads together. Hopefully, someone would knock his, too.

# Chapter 13

**She'd be a freakin' Emeril or die trying . . .**

It was a daunting task, and Joy didn't know if she'd be able to pull it off, but for some reason she wanted to prove herself to Brandr.

Thus, Joy started by convincing Liv to come down to the kitchen with her, promising that all she would have to do was sit in a corner and watch. As a further enhancement, she promised Liv that she could take one of the puppies for her own pet, give it a name, even bring it up to her own bedroom if she would be responsible for its care, including cleaning up its messes. Liv picked the smallest of the litter, a skinny black dog with oversized white paws, which probably indicated it would eventually grow to the size of a small horse. She called it Fenrir after the son of the jester god Loki and a giantess named Angrbode.

Luckily, after their initial surprise, the kitchen staff ignored her as she played with her newfound pet. But then the old lady, Gran Olssen, crooked her fingers at Liv, inviting her to come sit by her. Liv's eyes lit up at the sight of Gran Olssen. Apparently it was someone she had known in the pre-Sigurdsson days.

Lining everyone up, Joy examined their hands. "Okay, first thing we're going to do is scrub our hands with soap and water. Those with long fingernails will trim them. Those with dirt under their fingernails will scrape it out. In the future, at all times, there will be clean water, soap, and drying cloths over on that bench. Anyone going to the privy must wash their hands afterward. Is that clear?"

"Every time?" the bread-making girl, who identified herself as Helgi, asked.

"Every time. Also, after handling meat, especially poultry. Now, first things first: we're going to clean the cauldron and the kitchen table. Scrubbing won't work on the table at this point, so I'll need boiling water poured on it and then I'll scrape a couple inches off the top with a sharp knife."

Everyone was staring at her as if she was crazy.

To Brokk and Gandolf, the twin boys, she said, "Take that pot outside and dump the contents."

"Nay!" Gran Olssen exclaimed. "Ye cannot waste good food." At the expression on Joy's face, she quickly added, "We have been eating Kelda's broth for years. It will not kill us just this once more."

"Okay, everyone gets a bowl of slop . . . uh, soup for an early lunch. In fact, two or three, if you want. Tell the others, too."

Before she knew it, there were several dozen servants and a few of the soldiers who'd wandered in slurping up Kelda's slop. Meanwhile, she used a sharp knife to begin working on the table.

When the cauldron was empty and scraped clean, thanks to a rasp she borrowed from Osmund, she started the world's biggest pot of chicken noodle soup. With five chickens bubbling away and carrots, celery, and onions chopped, by Liv, no less—her puppy asleep at her feet—and ready to be added to the broth once the birds were cooked thoroughly and deboned, she asked Helgi, who had finished baking the day's bread, if she knew how to make noodles. While Helgi followed her grandmother's simple recipe of flour, eggs, and water, Joy told them all how, where she came from, chicken

soup was considered the be-all and end-all cure for colds
and other ailments. They just gawked at her. The dough was
soon rolled out and drying, to be cut into thin strips.

There were no potatoes, but she managed to commandeer
Ebba, Osmund's wife, when she made the mistake of wander-
ing into the kitchen, to begin peeling a huge pile of turnips,
some of which she would cut into cubes and toss into the soup
for a potato substitute, but most of which she intended to boil,
then mash with butter. That should go well with the venison,
which was already done and waiting to be sliced.

Gran Olssen was sticking a dozen defeathered and degut-
ted fat pigeons onto the now-empty spit. How she'd managed
to pluck and gut those little guys was amazing to Joy. The
dead duck, stuffed with an odd combination of chestnuts and
dried berries, was wrapped in wet leaves and put into the
hot coals.

It would be a bare-bones meal tonight in terms of variety, but Joy was aiming for quality, not quantity. If she
had time, she was going to try to make a bunch of apple
dumplings, her grandmother's recipe again, although she
would have to substitute honey for sugar. Covered with
fresh cream, the substitution shouldn't matter.

Joy was working so hard that at first she didn't notice the
silence around her. She did a double take at the tall, impos-
ing woman standing in the doorway. Her blonde hair, liber-
ally mixed with gray, was braided tightly and pinned into a
coronet atop her head. Her attire was the usual open-sided
apron, except it had gold trim on the edges, over a robe of
finest blue wool. Gold earrings dangled from chains looped
over both ears, and another chain ran from one museum-
quality shoulder brooch to the other, from one of which hung
a ring of keys. She must be the chatelaine, or whatever they
called it back then.

The woman's keen, grayish blue eyes took in Liv's presence downstairs with a nod, and then she noted the changes
already wrought in the kitchen. Her nose sniffed at the delicious aromas that wafted about, both the chicken soup and
apple dumplings now in the oven.

"Come," she said, motioning for Joy.

Joy looked behind her to see if she meant someone else, but no, she meant her, all right. She gave Ebba directions for taking the apple dumplings out when they were brown and told Liv to stay put 'til she got back. Then she followed the stately woman down a corridor she hadn't seen before 'til they got to a locked door. Taking off one of the keys, the woman indicated that Joy should go in first.

*Uh-oh! Don't tell me they're going to put me in a dungeon, after all.* But no, it wasn't a dungeon. It was another storage room, this time with shelf after shelf piled with fabrics and garments and bedding, not to mention candles, fine cutlery, silver goblets, wine, soaps. Plus pungent spices; among those she could recognize were dill, ginger, cinnamon, mustard, nutmeg, cloves, coriander, and sage, along with salt and pepper.

"I am Arnora Ingersson, his father's first wife, mother of Vidar, who should have inherited . . ." She stopped herself and bit her bottom lip to prevent herself from crying.

Joy put a hand on the woman's arm, although it probably wasn't welcome. "I have lost family, too. I know how it is."

"You are helping Liv, I hear. And you have put the kitchen to rights, as I should have done these many months. 'Tis too much for me, I must admit. My grief is too great."

"Maybe I could help you, too."

Arnora smiled at her indulgently. "Mayhap. Know this, the house, and, yea, the kitchen, were not always in such a state. The attack changed all of us, even Kelda. You must bear with her."

Now, that was going to take some patience.

"Here," she said, beginning to pull garments off the shelves and handing them to her until they were piled up to her chin. "You have taken one step. I will take the next. The thralls and servants alike must bathe and change their garments. I daresay some have not done so in a year or more. My fault."

"Where will they bathe?"

"You did not know? There is a bathing house on the far side of the bailey, a bow shot distance from the keep steps."

Arnora was gathering leather boots, slippers, and belts and tossing them into an enormous burlap type bag. "Once they have changed, send all the dirty clothing to the wash-house. We will have the north's biggest laundry day on the morrow." She smiled sadly at Joy.

"You were here when the assault took place?"

Arnora closed her eyes for a moment. "Yea, I was. Hid in the treasure room over the garderobe, I did, along with a few others. I will ne'er forget the screams. If I were a man, I would have gone berserk, too." *Like Brandr* was left unsaid.

"Man's inhumanity to man . . . it never changes."

"Well said!"

Joy barreled on, figuring she had nothing to lose by asking what she really wanted to know. "But I haven't seen evidence of Brandr being insanely violent . . . going berserk. Oh, he's grim a lot of the time, but that's not quite the same."

"You have been here a short time. Believe you me, it is there beneath the surface. And the least thing can set it off. A mention of the Sigurdssons. A vision he has when he is in the alehead. Punishment of a thrall for some betrayal of his loyal-ties. I saw him once almost flay the skin off a man because he dared question the continuing feud with the Sigurdssons."

*Flay? Like a whip?* Joy shivered with distaste, and, yes, apprehension. Hadn't he accused her of disloyalty?

"Ah, well, that is the way of life. And soon Brandr will take a wife. Mayhap he will be better then."

Joy gasped. "He's engaged to someone?"

"Not yet, but he knows his duty. This keep needs a mis-tress. Bear's Lair needs heirs . . . legitimate heirs."

Joy's face flamed.

"I would not have you hurt."

"We don't have that kind of relationship."

Arnora just smiled. "There is no harm in being a concubine."

"There is to me. Didn't you mind your husband having those other wives and mistresses?"

"Sharing is a good thing. Besides, we were much like sisters sharing the same meal."

"That remark doesn't even pass the giggle test."

Arnora blinked her surprise at Joy's words, then laughed. "You have the right of it. We were as jealous as cats fighting over one randy mouse. Still, Igor was faithful to me for more than three years when we were first wed."

"Men are as faithful as their options."

"Mayhap. For a certainty, he forgot me for a time on first seeing Fiona, an Irish princess, or so she claimed. But then Fiona learned good and well how I felt when Igor took a third wife and two concubines."

"Men!" Joy looked at Arnora with sympathy.

"Do not pity me. It is our way."

"Bull! By accepting this practice, you women enable men to wave their genitals like flypaper."

Arnora put a hand over her mouth to stifle a laugh. "Women have no power to change things."

"That's where you're wrong. Women have way more power than they realize." She went on to explain exactly what women could do.

After a very interested Arnora left the room with her, locking it behind them, Joy began to wonder if she'd said too much. That's all she would need to get even deeper on Brandr's bad side. A women's sex strike!

But Joy had bigger problems than that.

The longer she was at Bear's Lair, the more she was convinced this was no reenactment village. There were too many people playing roles that were downright authentic. Still, she couldn't believe that she'd traveled back in time.

Another thing: Brandr was angry because she'd tried to communicate with her team. If by some chance they were able to find her, they would indeed come in, guns blazing. In other words, an enemy, just like he'd said. Which made her his enemy.

She was so confused.

Pleased to see clean clothing laid out for them, servants, thralls, and free men and women alike, including the soldiers, went to the bathhouse in shifts that evening before dinner. They didn't want to put them on dirty bodies.

The meal was ready to be served shortly, and Joy was in the great hall, trying to scrub years of grease and dirt off the high table. It would take weeks to clean all the trestle tables, but she wanted to make a start. Unfortunately, she'd only managed to get about two feet done in the past hour, and she was bone tired.

Standing, she arched her aching back to get out the kinks. With a wide yawn, she looked to the right. Then looked again.

Brandr was standing there, hands on hips, his unhappy face on again.

What else was new?

"What in bloody hell are you doing?"

"That seems to be your favorite expression. By the way, that vein is standing out on your forehead again."

"I asked you a question. What are you doing?"

"Trying to clean the table, but it's going to take a looong time." She drew his attention to the section she'd scraped down to the raw wood.

"A good and much-needed chore, but why are *you* doing it? I told you to cook, not become a menial servant. Next you will be down on your knees scrubbing the garderobe."

"Actually—"

"Do not dare!"

"I did as much in the kitchen as I could, and I offered to help Arnora here. We were working side by side, but when she got a splinter under her fingernail, I told her to go supervise the clothing allocations."

"Arnora was scrubbing tables?"

"Yes. Why not?"

He rubbed the back of his neck, wearily, as if she was hopeless.

She tossed the rasp and cleaning rag into the half-filled wooden bucket of dirty water. "Well, I'll quit here for now. Time to serve the meal."

"You are not going to serve the meal."

"Why not?"

"Because you are falling over with exhaustion."

"A thrall's work is never done."

"That is not the kind of thrall you are."

"Oh? What kind am I?" She immediately regretted her loose tongue when she saw the evil grin on his face. "Never mind. By the way, I saved some of Kelda's slop . . . I mean, stew . . . for you to eat, since you are such a defender of her good work. Everyone else will get my grandmother's chicken soup."

"I swear, your tongue has a mind of its own. Blather, blather, blather."

"Yeah, well . . . yikes! What are you doing?"

He picked her up and tossed her over his shoulder, uncaring that the bucket was knocked over, saturating the rushes on the floor. Which was another thing to be done . . . sweeping up the dirty rushes. Really, what brainiac decided straw on the floor would be a good thing? But she digressed. With long strides, Brandr was moving down the hall toward the double outside doors where he grabbed a wall torch.

"This is getting to be a habit. I am not a sack of flour."

"I know that well and good. A sack of flour knows when to shut its teeth."

"That doesn't make sense at all. A sack doesn't . . . hey!" He'd placed his big hand on her rump with the fingers between her legs. "I don't appreciate your pawing me."

"I rather like it, myself." They appeared to be passing some men who'd been talking but stopped as they approached. She could only see as far as the torch's light and then only upside down.

"Greetings, Arnis. Good swordplay today.

"Erland, didst ask the smithy to fix that broken mace?

"Halldar, you are becoming quite the bowman.

"Oh, Tork, wouldst pour a cup of mead . . . or two? I will join you shortly."

"Uh, where are you going?" someone asked.

"Off to drown a wench."

**Steam heat, baby . . .**

Finally, Brandr arrived at the bathing house.

The wench sighed with pleasure at the change in temperature, from outside freezing cold to deliciously warm.

He inserted the torch in a wall bracket, joining several others along with some fat candles in soapstone holders. Setting her on her feet, he took her by the shoulders when she swayed with a mixture of exhaustion and dizziness. "Leave us," he ordered two nude men who were soaking in the small pool covered with a steamy haze. Without hesitation, they stood, dried off, dressed in clean garments, and left with their dirty clothes in hand.

Meanwhile, he undid the brooches that held her apron together, loosened the belt of her gunna, and lifted it over her head. She wore no undergarments.

"I can do it myself," she said but was too tired to physically protest.

Kneeling, he took off her half boots and stared up at her magnificent body. He must have seen finer, but in this moment he could not recall a one. Her eyes were closed, so he gave himself the freedom to examine her in detail. From her tousled flame silk hair, which was curling in the humidity, to her beautiful breasts, firm and uptilted, and the red curls below which his fingers itched to explore.

Later, he told himself.

Picking her up by the waist, he dumped her in the pool. A mean thing to do, but he was in a mean, and, yea, frustrated mood.

She came up sputtering in the water, which was waist-deep on her. "Jackass!"

"I have been called worse."

Finger combing her wet hair off her face, she sat on one of the steps, bringing the water level up to her breasts, which now floated on the top. A most enticing picture, if she only knew.

"Stay here," he ordered, even as he was dumping water over hot rocks, creating more steam. "I will go get clean garments. Do not fall asleep, or you will drown." She already had her neck on the lip of the round pool and her legs extended under the water.

"I don't suppose you have any bubble bath?" she asked sleepily. "Of course you don't. But how about a glass of wine? I love taking long bubble baths in my tub at home with a glass of wine."

He was cursing under his breath as he stomped back to the keep. The wine he could provide, but did she know there were going to be two in her "tub" before long? He would even blow bubbles in the water if that would make her more amenable.

He grinned at that picture, then almost ran into Tork who held the door open for him.

"What is that noise I hear?" Tork asked, cupping a hand to his ear in an exaggerated pose.

Alerted by Tork's teasing tone, Brandr declined to answer and shoved past him.

"Ah, 'tis the sound of a brave Viking knight being whipped by a woman's fleece."

# Chapter 14

**Splish, splash, they were (not) taking a bath . . .**

Even though Joy was half-dozing in the deliciously warm water, she was aware of Brandr when he reentered the bathing house, carrying a stack of clean, folded clothing.

And then he locked the door.

*Uh-oh!*

Leaning back against the edge of the small pool, a glorified hot tub, with her butt resting on one of the lower steps, her body submerged up to her collarbones, she kept her eyes closed. As she listened to the rustling sounds of him undressing, she controlled her raging impulse to look up and feast her eyes on all six foot four bare skin of him. With a sigh, he eased himself into the water, then began to wash and rinse himself. When she opened her eyes just a slit, he had just soaped his hair, slipped under the water totally to rinse, then came up, shoving his braids and long strands of hair off his face.

"I know you are awake," he said.

"I was not," she lied. "You woke me when you splashed around like a harpooned whale."

He leaned back on his elbows, grinning wolfishly at her. "You shaved."

"Yea, I did."

"I need to shave, too," she said, raising a leg and feeling the bristles.

He quirked a brow at her.

"Women shave their legs and underarms where I come from."

"As long as you do not shave other parts, as is done in some eastern lands."

"No, I don't do that."

He rubbed his fingers over his face. "I prefer to be clean-shaven after having lived one time in Jarl Hallstein's vermin-filled hovel of a keep. I got a good and healthy lice colony growing on every hairy surface of my body, including my nose hairs."

That was when Joy noticed that he was bare down to a very enticing belly button. The rest was indiscernible in the dim light cast by several torches and candles. But that was more than enough. The wide shoulders. Flat nipples. Even the slick, black body hair leading down in a vee. *I'd like to be a louse licking my way down that hairy water slide to . . . A louse? Oh, yuck! What a thought!*

"Dost like what you see?"

*Caught in the act.* "Oh, yeah."

"What else do you like?"

She laughed. "Fishing for compliments, are you?"

"And why not?"

"I like the fact that you haven't forced yourself on me."

He made a clucking sound of disgust. "As if I would! What kind of backhanded compliment is that?"

"I like your loyalty to family."

"There is naught to admire in that, either. Honor should be a given in any man."

"And your concern for your people."

"I have no choice but to be responsible. Dost think anyone asked me if I wanted to be leader of this wild clan?"

"I like your dimples."

"I do not have dimples." He tried his best to keep his lips tightly together so the traitorous dimples wouldn't escape.

"I like your concern for Liv."

"She is my sister. You had to know what a delightful creature she was before . . ." He choked up for a moment, then continued, "Liv was a pretty, lissome lass. Merry of heart. She laughed all the time. Never walked where she could skip. And dance . . . the little one could dance like a butterfly *drukkinn* on mead!"

"I like that you have a sense of humor just begging to emerge."

"You think I am funny?"

"No, of course not. But you have the gift of being able to laugh at yourself. For a man who prides himself on his grimness, you're doing a lot of grinning lately."

"Anticipation."

*Oooooh, boy!*

"Methinks you have a warped set of attributes you set for me. A man wants to hear that he is manly, and irresistible, and heroic, and—"

"Well, I must admit, I like your kisses."

He flashed her a full-blown smile, dimples and all. "Now we are getting somewhere." He stretched out one of his long legs and prodded her toes with his. Just that little touch was like an electric shock to her senses, and she could see by the way he jerked his foot back that he'd felt it, too. "What you do to me, wench!"

She didn't have to ask what he meant. "How about me? Is there anything you like about me?"

His eyes immediately went to her breasts, half-floating on the water.

She ducked a little lower. "Not that!"

"Why not?"

"Physical attraction. That kind of thing can happen with any woman."

"I beg to differ. I have not felt this kind of physical attraction in many a year. If ever."

"Really?"

"Truly."

It was probably just a line, but if so, she didn't want to know. "What else?"

"You make me laugh."

"Oh, there's a talent I aim for. Not!"

"I mean, in a good way. I have not had much to laugh about of late." He rolled his lips inward, studying her, then disclosed, "You lighten me."

*What an odd but wonderful thing to say!*

"You talk too much."

"Hey, we're supposed to be listing the things we like."

"You are brave to the point of stupidity. Like jumping out of a castle turret."

"I did not jump, and it wasn't a turret."

He winked at her, and, man, he had a sexy wink. "I like your wagging tongue . . . betimes. Of course, I have visions of said wagging tongue wagging in other ways."

"If you think I'm going to ask you what other ways, you're crazy."

"I like the way you cuddle up against me when asleep, and the way you snore."

"I do not snore."

"I like your gentleness in dealing with Liv. I like that you managed to coax her out of her bedchamber. I like what you did in the kitchens today, although you could have done so without insulting one and all."

"I didn't—"

"I like knowing that you are mine."

"No, no, no! Don't start the thrall nonsense again."

"I am not speaking of bondage. You are mine because I want you with a fierceness that cannot be denied, and you want me, too, though you resist your inner yearnings."

"So, you're saying you're mine, just as I'm yours."

He flushed. "Well, not precisely."

"Thanks a bunch! That's some one-sided relationship!"

"You missay me. There would be naught one-sided about it. Know this as well. I want you, and eventually I will have you."

"See, there's the difference between us. You mention taking me, while I want to make love."

"They are the same thing."

"Honey, they are miles apart."

"You called me honey."

"So? It's an endearment in my time . . . an endearment that's tossed about rather loosely, if you must know."

"You said *your time*. Why do you keep harping on that far-fetched idea?"

"It is far-fetched, but I'm beginning to think . . ." She paused, searching for the right words. "Brandr, when I was hit on the head in Germany, it was the year two thousand and nine." She held up a hand to halt the protest he was about to make. "When I woke up, I thought at first that I had landed in the model reproduction village of Hedeby that exists in two thousand and nine. Or that you were some lost tribe, like the pygmies that had somehow survived civilization undetected."

"Dost compare Vikings to tribes of pigs?"

"What? Don't be ridiculous. Oh, I see what you thought. Pygmies aren't animals; they're people who . . . never mind. Don't interrupt. When your brothers 'bought' me at the auction, I still thought it was part of some ridiculous charade, gone too far. Even when we arrived here, I tried to tell myself that it was just another model reenactment place. But then things started to get confusing."

"I do not like to hear you say such things."

"Why? Because then it would mean you're attracted to a nutcase?"

His flushed face gave him away. "Amuse me then with tales of your time . . . a thousand years from now."

She bared her teeth at his condescension, then figured it wasn't worth arguing over. "Well, people travel from city to city in cars . . . which you might consider horseless carriages, and from country to country in airplanes, which are very large metal objects that fly in the sky, carrying up to hundreds of people."

"Now I know that you jest."

"People don't hunt for their food, for the most part. We have supermarkets where a person can buy everything from fresh fruits and vegetables to meat of all kinds to hosiery to toothpaste to milk to hair brushes to . . . well, just about anything."

He shrugged as if that was no big deal.

"Floors are covered with wood or carpets. No straw on the floor, that's for darn sure. We have electricity to provide light and heat. The only way I can explain electricity is that all you have to do is flick a tiny lever on the wall, and lights come on."

"Magic?"

"No. It's done through wires and science and, oh, it's too hard to explain. We have armies in my time, but the weapons are vastly different. No swords or lances or maces. Instead, we have weapons that can shoot metal bullets rapidly. Rat-a-tat-tat! And we have tanks that can take down a building in one shot. Heck, we have bombs that can blow up an entire country."

His eyes were wide with wonder . . . and disbelief.

"Moving on . . . women got the vote in my country almost a hundred years ago, meaning we are equal to men in all ways."

"Why would they want to be?"

"Only a clueless idiot male chauvinist pig would ask that question."

"What of the Vikings? What are we Vikings doing whilst all these changes are taking place?"

"Actually, there are no Vikings anymore."

He gasped. "Our entire race has been destroyed?"

"No, not really. Instead, Vikings have blended into other countries by marriage and settlement. Women really liked Viking men over the centuries—"

"Of course they did," he interrupted with a smile of self-satisfaction.

If they were closer, she would have smacked him. "Mainly because they bathed more often than other men of the times."

"That, too, but it is incidental to our comeliness." He made an exaggerated gesture of preening.

"The closest that exists to a Viking culture in modern times is Iceland."

"Iceland! That gods-forsaken, frozen hunk of dirt is all we have left to us?"

"There is still a Norway, but the people there call themselves Norwegians, not Vikings. Same is true of Denmark, where they are Danes, and Sweden, where they are Swedes."

While he remained stunned, she went on to another subject. "Back to women, one of the biggest enablers of independence for women over the centuries was the invention more than fifty years ago of the birth control pill."

"Explain."

She did, and with each word his smile got wider. "I suspect men welcomed such an invention as much as women."

"They did . . . still do. And there are lots of other methods of birth control, too." She explained those, too. "But the greatest invention for men is the little blue pill call Viagra. Actually, their partners are thankful for it, too."

He hooted with laughter when she was done explaining erectile dysfunction. "A pellet that can keep a man's staff standing. Oh, this is too much! Of course, we Viking men do not need such."

"Ever?"

"Never."

"Don't kid yourself, Brandr. It happens to the best of men, especially as they age."

Once he was done laughing, he commented, "Please do not tell me that sex has changed over the years, as well."

It was her turn to smile. "No, not really, although women are much more uninhibited. And they demand satisfaction the same as their male partners."

"Now, that I would like to see. More uninhibited females. Mayhap you would like to demonstrate."

Joy's heart melted a little to see a teasing Brandr. This must be what he was like as a boy . . . or even as a man before his life went to hell in a Sigurdsson handbasket. That must be why she lost her mind and blurted out those infamous words that, once said, could not be taken back: "I think I love you."

Brandr froze in place and said nothing. *Nothing!*

"Well?"

"Well what?"

"The comment I just made is one that usually warrants a response." *Why can't I just shut my mouth and slink away?*

"What would you have me say? Those are women's words . . . a way of romanticizing what men know is . . . wait! Where are you going?"

"To hell for all you care!" She rose up in the water, unconcerned by her nudity, and was about to go put on some clothes . . . and hopefully a bit of common sense, as well. Really, what had she been thinking?

But then, swiping tears from her eyes, she fell backwards into the pool. Not of her own volition. Brandr had her by the hair and went under with her.

Sputtering to the surface of the waist-deep water, she turned and lashed out at him with fists and voice. "Let me go! I'm not going to stick around and make a fool of myself again."

"Shhh! I am the fool!" They were standing now, and he had her in such a tight grip, she couldn't move. She struggled and called him every foul name she could think of, and there were quite a few she'd learned while being around Navy men. Only when she went still, exhausted by her efforts, did he lift her by the waist with her feet dangling about a half foot from the bottom. Eye to eye, he told her, "I want you. More than I have ever wanted any other woman. I have never been in love, nor do I think I am capable of that kind of love. But know this: when you said those words to me, my heart bestirred with a yearning I cannot name."

"You're scared."

He bristled at her accusation, but then he shrugged.

She could feel his erection pressing against her in just the right spot. She could see the languorous, sensual fluttering of his lush eyelashes. She could hear the panting of his breath. "If you ask if you can tup me, like a barrel of beer, or swive me, like the last of the peanut butter in a jar, I think I might just scream."

He laughed, but then, in a voice so sex-husky a nun would melt, he said, "Wouldst make love with me, wench?"

What wench could resist?

**Older women, younger men . . . she was the ultimate cougar . . .**

A triumphant joy filled Brandr as he stared at her, knowing without a doubt, as Viking men have known through the ages, the wench was going to yield to his brutish urges.

He did not bloody well care if she was a thousand years old or a nubile sixteen. In truth, older women brought more to the bed furs, in his opinion.

"Joy?" he asked, his voice already thick with growing enthusiasm.

She lowered her emerald eyes with shyness under his steady gaze.

*Shyness? From the wench who is turning my life, and all at Bear's Lair, upside down and inside out? From the wench who claims to be a warrior, healer, and time traveler? From the wench who barrels in where others fear to tread? From the wench whose bravery defies good sense? Hah! I do not think so!*

"So, milady, wouldst demonstrate for me something uninhibited?"

"Huh?" Her eyes shot upward to meet his.

"You told me that women *of your time* are uninhibited in sex play."

"Aaah." He could see the shyness seeping out of her to be replaced by a sultry, teasing demeanor. "Do you mean like this?" He still held her by the waist, her feet dangling in the water, which was waist-deep on her, thigh-deep on him. Even so, she was able to put her hands on his upper arms and move her breasts from side to side across his bristly chest hairs, causing her nipples to harden. The surrounding skin, right up to her neck, bloomed with the sex-flush.

She gasped with shock.

He choked on his own gasp.

"Precisely like that," he said, though how he got the words out was beyond him. His enthusiasm licked through raw nerves and hot blood, turning him mindless with his need to plunge into her depths. But slaking his lust to the inevitable end was a long way off, he cautioned himself.

Raising her even higher so that her breasts were level with his face, he kissed one taut nipple, then the other, then scored the sides of each with his teeth, tugging 'til she mewled her protest. Nay, not a protest, he soon learned.

"Don't stop. Oh, God, don't stop now."

"As if I would!" *Or could.* Brandr cupped her bottom, forcing her legs around his waist, and walked her across the pool and up the steps. Without releasing her, he bent and picked up his cloak, tossing it down onto the stone floor, fur side up. Only then did he lay her down and arrange her the way he wanted.

Her lips twitched with a little smile. "Fur again?"

"And why not?" He came down over her, wedging his legs betwixt hers, then kneeling to see her body better. "Dost have something against fur for lovemaking?"

"Are you kidding?" She opened her arms to him.

"Not yet."

Her gaze shot immediately to his shaft, which reared up from his thatch of man hair, veins standing out in readiness, belying his "Not yet" message. "Oh, really?"

He chuckled and snatched her hand away when she reached for his manpart. "We play the game my way."

"Oh, really?" she said again, raising her hips so that her nether hair caressed his ballocks.

He about saw stars and almost spilled his seed way too early, like an untried youthling with his first maid. Joy would no doubt then be expounding on his need for those little blue pellets.

Knowing full well her effect on him, she lowered herself

and grinned. "I guess it's okay for you to lead . . . the first time."

"Vixen! I wonder if you will deliver all that you promise."

"I could say the same about you."

"Is that a challenge? Did you ne'er hear that there is naught a Viking man relishes more than a challenge?"

"Oh, yeah? You should know that my brothers have been playing the dare game with me for ages. As long as you don't double-dog dare me."

*Double-dog dare?* He was about to ask, but decided now was not the time to dwell on the odd words of her language. "I want to look at you first."

And that is what he did.

"I like to look, too," she said.

And that is what she did.

They examined each other hungrily.

"I like your hair." He rubbed a wet strand between his thumb and forefinger. "Like threads of red silk."

"Why do you wear braids on either side of your face?"

"War braids. Men with long hair wear them thus to keep unruly strands out of their eyes, or in one long braid tucked under a helmet, so the enemy cannot grab onto it. Do you not like them?"

"I like them all right. Especially with those colored beads."

"Mayhap I will braid your hair with them. Later."

"Not exactly appropriate for a thrall, is it?"

"Why do you keep jabbering on about that?"

"Because it's important."

"But not now."

"You're right," she purred. "Not now." In fact, she took hold of both braids and tugged him downward till he lay atop her. "They *do* come in handy."

He laughed, which was not all that easy with his manpart nestled betwixt her thighs, his chest pressing down on her breasts, his mouth within breathing space of her parted lips.

"I am too heavy," he said, brushing his lips across hers.

"No, you're just right." She brushed back.

Gripping her head with both hands, he molded her mouth to his in ever-changing patterns of soft coaxing to hungry hardness. Her pliant lips met his silent demands and satisfied her own needs as well. They were partners in every sense, anticipating what the other wanted.

He drew back and put his fingertips on the pulse point in her neck. "I can feel how much you want me."

She laughed and rubbed herself against his rampant erection. "I can feel how much you want me."

"Witch!" he said and nipped at the soft curve where her neck met her shoulder.

She put her mouth to his ear, flicked it with the wet tip of her tongue, then whispered, "I have never wanted a man the way that I want you."

Brandr wasn't sure whether to be complimented or upset over the men in her past. He shouldn't have asked, but he did. "Have there been so many?"

"No. Just a few. I'm twenty-seven years old, after all. Were you thinking there would be none?"

"Nay." *I just do not want to think about them.*

He began a slow, leisurely exploration of her body then, or as slow as he could, ignoring the driving pulse of a needsome cock. Her breasts especially he gave detailed attention. Shaping them. Massaging them with his calloused palms. Flicking the tips. Then kissing and suckling her 'til she cried out for him to stop.

"Brandr, you'll make me come if you keep doing that, and I want the first time to be when you're inside me."

Those tempting words prompted him to continue ministering to her breasts, in fact, intensifying his rhythmic suckling.

And then . . . and then, caught in the throes of an overwhelming passion, she arched her belly up to meet his abdomen. Her legs went rigid. And she began to keen out her peaking. "Oh, oh, oh, oh, oooh!"

Fascinated, he watched and felt her belly spasm against his skin.

"You rat!" She swatted him on the shoulder when her body was limp and flat against the furs once more.

"You were magnificent."

"I was?"

He nodded.

"Well, then, I guess it's okay." She eyed him through half-mast lashes. "Are your nipples as sensitive as mine?"

"Nay," he said, then flinched as she put her mouth to his flat nipples. Licking them to bigger nubs. Nipping at them with her teeth. Kissing them better. Much more of this, and there would be no actual intercourse.

He pushed her away, gently, then moved down her body. Kissing her belly. Stabbing her navel with his tongue. Rubbing his mouth against the tight curls that already exuded her musk of arousal. Only then did he separate her nether lips with his fingertips and let her anoint him with her honeyed dew.

"You are wet for me, dearling."

"Tell me something I don't know, *darling*."

"Always the smart mouth."

"Keep it up, and you may find exactly what a smart mouth can do."

*Does she mean what I think? Surely not!* "Is that a promise?"

"Brandr! I want you. Inside me."

When his fingertips meandered forward in her slickness to touch the pearl of her desire, she almost shot up off the furs. She would have knocked him aside if he had not been holding on so tightly.

"Now!" she demanded.

"Whate'er you say." He moved into position while she observed him closely, braced as she was on her elbows. Never had he met a woman so eager for the coupling, willing to watch up close what he would do. But, wait; he thought of something. "Joy, I must needs spill my seed outside your body when I peak. I would not breed a child on you." That is all he would need, his first son born of a time-traveling thrall, possibly taking him away to some unknown future place.

"Do you have any idea how unreliable coitus interruptus is?"

*Coitus interruptus? Holy Thor! The woman has a word for even that. And an opinion on every bloody thing in the world.*

"But that's okay. I'm protected for almost a year."

"Huh?" He could not believe his cock was at her portal, dripping his man-dew, and they were engaging in a conversation. Did the wench ever stop talking?

"I have a birth control implant."

"What?"

"See, there's an implant under the skin here."

He checked the thin skin inside her upper arm, and there was indeed a shaded area. "Another metal weapon?"

"No weapon. A birth control device." She took matters into her own hands then, reaching down to enfold his cock and guide him home. A hot, moist, pulsing slide to home.

He closed his eyes to savor the moment and gather his self-control for the long ride to come.

"Birth control implants are ninety-eight percent effective," she said then.

His eyes shot open. *Oh, my gods! She's going to talk again.* He was about to shut her teeth with a kiss but had to ask, "Percent?"

"Yeah. Like if you have sex one hundred times, the birth control would work ninety eight times."

"You intend to have sex with me a hundred times?"

She started to laugh, and he felt her laughter all the way to her inner muscles, which had already stretched to accommodate his size and were now convulsing with laughter.

"Who knew a woman's sheath could have a sense of humor? Amazing!"

That caused her to laugh even more.

But then the time for laughter passed.

Chest heaving with restraint, he began the long, slow strokes, almost leaving her body on each backstroke. Her muscles inside were tight and tugged at his cock in passing, coming and going.

Joy was thrashing and tossing her head from side to side,

making small sounds of growing arousal that fed his male ego. Slowly he drove her to the point of madness . . . and himself as well.

And then he stopped.

Until she stared up at him in question.

Then he started all over again.

Long.

Slow.

Strokes.

Again.

And again.

And again.

Then he stopped. And had to bite his bottom lip as Joy peaked again, clasping and clasping his manpart, nature's way of attempting to keep him inside and spill his seed.

Joy was blinking up at him now, knowing he had not yet reached the peak of his own enthusiasm.

"I learned a trick from a harem houri one time."

"Oh, no! Not the kinky stuff!" She tried to laugh but could not, so tense was her body, still.

"I plunge in slow and deep nine times with the tenth being hard and fast. Then I stop. Next time, it is eight and one. Then seven and one."

"What happens at the end?"

"Very hard, very fast for as long as I am able."

She smiled. "Sounds good to me." But then she proved that the path of all the sex games in the world could be diverted by one female deliberately and skillfully flexing her inner muscles, milking him to madness.

Even so, Brandr was a stronger man than most, though beads of sweat stood out on his forehead and underarms and chest. He counted and stroked, like a demented demon. And when he came to the end, thank you gods, he gripped her ankles and shoved them up to her chest, widening her knees so that she could take even more of him.

By now his cock was plunging fast through searing moist heat, the wet, slapping sounds a further impetus to his rush to peak.

Disjointed words came from both of them.

"Please."

"Now!"

"Yes, like that. Oh, my!"

"Spread wider, sweetling. Like so."

"I'm going to come. Again."

"Sweet torture!"

"Harder, dammit! Harder!"

His last rational thought before catapulting through the fiercest peaking was, *We are going to kill each other with an overabundance of Joy.*

Heat exploded in his genitals, rushing outward to all his extremities, and she screamed . . . she actually screamed her unending pleasure. Was there ever a greater gift from the gods than a man and woman peaking together?

Once sated, he rolled over to his back, taking her with him to his side, lifting one thigh over his. His chest was heaving still, and she panted her warm breath against his neck.

She rose up to look at him. The glow of wonder in her eyes humbled him.

"You are mine," he proclaimed. *I am never going to let you go now.* "Say those words you said to me afore."

She tilted her head in question. Then, "Ah."

He waited, heart pounding like a battle drum.

"I think I love you."

"Think?" He wanted all she could give, not some halfway declaration of mayhaps and perchance. And was that not odd for him? He should not care how she felt about him, as long as she was willing to spread her winsome thighs.

She smiled and put a gentle hand to his cheek.

The gentle hand was his undoing. He could almost feel the first crack in his dark soul. Lifting her hand, he kissed the palm.

"I love you, Viking, warts and all."

"What? I have no warts."

"Believe me, baby, you've got warts."

# Chapter 15

**There are bulls, and then there are *bulls*...**

Joy was neck deep in another of her quicksand *What was I thinking?* moments, and she could not care less.

Her lips burned in the aftermath of their lovemaking, her nipples felt raw, and there were muscles in some places between her legs that were screaming *Whaaaat the hell?*

She loved the damn Viking, no matter how bad an idea it was. But then, who said love came when and where it should? At the moment, she didn't want to think about the future and how this relationship would inevitably reach a dead end. For now, she wanted to hold her nose and do a huge belly flop into the unknown pool spread out before her . . . a very, very inviting pool.

"I do not have warts," Brandr said again.

"Yes, you do, honey."

"Show me."

"They're the kind of warts that don't show. Like your chauvinism."

"Show me what?"

"Chauvinism. It's another word for men thinking they are superior to women."

"Well, they are . . ."

"I beg your pardon!"

He pinched her butt for interrupting, then finished, " . . . in some ways."

"Another wart of yours is stubbornness."

"Is that not like the fjord calling the ocean wet?"

"I'm a little stubborn, but I never said I didn't have warts, too."

He kissed the top of her head where her hair was beginning to dry. It would soon be a curly bush without her necessary blow dryer and diffuser.

"Tell me more," he encouraged.

"Although I haven't seen any evidence of it yet, you're a berserker. I would think that's a whopper of a wart."

"That is beyond my control."

"Actually, it's not. I could show you—"

He kissed her quick and hard, no doubt to shut her up.

"That's another wart of yours. Always trying to shut me up."

"You are not going to cure me of berserkness, Joy. Forget about it."

"Okay." *Wanna bet?*

"I know where I have a big wart." He glanced downward.

"Honey, that's not a wart. That a bleepin' tree."

He chuckled. "Why don't you show me more of your . . . you know?"

"I do?"

"Uninhibitedness."

She grinned and moved so that she was half on and half off of him, one breast and one leg pressing down on him, not to mention a hand, which was meandering across his belly. He already sported a hard-on that could star in a porno movie. She wasn't going near that big boy yet. Still, it was past time to teach a Viking a thing or two about modern women. "Anything special in mind?" *Like I don't already have my game on!*

He grinned back at her, dimples and all.

Man, she loved the guy.

"Whatever you want, sweetling."

Yeah, right. "Listen, you had a great time torturing me with that start, stop, start, stop teasing. Time for a little reverse torture, I'm thinking."

"Me?" He put both hands to his chest in fake affront.

"I didn't see anyone else having sex to a count. You were practically shouting, 'One tickle tummy, two tickle tummy, three tickle—'" She flicked her fingertips over his tummy for emphasis.

Instinctively, he sucked in his belly, and his "tree" grew another inch or five. Okay, she was exaggerating. But not by much.

He burst out laughing. "I must say, I never knew sex could be so . . . fun."

"Hey, you know what they say, there's nothing sexier than a man who can make a woman smile in bed."

"How about a woman who can make a man smile in bed?"

"That, too." She swung her leg over farther so that she straddled him, her butt on his thighs, Mr. Big Boy standing up in front of her like a neon sex sign blinking *Here I am, here I am, here I am, just in case you hadn't noticed*. Yeah, like anyone could miss *that*.

His eyes roamed her body in the most delicious way. She could tell he liked what he saw. He was probably viewing her through the rose-colored prism of sex, not seeing her flaws. But right now, she didn't care. She would take his adoration any way she could get it.

"In my country, they have what they call cowboys." She twirled the hair on his chest with seeming nonchalance. "Do you know what that is?"

"Nay," he said, at the same time he was running his calloused hands lightly over the outside of her arms—shoulders to wrists, back up, then down again, over and over—in a feathery caress.

"Well, they are men who ride horses to round up cows

that are left to roam on the open range. Sometimes cowboys ride wild bulls in rodeos, too."

"Your point?" His wicked fingers had now moved to the outsides of her breasts. Not under. Not between. And definitely not the aching centers. Just the outsides.

"My point is that there are cowgirls, too."

When he finally understood, a mischievous smile split his lips. "Am I to be the horse or the bull?"

"Both, I think. First, a little easy riding. Then maybe some wild bronco busting. Are you up for it?"

He glanced once again at his erection, then up at her. "More than up, I would say. In fact, I dare you to do it and last for, oh, let us say, a half hour."

"How will we know when a half hour is up?"

He lifted her up and slowly, agonizingly lowered her onto his huge staff, which she could swear was pulsing. "We will know because that is the longest I will be able to hold off my peaking."

"You mean orgasm?"

He nodded.

She pretended to consider whether she was interested in his challenge or not. Meanwhile, she fought the impulse to move herself on his marblelike penis, to have her way with him in her own way, to prove a point. Though she was having an increasingly harder time remembering what that point would be.

But then he said those magic words. "I double-dog dare you."

The Viking was a quick learner.

**Even Vikings need a break once in a while . . .**

Three hours had passed since Brandr took Joy to the bathing house. He knew because he checked the time candle in the clean, empty kitchen as they passed through just now.

With an arm looped over her shoulders, he had her tucked close to his side. For once, she was quiet and docile. He liked to think he'd worn her down to acceptance of her lot with their strenuous love play, but he was not such a fool. Her meekness would not last long.

He wished he could have kept her in the bathing house all night, but both of their stomachs had started rumbling with hunger. Sex, satisfying as it was, could only feed one hunger. Besides, his bed would be more comfortable.

They peeked into the great hall and saw that dinner was over and many of the folks were already abed. A few of the men were playing *hnefatafl*, a board game, whilst others threw dice for coin. "Let's go back to the kitchen and get something to eat," he whispered in her ear.

"As long as I don't have to serve you."

He pinched her bottom. "I will serve you. This time."

"Oh! I don't believe it!" Joy exclaimed, then shot out of his arms and across the hall.

"What in bloody hell . . . ?" He followed after her to where Tork had a maid up against the wall, tupping her, he assumed, or about to. It was the new thrall, Ebba. Was this what had Joy in an uproar?

He caught up with Joy just as she kicked Tork in the buttocks.

"Whaaat?" Tork spun on his heel. Luckily, he still had his braies on, but they were unlaced. The tupping had not yet commenced. Otherwise, he might be suffering pain from both sides.

"You rat! Can't you find an unmarried woman to boink?"

"Huh?" he and Tork said at the same time, turning to the flustered maid, whose huge breasts were exposed by the lowered bodice of her gunna.

He pulled Joy back. "Behave! The wench does not appear unwilling."

"She came freely," Tork said indignantly.

"How would you know? Did she have a choice? Did anyone ask her husband if he objected to sharing? Men!"

She was about to stomp off, but Brandr grabbed her by the upper arm. "Oh, nay! You are not going to brew up trouble, then leave the mess you make." Turning to Ebba, he asked, "Are you married?"

Her eyes shifted from side to side, worried. Over to
the side, he saw a man rising from his sleep pallet, walking toward them. It was the Saxon thrall Osmund, the
woodworker.

"Is that your husband, Ebba?" Brandr asked.

She nodded, even as she cast accusing glares at Joy. "I
ne'er complained to her, Master. I know me place." Then
she burst out bawling, huge sucking cries accompanied by
a running nose.

"Ebba, even thralls have a choice here at Bear's Lair. Especially if you are married to another man."

"Hey," Tork intervened. "Do I not have some say in the
matter?"

"Shut up," Joy said, then ducked behind Brandr.

"Can you not control your bed thrall?" Tork spat out.

Joy peeked around his side. "Bite me!" she taunted, then
stuck out her tongue at Tork.

Everyone, himself included, just gaped at her.

"Well, he deserved it." Joy was at his side once again.

Osmund, the woodworker, joined their group. "Ebba?"
Seeing her tears, he scowled at Tork. "What did ye do to
me wife?"

"Oh, my gods!" Tork threw his hands out in disgust.

"Come," Brandr said to Joy. "Let them resolve this
themselves."

"Where are you two going?" Tork demanded to know.

"To the kitchen. To eat."

They soon discovered Tork following them. When Brandr
turned to confront him, Tork said, "If I cannot fuck, I may as
well eat. Unless you want to share your wench."

Brandr held Joy back before she could fly at Tork, who
was grinning at his success in goading her. Brandr picked
her up from behind and walked them both into the kitchen,
where he sat her on a bench. "Do not move!"

Tork, still grinning, was about to sit on the bench on the
other side of the table when Brandr ordered, "You will help
me gather some food."

"Why can the wench not serve us?"

"Shut your teeth, Tork, afore she kills us both."

"Fleece whipped, that is what you are," Tork muttered under his breath as he accompanied Brandr down the steps to the cold cellar.

Brandr elbowed him. "Enough! Joy cannot hear your provocative remarks down here."

He and Tork gathered up milk, cheeses, leftover venison, a heaping dish of something that resembled mashed-up turnips, which did not taste too bad, he decided after sticking in a finger and licking it off. And Joy's grandmother's soup, too.

"Where are those apple tarts I smelled earlier in the kitchen?"

"Apple dumplings," Tork corrected. "They are gone. Mayhap you should order your wench to make double the number on the morrow."

"Lot of good that would do me," he murmured.

Tork smiled at him. "You and the thrall were gone a long time."

"So?"

Tork waggled his eyebrows at him.

"You are such a boyling at times."

"Are you saying I am immature?"

"You said it. Not me."

When they got to the kitchen, they saw that Joy was still sitting on the bench, dozing, her chin down on her chest, little snoring sounds coming from her mouth.

"Wore her out, you did," Tork congratulated him.

"Shhh. She will start talking if we wake her."

"I heard that," she said, sitting upright.

Brandr figured he had best cover his tracks if he wanted any more bedsport tonight. "I just meant that we should spare you, after all the good work you did today."

"Nice try, Brandr. You've already told me a number of times that I talk too much."

He cringed as he sat beside her on the bench, uncomfortable at having his words thrown back at him. "Here, dearling," he said, placing a wooden dish in front of her.

"What is it?" She stared at the block of hard, congealed broth into which pieces of something resembling meat had been mixed.

*"Hrútspungur."*

" 'Tis a favorite of Brandr's," Tork inserted, then cast a shark smile at Joy. "Ram's testicles."

"It is *not* a favorite of mine . . . any more than gammelost is a favorite of yours," he countered to Tork. Gammelost was a stinksome cheese that was said to drive some men berserk. He did not need to be any more berserk than he already was at times.

Joy surprised them both when she took a big bite of the loathsome dish and said, "Yum! Tastes like my great-aunt's headcheese or souse. She married a Pennsylvania Dutchman. This batch needs more salt. If we run out, I know where I can get some more balls I can slice off and cook up into a tasty gelatin."

She was looking at the two of them.

"Does she have something to say about everything?" Tork asked him.

Brandr nodded. "Talking is her second best talent."

"Be careful, or you won't be the recipient of my best talent anymore," Joy cautioned him.

Mostly, they ate in silence as they shared the platter of cold meats and cheeses. He and Tork drank milk, which Joy disdained, choosing water instead.

He peeled and sliced a pear for them to share.

She hesitantly tasted some skyr, then put a dollop on her plate over several pear slices. "This tastes like cottage cheese," she told him. "Are these pears from an orchard here?"

Brandr nodded. "From a tree my grandfather planted afore I was born."

"Remember the time you hid in its upper branches for one whole day and night?" Tork reminded him, a mischievous gleam in his brown eyes.

"What did you do?" Joy asked him.

"I do not recall."

"Hah!" Tork said. "He put worms in his aunt Siv's sleeping pallet."

"She always was a waspish one, if you ask me. She deserved more than worms."

He and Tork grinned at each other.

"What happened when you came down from the tree?" Joy wanted to know.

"I could not sit for a sennight after my father was done with me. And he made me sleep in the cow byre."

"By the seventh day, you smelled like Ulfar's codpiece. Phew!" Tork remarked.

Joy plopped huge gobs of the grayish turnips on their plates, insisting, "Eat. Vegetables are good for you." Then she asked, "How long have you two been friends?"

"Since birth, or soon after," Tork told her. "My mother and his mother were distant cousins."

"We grew up together, learned to swim and wield a sword together, fought battles side by side, even tupped our first maids together," Brandr elaborated.

"Together?"

"Dost really want the details?" He smiled at her.

She seemed to ponder, then said, "No."

"The only time we were apart was when Tork wed. Two years you were gone, is that not right?" he asked his friend.

"You're married?" Joy appeared surprised. "Where's your wife? And why are you screwing other women if you're married?"

"I *was* married."

She tilted her head in question.

"His wife divorced him," Brandr told her.

"I didn't know there was divorce in Viking society, or that a woman could be the one to initiate the divorce. Can I assume it was adultery?"

"Nay," Tork said. "Well, Dagny did divorce me because I happened to stray. Just one time, mind you, but it was not my fault. The dairymaid kept flaunting herself at me. But adultery is not grounds for divorce in our society, leastways not by the male."

"That figures," Joy said.

Brandr chuckled. "Dagny accused him of fornicating with goats."

Joy choked on the water she had been sipping. He clapped her on the back 'til her passages cleared.

"You screwed goats?"

Tork made a clucking sound of disgust. "Nay, I did not do *that*, but Dagny wanted to embarrass me, and she did."

"So?"

"So I left."

"And where is this Dagny now?"

"Enjoying herself at my estate in Vestfold."

"You allowed her to keep your home? I mean, do you have more than one?"

"Only one. And, nay, I bloody hell did not give it to her. But she will not leave. So I left."

"Forever?"

"Nay! She will give up eventually, take another husband, and go to his holdings. When she does, I will return. In the meantime, we play a game of who will give in first, and I assure you, it will not be me."

"How long since you've seen her . . . or your home?"

"Five years."

"I think I like your wife." Joy grinned. "Did you love her?"

Tork's face bloomed with red patches. Brandr had not known his friend could blush. How interesting!

"I thought I did, but I was young and lackwitted."

"When did you see her last?" If anything, his wench was persistent.

"Five years past."

"Did you have children?"

"Nay! Thank the gods! During the two years of our marriage, we were only together on the odd sennight or so."

"Because?"

"Because, of course, I was off a-Viking, or trading, or fighting one war or another."

"Or committing adultery. Men!" Joy turned and glared at Brandr.

"What did I do?" Brandr asked.

"You men are all the same. Dumb as dirt!"

"I have a philosophy about marriage," Brandr said. "Seems to me marriage is like a besieged castle. Those outside are trying their best to get inside. And those inside wish they could escape. Battering rams in. Ladders out."

"Oh, you!" Joy smacked him on the arm.

He got up to fill three mugs with the chicken soup heating over the low fire, and Tork said in a low voice to Joy, "Do not hurt him, or I will kill you."

"Whaaat? Who?"

"Brandr."

"I beg your pardon. How could I hurt him? I have no weapon."

"There are weapons, and there are weapons. I saw him smile tonight, the first in a long, long time. You have brought him out of the darkness. If you do aught to hurl him back into that pit, I swear by Thor's hammer Mjollnir, you will suffer."

Brandr was both touched and amused by his friend's words. "I can speak for myself, Tork. There is no need for you to defend me with a mere woman."

"Mere woman?" Joy started to rise. "Maybe this mere woman will go up and sleep with Liv tonight."

He shoved her back down. "Sit, and do not be so quick to take offense. I am the one who should be offended that you two speak of me as if I am not here, as if I am a weakling who cannot take care of himself."

"That is not what I meant," Tork mumbled.

"And, truth to tell, if I want to languish in darkness, it is my decision and mine alone."

"That is all well and good, Brandr, but I know more about women than you do, and you should take heed of my advice. Fuck them and leave them, is what I always say."

Joy made a scoffing sound. "I can see how well that's working for you. No wonder your wife divorced you."

"Joy loves me," Brandr said before he could stop himself.

"I cannot believe you repeated that." Joy slapped him on the arm, then slapped him again for good measure.

It did not hurt, but, really, he did not understand the woman. He had been defending her . . . in a way.

Tork eyed her suspiciously. "I am wary of women who spout love nonsense. They usually want something."

"You are an idiot."

"That is the selfsame thing I said to him this morn when he was bragging about his sword luck," Brandr told her.

Joy looked from him to Tork and back again, as if they were both idiots. "You two are so different in appearance. I thought Vikings were all supposed to be blond."

It was true; Tork was as light as he was dark. In stature, they were the same height and breadth, but his hair was black and his eyes dark blue, whereas Tork had pale hair and honey colored eyes.

"Norsemen are light *and* dark," Brandr told her. "In fact, the Irish distinguish betwixt us as Finn-Gaill and Dubh-Gaill. White foreigners and black foreigners."

"Whilst the Irish are just plain afraid of us," Tork observed.

"That goes without saying." A wide yawn escaped Brandr's open mouth then. Tork and Joy did the same, following his lead. They had finished most of the food they'd brought forth, so he said to Joy, "Let us leave this for the kitchen maids to clean up in the morn. And, nay, I do not mean you, afore you get your hackles in a huff."

They all rose.

Tork said, and he was serious, "What are we going to do now?"

Brandr was stunned into silence. Did his good friend really think he was going off with him to drink or chatter 'til the wee hours? That was taking friendship a bit too far, in his opinion.

It was Joy who broke the silence with a laugh.

He took that as a good sign.

# *Chapter 16*

**From the mouths of babes . . .**

Joy felt as if she were floating on a cloud of happiness the next few weeks. She was like a teenager in the throes of a first love. But then, this was a first love for Joy, and there was nothing immature or transient about it.

She should have been worried about her situation here. Wherever here was. And why she was here. And how she was going to return home.

She should have been distraught over the prospect of time travel, which Joy was increasingly having to accept.

She should have hated, not loved, a man as crude and brutal and chauvinistic as Brandr.

She should be missing her old life.

Instead, she had settled into life at Bear's Lair with a happiness she didn't dare question for fear it would disappear.

Working with Liv, she'd managed to get the girl to speak, and once she started, everything spilled out of her. All the horrors of the Sigurdsson attack, what had happened when she'd been captured, her fears for her future. She even mentioned with regret her lost love, Einar Egillsson, whom she had expected to marry. While still reticent in crowds, especially around men, she moved freely around the keep now, helping Joy in the kitchen until Kelda resumed her duties, then taking up embroidery duties in the solar.

There had been only one problem. One of Brandr's soldiers, Sven the Scowler, had made a coarse remark to Liv. When he'd reached out a hand to touch her breast, Liv had gone into hysterics. Her screams had reached Brandr, who was outside. When he'd come in, taking in the scene in a glance, he'd gone wild with fury. And Joy got her first glimpse of how he would be as a berserker. In the end, Tork and Brandr's other men had to pull him off of Sven, whose nose was broken, his face covered with blood, and several ribs broken. Even though Sven had apologized to Liv and Brandr, it had taken Tork more than an hour to calm Brandr down, and even then Brandr refused to talk with anyone, even her. In fact, he shoved her aside at one point, knocking her to the floor. "Leave be, wench!" he'd howled. "This is who I am. Do not try to change me." Instead, he went off to the far end of the hall and began drinking, continuing the entire day.

Until he came to her near midnight, reeking of ale. She would have shoved him out of bed and told him to go sleep it off somewhere else. But she'd seen the bleak look in his eyes, and she opened her arms to him. Despite his inebriated state, he was gentle with her, showing her without words how sorry he was for his behavior.

Although Brandr still referred to her as thrall when they were alone, and he still insisted she wear his thrall amulet, he allowed her to dress "above her station" and move about as a free woman. Otherwise, she would not make love with him, and he knew it. And make love they did. A lot. And not just at night under the bed furs. He came to her at the oddest times. Once midday in one of the bed closets, with the door closed. Once up on the ramparts during a snowstorm. Once against the wall in the cellar.

And what a lover he was! Sometimes gentle, often hard.

He demanded much of her in making love, forcing her to do some things she never would have considered, but then he gave much in return.

Even when they weren't making love, he touched her often in passing, or just conversing. Skimming stray hairs off her face. Caressing her arm. Patting her rump. And she did the same to him. She couldn't help herself. Just catching his eye across a crowded room made her heart race.

She was so much in love that she couldn't imagine ever leaving him, even if it meant living here in the past.

Thus it was a shock when she made a discovery that changed her view of everything, even the man she loved.

Joy was still barred from going outside the keep, but that didn't stop her from trying, even though the days were mostly dark at this time of the year. By her guesstimate, it must be about the middle of October, and it may very well be this way until late January. Christmas must be bleak in these parts, if they even celebrated Christmas. Although Brandr had told her one time that he practiced both Norse and Christian religions. Jeesh! That was like a man saying he both did and didn't believe in God. But then, she knew of soldiers who got bunker or deathbed conversions, and others who didn't really believe in God but went to church anyway, as insurance, just in case.

One morning, wanting to alert Bergdis, the dairymaid, that they would need more cream the next day for a special mousse she was experimenting with, Joy slipped past the guard. He was flirting with Ebba, who was still misbehaving, despite her being with her husband now.

Once she rushed into the barn, then held her nose against the pungent odors, she glanced around, even into the various stalls, unable to find either Bergdis or her husband Randulfr, who was in charge of the stables. But then she heard an odd mewling sound.

*Cats?* she wondered.

Taking a wall torch in hand, she crept toward a far stall where she discovered not a cat but a whimpering baby. By the tear tracks on its face, the baby, no more than four or five months old, must have been crying for a long time and was petering down to a whimper of distress.

"Hello!" she called out for help. "Bergdis? Are you here? Randulfr?"

No answer.

But her voice must have alerted the baby that someone was nearby.

Opening its blue eyes, the baby gazed up at her and then let loose with an unending howl.

"Now, now," she said, setting the torch into a holder. She knelt in the straw and picked up the child. "Shhh. It's okay. Shhh." She noticed a pottery jar of milk nearby and a twisted cloth that must be used for feeding the baby. Resting the baby in the crook of one elbow, she began to feed it in this primitive manner.

Its little mouth latched onto the cloth nipple and sucked greedily. She kept dipping it in the milk and returning it to its mouth. The whole time, the baby's bright blue eyes stared up at her. It probably had blond hair, but it was hard to tell with all the grease and grime that covered it. Its body appeared too thin, but then she didn't know much about babies.

"Oh, sweetie! You are a darling. Who do you belong to, huh? And why are you lying here all by yourself? Someone is going to answer for your neglect. Yes, they are."

Once fed, she laid the baby back down on the straw and lifted its little gown and its cloth diaper, which was sopping wet and filled with feces. The child couldn't have been changed in more than a day, further evidenced by its raw and chafed bottom. It was a little boy, she soon found out when it squirted up at her, dampening her apron, then smiled.

"Oh, my gods! Oh, my gods!" Bergdis said, as she rushed up to the stall. "What are you doin' here? The master is gonna kill me. Here. Give the bratling to me."

*Bratling? I don't think so!* Joy stood and refused to relinquish the child. "Why is the baby lying here in this filth with no supervision?"

"I had ta go help me husband birth a foal."

Joy flinched at the woman's blood-covered hands and apron. And she had been about to pick up the baby like that? No way! "Are you saying this is your baby?"

Bergdis shook her head vehemently. "He was given ta me and Randulfr ta care for."

"What's his name?"

Bergdis's already flushed face got redder. "It ain't got no name."

"What?"

"Oh, please, mistress. Give over the child. There will be such trouble."

"Whose child is this?" Joy demanded to know.

"I cannot say. I cannot say." She lifted her apron up to her face and began to wail.

Meanwhile, the bright little baby's head moved from side to side, as if following the exchange.

"Well, if you won't tell me, Brandr will."

Bergdis wailed louder.

And there he stood, hands on hips, his eyes blazing midnight blue fire. "What in bloody hell is going on here?" His eyes went wide as Joy turned. Whether he was shocked at her being outside the keep, or that she was holding a baby, she wasn't sure.

"Brandr? Look. This little baby was lying out here, crying. It needs changing and a warm cradle and . . ." Her words trailed off at the expression of outrage on his face.

"Put the baby back where it belongs," he said icily.

"What? Where? In the straw?"

"I do not care where. Just put it down and get your arse back in the keep."

"No!"

"What did you say?"

"I said no. I will not abandon this baby here. And I don't understand why you would even think I would." Tears filled her eyes.

"The child is Liv's."

As understanding seeped in, she said, "Oh."

"Now will you give the babe back and return to the keep?"

"I can't."

"And why not?"

"It's not being cared for properly." She lifted the diaper to show him the flame-red bottom.

He sniffed at the stench, then turned to Bergdis. "You were given care of the baby."

"But, Master, I had to help Randulfr."

"Give the child back to her," he told Joy.

"Brandr, this is your nephew. How can you be so heartless?"

"Heartless? I could have . . . *should have* . . . left the child out on the cliffs to die. It is a Sigurdsson whelp, born of rape."

"It also carries your blood. And it's not his fault."

"I could kill the babe now and care not a whit."

"If you do, I could never forgive you. Never."

"Liv does not want the baby. She could not bear to see it. Dost want to reverse all the progress she has made?"

He was probably right. It would be traumatic for Liv, especially if she was forced to see him. Still, Joy couldn't abandon this little scrap of humanity.

With a gurgle of pleasure, its little grubby hand reached out and tugged on a strand of her hair. She closed her eyes in an attempt to stem the tears that burned behind her lids.

"Come," he urged in a softer voice, holding out a hand toward her.

She opened her eyes and stared hopelessly at him. "I can't."

"So be it. Stay here in the barn then. See how long you like sleeping with cows."

"It can't be any worse than sleeping with a pig," she snapped out and instantly wished she'd kept her mouth shut.

He turned slowly, cast her a withering look, and then he was gone.

**She took a stand for motherhood . . .**

"Your name is going to be Matthew. What do you think of that, little one?"

The baby just stared up at her from his fur bed laid out on the straw. He was fed and bathed, and what a beautiful blond-haired angel he was! His little feet pumped, and his arms windmilled, now that he was free from all the binding covers.

He was too skinny, but that should take care of itself with proper feeding. She would have to ask someone how soon he could take solid food. His bottom and the area around his tiny penis were still raw, but hopefully Bergdis would bring some ointment when she came back with clean cloths and blankets.

"Yes, Matthew, you are going to be just fine, aren't you?" She tickled his tummy, and she could swear he nodded his head at her.

"Matthew? 'Tis an odd name fer a Viking," Bergdis remarked, having just come back. Almost grudgingly, she handed her a pile of fabric, a pottery jar, which smelled like lard, and a fresh torch to light when the current one sputtered out. Surely, she could have done better than that for diaper rash, but Joy wasn't going to complain, since she'd already promised to do Bergdis's chores in return for these favors.

"Well, he's not really a Viking, I guess, since nobody wants him. I'm adopting Matthew." Joy didn't know where the idea to name him Matthew had come from or why, but it just seemed right that this little miracle be her dead brother's namesake. She probably wouldn't have any other children, stuck here in the past as she was, and, yeah, she had to accept that was what had happened, unbelievable as it was.

"Will ye call 'im Matthew Brandrsson or Matthew Igorsson or Matthew Sigurdsson or Matthew Bastardsson? Hee, hee, hee."

"None of those. He'll be Matthew Nelson," Joy replied to Bergdis's snide question, although she hadn't really thought that far until this moment. "The ignorant people here don't deserve this precious gift from God."

"Yer barmy if ye think a child of rape is a gift."

"I understand the attitude of Liv and the rest of you about the rape and about a child resulting from the rape. But the baby is here now, and it's not his fault."

"Make sure ye muck out those stalls." Bergdis left in a huff.

An hour or so later, Mattie was sleeping in his new toddler gown and clean nappy, which she'd had to tie on the sides since she had no pins. And she'd just raked out one smelly stall. Holding her breath, she kept reminding herself that she could do this if it meant that Bergdis would continue to provide her with the things she needed to care for the baby.

Bergdis returned then and tossed more fabric at her. "The master says ye are ta wear these from now on." Joy didn't need to open the material to tell it was the damn thrall gown. So they were back to that again. Well, so be it!

Wringing her hands, Bergdis continued to stand there. "Ye should return the babe to me care. Ye should go back ta the keep and yer proper place."

Joy straightened and put a hand to her aching back. "Why should I do that?"

"The master, he be in a berserk rage. Yelling and throwing things. He almos' killed Dar Danglebeard when he said somethin' 'bout how the master been spoilin' his bed thrall, an' it took five men ta pull 'im off, an' Tork had ta knock 'im out with a blow ta the noggin with a wooden shovel. Then Liv heard about you and the babe, and she went screamin' ta her bedchamber and willna come out. Now Kelda is havin' a fit 'cause she doan know how ta make apple dumples."

"Dumplings."

"Dumplins, then. And Tork is tellin' ever'one 'The bitch is trouble. We oughta toss her in the fjord.' "

With that in mind, it was a bit alarming a short time later to see Tork staggering into the barn, drunk as a lord.

"Where is she? Where's the bitch?"

"Shhh! You're gonna wake up Mattie." She rose from the straw where she'd been lying with the sleeping baby under a warm bed fur. It was getting darn cold in the barn now that nightfall had come, although it was hard to tell night from day this far north. That's why she'd had to keep a torch burning all the time.

"You!" Tork stormed up to her, pushing her up against the stall door with his hands pressed to her throat.

*Oh, my God!* she thought, choking. *He's going to kill me.*

"I warned you. I told you not to hurt Brandr. But did you listen? Nay, you are like all the other faithless women."

She heard a rustling sound behind her and knew Mattie was about to waken from the noise. A reminder. If she died, the baby would probably be left to die, too. With adrenaline-triggered force, she shoved Tork away and kneed him in the crotch.

"Ouch, ouch, ouch!" Tork was holding his goodies, bouncing from foot to foot. And a lopsided bounce it was, too, since he was half-crocked.

"You should talk about faithless, you . . . you adulterer."

Mattie decided to let out a howl of protest then.

They both turned to him.

One howl appeared to be enough. Now that he'd gotten their attention, he yawned and went back to sleep.

"Bloody hell! He looks just like Liv." Tork appeared stone cold sober, which wasn't possible, but he had suffered a shock.

"Of course he looks like Liv," she said gently. "What did you think he would look like? Godzilla?"

"Which god?"

"Never mind." *Forget about being gentle with the clod.* "Are you happy that you almost killed me?" She put her fingertips to her neck. There was no mirror available, but she would bet she had finger marks there already.

"You kicked me in my manparts," he said indignantly.

"Kneed. I kneed you in your nuts. Don't worry. You'll live to commit adultery again."

He growled and turned his fists into claws, probably contemplating another assault.

She backed up so she was on the other side of the half door.

"You have the mouth of a stinging wasp."

"Compliments will get you nowhere."

"Come back to the keep. Brandr needs you."

"Can I bring the baby with me?'

"Are you demented?"

"I can't leave the baby."

"It's colder than a polar bear's tit here."

"It's not so bad under the furs. And the cows provide some heat."

Tork stared at her as if she was crazy, then swaggered off, muttering, "I told him so. I told him she would be trouble, but did he listen to me? Nay! Nobody listens to me. And she is not even comely."

"Why don't you go screw a goat?" she called after him.

She thought she heard him chuckle.

No more visitors came until the next morning when Arnora showed up. There was a stern expression on her face, but she carried supplies, for which Joy had to be thankful. A flower-scented ointment, more clean nappies and baby gowns, a bone rattle, of all things, and an extra fur blanket.

"Girl, you are creating a stir."

"Tell me about it."

"Let me see him."

Joy carefully picked up the sleeping baby, cradling him in the crook of her elbow, up against her chest. "Isn't he beautiful?"

"'Tis true then. He resembles Liv."

She nodded.

"I thought you cared for the girl."

"I do."

"Then how can you cause her such pain?"

"Liv is an adult. In time, hopefully, she'll get over her trauma. She certainly has enough family and friends to help her through that stress. But Matthew has no one. Just me."

Arnora bit her bottom lip. "I do not know where this will end."

"I'm not asking for anything special. Just let me care for him here."

"'Tis not that simple. Even though you are out here, your presence and what you are doing hangs over us all. A pall of sorrow."

"I never intended to hurt anyone."

Arnora sighed and was about to leave.

"One thing, Arnora . . . do you know at what age a baby takes solid food, like porridge? Matthew is so skinny."

Arnora put a fingertip to her lips, probably counting mentally how old Matthew would be. "I will send some thin porridge. You can try and see if the baby will take it."

Kelda came later, carrying a bowl of watery porridge with honey drizzled on top, with a wooden spoon, on Arnora's orders, she was sure. "A fine mess ye have created up in the hall!"

"I never intended—"

Kelda waved a hand dismissively. "How do ya make them damn apple dumples? Ever'one is askin' fer 'em, and I fergit how much flour ya said ta use."

"Dumplings."

"Huh?"

"Apple dumplings, not dumples." She repeated the recipe to her.

Soon Kelda was storming off, too, but in her wake she called back, to Joy's surprise, "I'll send some stew and bread fer ya later."

During the "night," as Joy shivered under the bed fur, her nose feeling like an icicle, she felt someone slide under the fur on the other side of the baby. There was no light. She was saving the torches for those times when the baby was awake or she had work to do. "Who is it?" At first, she was hopeful that it might be Brandr, but she almost immediately dismissed that idea. He would have made more noise, and his weight would make more movement under the cover.

"'Tis me. Gran Olssen. I figger two bodies kin make more

heat than one, though this ol' body is mostly bones. No fat ta speak of. Besides, ye will need someone ta watch the wee one when yer muckin' and milkin'." She was right. Bergdis had taught her how to milk a cow, and it was hard working with the child next to her, demanding attention.

Still, she couldn't accept help from the old lady. "Oh, Gran, you shouldn't be here. Brandr will consider it a betrayal."

"The boy is a fool. And he is surrounded by enough like fools. Yer not ta worry, girl. All things work out in the end."

"Why don't you resent the baby, like everyone else?"

"I have seen too much hatred and fighting over me years. Mayhap 'tis time ta make peace. Mayhap this child could be the first step."

On those encouraging words, the old lady was soon snoring.

Unfortunately, two more weeks passed by with no change, except that the winter winds brought more snow and cold. She found herself crying whenever Gran was not around. Except for Gran, visitors stopped coming. She was lonely and hungry and cold all the time.

It was hopeless.

She needed a knight in shining armor, and there wasn't a damn one in sight.

# Chapter 17

**His armor wasn't shiny, but he could be a knight, dammit! . . .**

It was late one night, three sennights after the wench from hell had chosen a barn and a babe over him. He was sitting alone before the hearth fire in the great hall. Ale no longer brought the stupor he needed for numbness. Everyone else was asleep or pretending to be in order to avoid his out-of-control temper.

So he was not in the mood for Gran Olssen, who hobbled up to him on her cane and sank down beside him on a bench. He was hurt and angry that the old lady, who had been at Bear's Lair for more than half a century, had chosen to disobey his orders that no one was to help the wench or babe in the barn.

"The girl is ill." That is all she said.

"What girl?" he asked after a long pause, although he already knew, and he did not care. Leastways, he did not want to care.

When he said nothing more, the old lady sighed and began to rise.

"How ill?"

"Very. She has been fighting a running nose and head pains and body aches fer two days. Now the fever has taken over."

"Fevers come, and fevers go."

"And some lead to death."

*Death? Nay, it cannot be!*

"Ah, well, 'tis in the hands of the Norns of Fate now."

The wily old witch! She knew he would not leave Joy's fate to the gods. Not when he could help.

Standing, he stormed through the hall, grabbing a wall torch on the way. Tork glanced up with a question, from where he'd been dicing with Sven the Scowler. He began to rise, as if to come help Brandr with whatever was distressing him.

Brandr motioned him to stay and was soon out in the bitter cold. How was Joy standing it? Surely, the barn was not warm enough, even with the bed furs he'd seen Arnora and Gran Olssen dragging out. Why had he not thought of this afore?

Into the barn he went, letting the door slam behind him. In the pitch-black, he could not tell where she was, although he recalled that the babe had been in a far stall. Making his way there by light of his torch, he could only think, *It is so cold in here. How could I have left her here? What kind of man am I? I should have forced her to return with me.*

At the last stall, he put the torch in a wall holder and went in. Joy was rolling about, uncovered, whilst the babe was wide awake, only its little face peeping out of the bed furs.

Kneeling, he put a hand to her burning forehead.

"Brandr? No, you can't take the baby. You can't." Even in her delirium, she rolled over and took the baby in her arms, clutching him so hard the baby began to cry. Did she think he would hurt the babe? Well, of course she did. Had he not left the babe out here to survive or die on its own? He had known when he entrusted the baby to Bergdis that it would be neglected. It had been his halfhearted attempt at humanity. And, truth to tell, he had never asked after its welfare once in the past five months.

"You must come inside. You are sick, Joy."

"No, no, no! I won't leave my baby."

*Her* baby?

"You can't make me." Tears were rolling down her face. Her eyes were glazed with fever as they implored him.

"Shhh," he said, picking her and the babe up and tucking a fur over them both. He kissed her damp forehead. Suddenly, he noticed that the babe had stopped crying, and blue eyes as crystal clear as Liv's gazed up at him, trusting. In fact, it shook a bone rattle in its one fist, then whacked him a good one on the chin with a giggle. He supposed he deserved it. A vise tightened over his heart 'til he could scarce breathe. "I will not leave the child, Joy. I promise."

Though, gods help him, he did not know what he would do. He just knew he could not let her die.

He loved her. Three sennights of his madness had convinced him that he could not live without her. Forget pride and hatred and stubbornness.

But was it too late?

### The miracle of a mother's love . . .

For two days, Brandr sat by Joy's bedside as she struggled to live. The fever just would not break.

Every time she became remotely lucid, and there were only a few instances of that, she worried over the baby. And he would have to pick up the little mite from the cradle Osmund had hastily built and hold him in front of her face to prove he had not tossed him off a cliff or drowned him in a fjord, as she seemed to think he would, from her feverish ramblings.

And the damn baby kept smiling at him. Did Matthew not sense how Brandr hated him? And what kind of name was that for a Viking baby, anyway? Sounded like a Christian apostle.

Folki was the closest they had to a healer here at Bear's Lair, and he would be damned if he would let the incompetent old man near her. Instead, he and Arnora had taken turns swabbing her down with cold cloths and caring for the baby. The baby who was crying once again.

Today was the worst. He just could not get the baby to sleep. If he was not crying, he was fussy, wanting to be picked up. Brandr had sent an exhausted Arnora off to sleep. With a sigh, he went over and checked the baby's nappy. He was dry, for once. By Odin! The baby did piss a lot. So Brandr picked him up and held him up to his shoulder, walking around his bedchamber.

"You are a pain in the arse, do you know that, Matthew?"

Matthew grabbed for one of his war braids and yanked. Hard.

He laughed. "Yea, I can be a pain in the arse, too."

"Gaaa," the baby said.

"What are we going to do about Joy, you ask? Your mother Joy, I mean. Leastways, that is what she says she is. Bloody hell, what a mess! Ooops, I should not swear in front of you, should I?" He leaned back to better see the drooling baby, who favored him with a toothless grin.

There was a soft knock at the door followed by, "Brandr?"

It was Liv.

He tried to disengage his hair from Matthew's fist, to no avail. But then it was too late.

Liv opened the door and came in. It was clear by her bloodshot eyes and red nose that she had been crying. Nothing new there.

"Liv, dearling, come back later."

"Let me see him."

"Are you sure?"

She nodded and stepped farther into the room.

He turned the baby in his arms, and it was the most amazing thing. The baby stilled and stared at Liv as if he recognized her.

"Arnora says he looks like me when I was a baby."

"He does."

"Do you see aught of the Sigurdssons in him?"

"Nay, they are mostly red-haired, as I recall."

"Is he smiling at me?"

"No doubt he is about to fart in my hand."

"Oh." Liv's lips twisted with a grin she tried to hold back. "How is Joy?"

"No better. No worse."

"Is she going to die?"

"Not if I can help it."

"The baby is important to her?"

"Very."

"Is it my fault she is so ill?"

"Liv! Why would you ask such a thing?"

"If I had been willing to care for my own . . ." With a long sigh, she held her arms open for the baby. "Let me."

"What?" He was shocked. "Liv, you do not have to do this."

"It might help Joy," she said. Then in a smaller voice, she said, "And it might help me, too."

The baby went gladly into her arms, staring avidly at her face.

Liv smiled down at him. "What do you see, my pretty one? Do you see your mother?"

Brandr plopped down into a chair, too stunned to say or do anything.

"Can I take him to my bedchamber?" she asked.

He helped move the cradle and baby clothing and nappies to her room. When he came back, he sat on the edge of the bed, still stunned at how easily Liv, after all this time, had taken to the baby. He could only hope the rest of the folks at Bear's Lair would be so receptive. Well, they would have to, he decided in that moment, or they would answer to him.

He smiled to himself.

And that was when he noticed Joy's eyes, wide-open and staring up at him.

"Hi!" she said.

*What kind of greeting is that?* he thought, but then chastised himself. *She is alive, and she is awake.*

"Hi!" he said back.

She tried to smile, but even that was too much for her cracked lips. Then, almost immediately, panic filled her green eyes as she tried to sit up. "My baby . . . where's my baby?"

He forced her to lie back down. "With its mother."

"What do you mean?"

"The baby is with Liv. Is that not wonderful news?"

She gasped. "You took my baby."

"It is not your baby, Joy. Not anymore."

She whimpered.

He had meant his words to be of comfort, to assure her that all would be well with baby Matthew now that Liv had taken him to her bosom, but instead tears filled her eyes and began to trickle down her face, a face that was gaunt from all the weight she had lost. "You took my baby."

"It is for the best, Joy. Once you are well, you will see—"

"I hate you. You are an unfeeling monster. I hate you, hate you, hate you."

### She wasn't jealous. She must have eaten something green . . .

Joy had not spoken with Brandr in more than a week, and she was ready to climb the walls or scream in frustration.

It didn't help that it was dark so much of the time, the winter solstice was approaching, and the days would not become longer for weeks, maybe months yet. They were all suffering a bit from SAD, seasonal affective disorder, where lack of sunshine caused depression.

Ever since she'd overreacted and vented her anger on first coming out of her fever, Brandr had made himself scarce. The first two days, she'd floated in and out of her feverish state, her climb back to normal health slow and painful. Arnora nursed her as best she could, and Liv came in occasionally with the baby. And she'd drunk so much chicken noodle soup she was about to cluck, the kitchen staff having recalled her words about the healing properties of that modern medical standby.

It was unreasonable, she knew, but Joy was jealous of Liv and heartsick that little Matthew would no longer be her baby. The zinger had been when Liv told her she'd named him Erik after a favorite uncle. Didn't matter that Joy had already named him Matthew. She was in no position to argue.

On the second day, Arnora came in with one of the male servants, and they removed her and all her belongings, meager as they were, to Liv's bedroom, which they would share with the baby. Brandr didn't want her anymore. Afterward, she was forced to endure the double pain of seeing Liv bond with her child and no longer having Brandr in her life. To reinforce her agony, the amulet that read in runic letters "I belong to Brandr" had been removed from her neck. How crazy was that, being upset about a thrall collar taken off?

Despite her efforts, he refused to speak with her. Instead, he relayed, secondhand, that she should take any of her problems to Arnora or Tork. As if her love for him was a problem! When she'd waylaid him in the storage room yesterday and started to say, "I'm sorry," he'd put up a halting hand. "I am not interested." And he walked away.

Even worse, this noon she'd seen him chatting, up close and personal, with a young woman, early twenties, whom she hadn't noticed before. Liv told her that Inga was the widow of one of the men killed during the Sigurdsson assault. She had been away visiting her mother in Hordaland at the time with her twin sons, the ones Joy had met in the kitchen.

"She is an upstairs maid. Brandr is probably just giving her directions for cleaning the bed linens."

Joy looked at Liv.

"Well, mayhap not."

Right now, Liv was rocking the cradle where Matthew—rather, Erik—was about to fall asleep, his little thumb in his mouth. Joy had to admit, the baby was better off with his mother, now that she'd had a chance to be more rational. Better for both the mother and child. Not that Joy's heart didn't ache just a little bit when she held him occasionally.

As she tidied up the room, putting soiled nappies and

clothing on a pile to take to the laundry, she said, "I don't understand why Brandr won't at least talk to me. I know he wasn't in love with me, but he seemed to care. How can caring turn to loathing so quickly?"

"My brother spent an entire sennight at your bedside. Little did he sleep. His only concern was pulling you back from death's door."

"And I said I hated him."

"More than that. You called him a monster, reaffirming what he already thinks of himself."

Ah, now Joy understood. With just one word, *monster*, she'd flung Brandr back into the black hole of berserkness where he'd been when she arrived.

"I don't really think he's a monster," she said. "It was my fever speaking."

"Betimes true sentiments come out with ale or fever."

"No! That's not true. I love him, and I could never love a monster." In that instant, she realized she had a long row to hoe to get back into his good graces, but she was the one who would have to do the hoeing. Where to start? Where to start?

"Can I go down to dinner with you tonight in the great hall? I'm sure Arnora would watch the baby, or you could bring him with us."

Liv shot her a glance of suspicion. "Of course." Then, "Why? You have disdained mixing in company thus far."

"I've got a plan."

### The score was one-one . . .

Brandr's jaw dropped with disbelief as Joy strolled into the great hall with Liv that evening. The nerve of the woman!

She was wearing a red gown with a white apron trimmed in red. The red should have clashed but did not with the wildly curly flame hair, which was held down with a braided silver circlet over her forehead, all thanks to Liv, he was sure. She looked like a bloody Viking queen, not a thrall.

Which everyone must be noticing. But he did not have the heart or inclination to protest.

Even worse nerve had she to walk up onto the dais and sit down beside him. "Hi!" she said.

*Hi? I will give her hi! And how dare she smell like roses! The soap Arnis and Erland had brought for Liv, no doubt!* "I hate roses," he said, like a lackwit. With a grunt of disgust, he rose to his feet, picked up his wooden mug of mead, and walked to the other end of the table to sit beside Tork. He did not need to see her face to know that she was hurt. Well, he was hurt, too. Nay, he was not hurt. He was angry. Bone-deep angry. Besides, it was for the best.

Liv sat down beside him. She looked lovely, like her old self, except more mature. Hard to believe she was barely fifteen, so much having happened to her. She wore clothing similar to Joy's, except hers was blue to Joy's red, and instead of a circlet her blonde hair had been plaited into a single intricate braid that hung down her back. Earrings with blue stones dangled from chains twined round her delicate ears.

"How is the little bratling doing?"

"Brandr!" She smacked him on the arm. "Erik is doing fine, getting fatter every day."

"Are you sure about this?" He feared that Liv felt forced into accepting motherhood of the bastard child. And, yea, that is what he was, no matter how they skipped around the subject.

"Very sure. Joy and I have talked about it. She has worked with rape victims in the past, and my reaction was not uncommon. Women who breed after rape either love the child or do not. Many of them terminate the babe whilst still in the womb."

He stiffened at her first mention of Joy. He did not want to discuss the witch. Not with Liv. Not with anyone.

"It will be hard, little sister. I can protect you whilst here at Bear's Lair, but there will always be those who . . ." He shrugged.

". . . who think I should have killed myself," she finished for him. "As if I had any chance to do that, even if I wanted to! I know there are also others who will not treat Erik well. I guess I will just have to work hard, with your help, to make him strong."

He squeezed her hand. "How did you get so mature?"

"Joy helped me."

He stiffened once again. "Do not mention her name to me."

"Why? She loves you."

"Pfff! She does not. Nor do I want such from her."

"What do you want?"

"Not a thing."

That was when he saw her talking, with seeming intimacy, to Tork. And laughing.

*She laughs while I am like ice inside? She flits so easily from one man to another?*

Slamming his empty mug to the table, disdaining the platters of food being placed on the table in front of him, he stood and stormed out of the hall.

*Out of sight, out of mind,* he told himself.

Even he knew that for the false notion it was.

# *Chapter 18*

**She made an offer he had a hard time refusing . . .**

Joy was a fighter. She'd forgotten that for a while, but no more!

Okay, so Brandr had won the first round by walking away.

This was day two, second phase of her plan. So Brandr thought he could escape her presence by shuffling chairs, huh? Or shuffling himself out of her presence? Well, she would see about that.

That night she waited until the meal was already being served. In fact, the dessert course, her apple dumplings with fresh cream, which had become a favorite of the Vikings.

All the chairs at the high table were filled, except one at the far end. Liv was seated between Arnis and Brandr, who watched her warily as she approached the stairs at his end. At the last moment, Liv rose and moved to the far end, making some lame excuse, and Joy was able to slide into the chair next to him.

"Well done!" he remarked, his eyes taking in the same gown and apron she had worn the night before. Hey, she didn't get that much of a selection. Besides, she thought she looked pretty good. "But have I not made it clear I do not want you near me?"

She placed a hand on his. He turned it, reflexively, and her fingers pressed against the inside of his wrist where she could feel his rapid pulse rate. So, he was not an unaffected as he pretended.

He jerked his hand out from under hers, as if with distaste.

"Actually, I think you *do* want me near you, and that is your trouble."

"Are you going to sigh-co me, or whatever you call it?"

"Psychoanalyze."

He shrugged as if to say *Whatever!* and turned to speak to Erland on his other side.

"What an ass!" she remarked to Arnis, who was grinning at her.

"Dost refer to me or Brandr?"

"Brandr," she said, "though I'm beginning to think all men are asses."

That was reinforced when Brandr stood and held up a hand for silence. When everyone was quiet, he announced, "We have new entertainment tonight. Mistress Joy is going to favor us with tales of the future and how we Vikings are going to fade from the earth. Oh, and mayhap she will tell us about a little blue pellet that can make a man's staff stand to attention for a sennight and more."

Everyone began to call out their approval of their new skald. The old skald was dead drunk at the back of the hall.

Red-faced with embarrassment and displeasure at being put on the spot, she glared at Brandr as he sat down again and reached for his mug of ale. "I will get you back for this."

"I would like to know how. There is naught you can do to affect me anymore." He snickered. He actually snickered at her.

"Well, you see, Brandr, we never got around to engaging in all the different kinds of sex I wanted or planned." She put a hand on his thigh, high up.

His face filled with color, but he didn't shove her away.

So she plowed on, "For example, I could slip under the table when no one was looking, kneel between your legs, and . . ." She told him in detail what she could do. Only when she was finished did she lick her lips and smile at his astounded and, yes, interested, face.

Then she squeezed his thigh, stood, and sashayed across the dais and down the steps, not giving him a backward glance. But she knew that he was watching her.

When there was silence in the room and some of the people had moved closer so they could hear better, Joy began:

"Once upon a time, in the year two thousand and nine . . ."

### Some forms of dining can only be done in twos . . .

Brandr was able to evade Joy for two whole days.

But that did not mean she was not on his mind. Oh, nay! She had managed to implant herself in his brain like an erotic splinter with those images she had suggested at dinner two nights past.

So he decided not to eat in the great hall . . . for the time being. Which was silly, he knew, and cowardly, but he could not stop himself. Or he pretended an interest in Inga whenever he saw Joy approaching.

"It is a defense mechanism," Tork told him, slipping down into the bathing pool beside him.

"Huh?"

"Joy asked to have a chat with me tonight."

"A chat?"

"Yea, that means a talk."

"I know what a chat is. Why are you chatting with the wench?"

"Because she asked me to."

"What kind of friend are you, that you go chatting behind my back?"

"Will you stop interrupting me? I am trying to tell you that Joy believes you avoid her as a defense mechanism."

"I assume you are going to explain."

"You avoid her to prevent yourself from being hurt."

"Mayhap I am just bored with the wench. Didst ever think of that?"

"Ah, well, then, you would not take exception to my tasting the wench's favors?"

He turned slowly to take his friend's measure.

"I was jesting, Brandr. Holy Thor! Do not be so sensitive."

"Sensitive? Nay, do not tell me. Another Joy word."

"Once I find my female side, I will show you how to find yours." He grinned at Brandr. Then they both burst out laughing.

"She has certainly been entertaining one and all with her nightly sagas. Didst know that Rolfr the Ganger in Norsemandy will breed sons and grandsons leading to one called William the Conqueror, who will win a great battle for all of Britain?"

"Truly?"

Tork nodded.

"When?"

"About fifty years from now."

"Do you believe her tales then?"

"I do not know. How about you?"

"Same here. She sounds believable, but how can it be? Time travel? Pfff!"

"Well, the old ones tell fanciful tales of giants and dwarves and dragons and such. How much different would future marvels be? I do not know if she speaks the truth or is just a good storyteller. I do know this, Brandr. She loves you."

"I do not think so, but even if it 'twere so, I do not care."

Tork raised an eyebrow of disbelief.

"'Tis for the best, Tork. Do not join the wench in her games. Yea, I still want her, but it was always going to be a dead end. Either she will go away in a poof, or I will wed some suitable Norse maiden, and you know she is not the type to share."

"She would probably cut off your manpart and make it into some gel, like ram's testicles.

He winced but then grinned at his good friend.

"Do you think there is any of those apple dumples left?"

"I was thinking more of a tun of ale."

"Perfect. Beer and apple dumples."

But, truth to tell, Brandr was thinking of a different kind of eating . . . one Joy had planted in his head. And no amount of beer or sweet dishes was going to make it go away.

### Dressed to kill . . . with temptation . . .

"Liv, can we go up in the treasure room and see what we can find?"

Liv straightened with shock from the gown she was edging with embroidery in the form of twining acanthus leaves. "You would steal from Brandr?"

"No! I just want to see if there's any clothing there, other than these sexless apron outfits you women wear here."

"Sexless?" Liv lifted her own apron, not understanding.

"You'll see." Later she was the one sitting in Liv's bedchamber, wielding a needle. She'd found a gown "in the Saxon style," according to Liv. It was long-sleeved velvet in a midnight blue color, like Brandr's eyes. Very plain except for some gold silk banding on the wrists and hem, and a very wide gold cloth belt, almost like a bustier. It had a rounded neckline, but it was above the collarbone. Joy was lowering it a bit more to expose some cleavage. Not that she had the breasts for cleavage, not without help anyway. So, with a little creative binding, aided by Liv, she was going to create the impression that she did. It would be the medieval version of a Victoria's Secret push-up bra.

Liv couldn't stop giggling. "Will you not be embarrassed to go out in front of one and all in this wanton garment?"

"You think this is wanton? Honey, you should see what they wear in my time. Dresses so tight they could be painted on, and the hems up to here." She pointed to a place high on her thigh.

"You jest?"

"Nope."

"Do you . . . did you dress like that?"

"No, but not because I thought it was objectionable. It just wasn't me. Besides, I've been in WEALS training where such clothing would be unacceptable. Men and women dress the same there. *Blah*, being the key word."

"I cannot believe you shaved, as well."

"Almost all women do, in my time. It feels great."

Liv looked skeptical but then she asked, "Mayhap I will try it when I bathe on the morrow. Will you show me how?"

"Sure." *Why not?* Joy figured. She'd already gotten herself in trouble for a dozen other reasons. Helping Viking women to get clean-shaven shouldn't be a big deal.

All her high hopes didn't last long, though. No sooner had she entered the hall than Brandr confronted her. "Oh, nay! Never! You will not be going in front of my men dressed like that."

"What's wrong with how I'm dressed?"

"Have you totally lost your senses? Not only are you a thrall, but now you would sell your wares."

"Thrall, thrall, thrall! I'm sick of hearing that word." She went rigid with affront. "The only man I was trying to interest was you, but then you're right. I've lost my senses to think you are worthy of my *wares*."

"Is that so?" They were both glowering at each other. "And, by the by, where have you been hiding *those*?" His eyes were about bulging out at her bulging breasts.

"I don't know what you mean." She straightened, which caused her breasts to be even more prominent.

He used a fingertip to trace the edge of the bodice, which caused her nipples to rise and harden, evident under her dress's thin fabric.

By his grin she knew that he had noticed. "Do not think you can entice me with these beauties. I have seen better."

"Bite me!" she said, spun on her heel, and went back to

Liv's bedchamber, tears of hurt—and, yes, frustration—filling her eyes.

She was already gone before he muttered, "I would like to. Gods help me, I would like to bite you, every blessed wanton bit of you."

## Hit me with your best shot . . .

"Uh, Brandr . . ."

Brandr was just breaking fast the next morn when Tork approached him. "What?" he snapped.

"In a sour mood, are ye?"

"Bite me!" he said.

Tork just laughed at the expression he had picked up from Joy. An appropriate one, he had to admit.

"You might want to come out to the exercise room and see how bow-skillful our newest archer is." Brandr's father had built a huge annex onto the keep where he stored weapons. In the winter months, soldiers repaired and sharpened their swords there, but they also engaged in exercises of sorts.

"I will be there soon enough." He'd been up for three hours and had worked up an appetite, not just engaging in swordplay but setting up wrestling matches betwixt some of his men to build muscles and raise spirits, helping to cart deadfall limbs from the forest for firewood, and riding his horse down to the fjord and beyond, checking the ice fishing nets. At this time of year, they had to make use of every daylight hour they had.

"Whate'er you say." Tork grinned as he reached for a piece of manchet bread with a slice of hard cheese.

"I assume that grin means you are up to some mischief."

Munching on his bread and cheese, Tork did not answer immediately. After swallowing, he said, "Not me. Your new archer."

Fine hairs rose on the back of his neck. "She would not."

"She would."

"Bloody hell!" he swore, shoving his own food aside,

stomping down the steps, across the hall, and through the long corridor leading to the adjacent room, which was huge, as big as the great hall, though not heated. Men in the heat of exercise needed no hearths.

And there she stood, dressed in men's—rather, boyling's—braies and tunic with a longbow raised to her shoulder. And, with a whoop of delight, she let loose an arrow, which whizzed through the air with a direct hit to the target.

His men—traitors, all—were laughing and cheering.

"Luck," he declared under his breath.

"She has been doing thus for the past hour."

"And you just now came to tell me?"

"I was enjoying the view too much."

Which Brandr understood when she bent over to pick up a new arrow from the ground, exposing her rounded arse in the tight pants to several dozen lustsome, appreciative male eyes.

*"Joy!"*

She straightened so quickly she almost slipped on the rush-covered floor. "Hi!" she said to him.

His eyes almost rolled back to the whites with fury at her blithe greeting.

Without further words, he took her by an upper arm and nigh dragged her back to the hall, ignoring the laughter behind them and her squeals of resistance.

"What is wrong with you?"

"Everything," he said through gritted teeth. "E'er since you arrived on the scene, everything is wrong."

She tried to wriggle out of his grasp, but he was having none of that. Noticing the gawking folks who began to gather from the kitchen and then the great hall, he continued to drag her toward the stairs, then picked her up and carried her to his bedchamber, slamming the door behind him. Only then did he release her to stand.

"You are two bricks short of a full load, buddy. What did I do wrong now?"

At first he could not speak over his fury and, yea, his fascination with the tempting picture she made. Chest heaving under the tunic, which was belted, thus outlining her female assets. Hips, buttocks, and long legs clearly defined by the slim braies. Her red hair was braided and tucked under a fur hat, which drew attention to her creamy skin flushed from the cold, or more likely, embarrassment over his treatment of her.

He shook his head to clear it and said, "What gave you the idea I would countenance your engaging in military exercises?"

"I'm a soldier. Bows and arrows are not my weapons of choice, but, hey, I've got to practice with something to keep in shape."

"Keep in shape?" he sputtered.

"Military shape. Readiness."

"Readiness for what?"

"Battle."

He threw his hands out in disgust. "See. You prepare for fighting like an enemy. And you wonder why I say we have no future."

"What makes you think I wouldn't fight *for* you?"

"Would you?" he asked, then immediately regretted his question. "Who asked you to?"

"You're impossible."

"*I* am impossible? *I* am impossible?"

"You're repeating yourself."

"Why can you not sew or do normal things like other women?"

"I sewed yesterday, and you didn't like the result."

"What am I going to do with you?"

A wily, siren expression crossed her face then. "I have a few ideas."

"Would any of them involve this?" He lifted her by the waist, pressed her against the wall, then moved betwixt her dangling legs. With his raging erection pressed against her woman's folds, he nigh exploded in his braies, so high was his enthusiasm.

"Brandr . . ."

"Nay, do not talk." He lowered his mouth to hers, hungrily. Meanwhile his hands moved everywhere over her body, settling on her braies, which he soon tugged off, along with his own, never breaking the kiss. Without further foresport, he slammed himself into her slick sheath.

She was in no better condition as she closed her eyes and moaned her own enthusiasm. Was there ever a prettier sight than a woman in heat? Already her inner muscles were clenching and unclenching him, goading him to spill his seed. But not right now. Not if he could hold off. The wench had been torturing him for days. Time to wield a little of his own torture.

Because her braies were caught in her boots, as were his, and she was unable to lift her legs around him in this lack-witted position, he controlled the action. It took every bit of holding power he had, but he managed to employ long, slow strokes on her unending peaking. A remarkable feat, since her woman's channel was fighting a muscular tug of war to keep him in. He had never experienced anything like it in his life.

"Please . . . now . . . oh, Brandr!" She was mindless in her throes of ecstasy, her hands flailing, then tunneling in his hair. Kissing him with mouth and tongue and teeth. Once, she even bit his shoulder.

In the end, when he was pounding into her, hard and fast, she let loose a loud, keening howl of bliss. He might have roared himself, so great was his sex pleasure.

Once the madness had passed, he withdrew from her with sweet pain and yanked up his braies. Only after he'd laced them did he allow himself to look at her.

She was on her feet now but still braced against the wall. Her braies were still down to her ankles, but her legs were spread slightly, and he could see his man seed glistening on her inner thighs. Why that should touch him so, he did not know, but it did.

"A wall banger . . . I cannot believe I engaged in a wall banger with you."

An appropriate expression, he decided, because for a certainty his knees were still trembling. "This was a mistake," he said, wanting to reach for her and hold her through the aftershocks of her peaking but knowing it would be a sign of further weakness. After all, he had already given in to her temptation, despite his best efforts.

Through limpid green pools, her eyes met his. "Why?"

"Are you willing to stay here in this land?"

"Forever?"

He laughed. "A lifetime."

"I'm not sure I can, but I want to . . . I think."

*She thinks? And I am to lay myself open to a woman who thinks she might like to stay with me?* "As my concubine?"

"What? No! I mean, I don't know."

He arched a brow at her.

"If we were in my time, we would be lovers . . . in a committed relationship."

"Committed relationship? What is that?"

"Exclusive. No other partners. Possibly leading to marriage."

"Joy! I cannot wed with you."

"Why?"

"Because . . . because . . ."

She sighed heavily and turned away from him and pulled up her pants, taking time to lace them tightly. "Because I'm a thrall," she finished for him. Then she raised her head and turned to stare at him directly. "Here's a news flash, buddy. Unless you're willing to be open to that possibility, I am no longer going to have sex with you."

"You dare to offer marriage to me? Even if you were a freedwoman, a high jarl does not wed that far below himself."

"No, you idiot! I wasn't asking you to marry me. I was saying that it has to be a possibility. We have to be equal playing partners." She thought a moment. "Below yourself! In what world?"

"What is wrong with being a concubine?"

"How would you feel, if I were a free woman of rank and you asked me to marry you, but I said that I only want you for sex?"

"Huh? What kind of dumb female argument is that?"

"Suffice it to say: the candy store is closed for now, until you come up with the key."

"Does that mean you will no longer be torturing me by flaunting yourself?"

She smiled, and it was not a nice smile. "No. Actually, it means that I will be ramping up the torture."

"So be it," he said, but what he thought was, *I cannot wait. She will see reason in the end. She has no choice.*

## There are wars . . . and then there are "wars" . . .

Joy was running out of ideas.

So it was a surprise to her when Brandr turned to her at the dinner table that night and asked why she had such an odd expression on her face . . . and was flushed. "Have you finally given up the fight and now accept your lot in life?"

He actually had a gentle expression on his face. No, not gentle. Self-satisfied. Overconfident. The jerk!

At first, she was going to say that, yes, she surrendered. He won. She wouldn't be pursuing him anymore. Not that she was going to fall into his bed as a freakin' concubine until someone better, more suitable, came along.

Then something occurred to her. Maybe she was giving up too quickly. "I'm practicing my exercises. Kegel exercises."

"I do not want to know what you mean by that."

But she told him anyhow.

And, although he said nothing, that vein in his forehead looked like it was about to pop. She wondered if something farther down was about to pop, too, but she wasn't going to push her luck by actually looking.

But then the louse turned the tables on her. "Didst know we Vikings have a secret sex trick that we employ on special occasions?"

He was probably kidding. "The times we were together weren't special enough?"

"I was saving it."

"Lucky me! Sounds like you saved it too long. So what is this super sex secret?"

" 'Tis called the Viking S-Spot."

"You mean, like the G-spot?"

"I know naught of a G-spot."

She thought she would get him off balance by explaining, graphically, what it was.

Instead, he said, "Nay. The S-Spot is down in that region, but much more intense and pleasurable for both partners. And it cannot be found with the fingers."

She stared at him for a long moment, waiting for him to explain more. When he didn't, she got up in a huff, stepped down off the dais and, without even being asked, began her nightly skald duties.

"Last night I told you about Hitler and the Holocaust and what we refer to as the Big War. Tonight I am going to tell you about 9/11, one of the worst terrorist attacks in history, which led to war in Afghanistan and Iraq, what you call the Arab lands."

Having the total interest of her audience, Joy talked, but as she talked, she cast a glance Brandr's way every once in a while. He was as intrigued as the rest, but she knew instinctively that part of the attraction for him was herself. The question was how to win this inner war he was waging . . . a war in which she could only be the loser.

## This last cut was the deepest . . .

Joy was sitting at the kitchen table one afternoon, several days later. It was a cozy setting with the warm fire, the puppies asleep in the corner, including Liv's growing Fenrir, who was already earning his name. The hectic morning's work was done, and dinner was many hours away.

The women were intrigued by the practice of tea drinking she'd introduced them to. The raspberry tea she'd brewed yesterday, made from dried raspberries with some leaves still intact, sweetened with a little honey, went over big.

Today, they were not so sure about the gingerroot tea. But she loved that they were game to try all the new things she tossed their way.

She was making apple dumplings *again*, the Vikings not yet tired of that dish, though she'd tried to entice them to puddings, to no avail. Liv was sticking cloves into a smoked ham, which would be baked after the dumplings were done. Kelda was stirring a venison stew in the cauldron, which had been scrubbed this morning, as it was every morning, to Kelda's chagrin but acceptance. Ebba was chopping vegetables.

"Eeeew! That eel is turnin' me stomach," Ebba said, staring at the concoction Inga was preparing with chopped pieces of eel swimming in cream, dill, sliced onions, salt, and pepper. Ebba got up and rushed for the downstairs garderobe, the one off the great hall. When she returned, everyone watched as she went over to the bench to wash her hands and gargle out her mouth, spitting into the slop bucket.

"Are ye breeding?" Kelda asked bluntly once Ebba sat down.

"Methinks so, but 'tis a miracle how it could happen now and not all those years I was with Osmund back in the Saxon lands."

*Maybe because the baby isn't her husband's.* Joy's thoughts must have shown on her face, because Ebba quickly said, "I be four months along. It be me husband's bairn, that is for sure. Unfortunately."

"Why unfortunately?" she asked.

"Well, the child of a thrall is a thrall. That goes without sayin'. Now Osmund will not only have ta earn his own freedom and mine, but our child's as well. It will take many years more."

"That's horrible."

Everyone glanced her way.

"Well, it is. Babies born into slavery . . . how barbaric is that? Explain this whole class system to me."

"There be jarls or high chieftains, like Brandr. The Saxons call 'em earls," Kelda explained. "Then karls, which be wealthy freemen, like Tork. Then reg'lar freemen. Then freedmen. Then thralls."

"What's the difference between a freeman and a freedman?"

"A thrall can buy or earn their freedom, or have it gifted fer some service," Kelda told her. "Then they become freedmen."

*So I could be freed.*

"But even then, a freeman has higher status than a freedman," she continued.

"How so?"

"Let me explain," Liv said. "For every person, the law levies a wergild, or a man's worth or a woman's worth. The amount to be paid in the event of murder, for example. For those higher up, the wergild is significant. For those lower down, it is a pittance. But for everyone there is a wergild. Even animals are assessed a wergild."

"Oh, my God! You're saying that thralls have the same worth as a cow or a horse?"

Liv's face bloomed with color. "I did not mean . . ."

"Sometimes less," Ebba said. "Sometimes more if they have special talents, like a blacksmith."

Joy was stunned and crushed. How many cuts was she going to suffer before she bled to death inside? "Liv, is your child going to be a thrall? I'm sorry . . . I shouldn't have asked that. Really, I didn't mean to offend you."

Liv waved a hand to show she wasn't offended. How far the girl had come! "Nay. Erik is free, as am I."

As was his father, whoever that was, Joy surmised. "And if Ebba's child's father had been one of the Vikings here"—*like Tork*—"would the child be free?"

Everyone at the table shook their heads and glanced at her with sympathy.

The implication was clear. Even though no one referred to her as a thrall, they all considered her one . . . a favored thrall, but a thrall nonetheless. And if she should get pregnant with Brandr's child, that baby would be a slave.

What kind of society had she landed in?

Sensing her distress, Kelda displayed a kindness Joy had never expected and changed the subject. "Inga, I seen ya go off with Baldr the Braggart these last few nights. Mayhap there will be a weddin' come winter solstice?"

Inga—the woman Brandr had been talking to on several occasions, the one Liv said was widowed during the Sigurdsson assault—fidgeted, apparently uncomfortable with the question. "Baldr is a good man. And brave, too. He served with Brandr in the Jomsvikings afore coming to Bear's Lair. Still . . ."

"What holds ye back?" Kelda persisted.

Inga blushed and mumbled, "He is not very big . . . down there."

The rest of them frowned with confusion until Gran Olssen, who had appeared to be snoozing in her corner chair, cackled and said, "She means his manroot is more of a man stub."

They all burst out laughing, including Inga, who quickly added, " 'Tis not that bad."

Of course Joy had to open her big mouth and say, "You know, size isn't everything."

To which Gran Olssen added, "It ain't the size of the stick, 'tis the magic in the wand."

They all laughed some more but then launched into a detailed discussion of exactly what could be done in a situation like that. Which led to a discussion of orgasms, which the Vikings referred to as peakings, and enthusiasm, which was arousal, as in "his enthusiasm was high." Joy had to smile at that, wondering if she had been "enthusing" Brandr much lately.

The women were particularly interested when Joy mentioned multiple orgasms and women's right to demand as much pleasure from sex as the men. And then she told them about their clitorises, which was probably a big mistake. She suspected there would be some spread legs before brass mirrors that night.

Oh, well! Joy had bigger problems to worry about.

Not only was she fighting a battle with Brandr over the

class system here, which would preclude him from any really committed relationship, but now she found that if she ever got pregnant, the baby would be a slave.

A deal breaker, if there ever was one.

Okay, she told herself, she had a birth control implant that had been put in last June, which meant she had roughly six months or so to engage in sex without any consequences. So she could make an agreement with Brandr. Lovers for now, but an end in sight next spring when the fjords were open and she could leave for Hedeby, where she might be able to return to the future. If not that, freedom so she could make a life for herself here with someone else.

*Let's see how enthused he is now.*

# Chapter 19

**Let's make a deal ... or not ...**

The wench trapped him on the way back from the below stairs garderobe that evening. He had been washing his hands at the pitcher and bowl set on a bench out in the corridor, another of her "improvements" to his keep.

"I have to talk to you."

"Is that aught like the talk you gave me against the wall in my bedchamber?" He was in a teasing sort of mood. Good sex does that to a man betimes. Mellows him, despite his best intentions.

"Talk. I mean T-A-L-K."

Apparently she was not like-mooded. In fact, the seriousness of her expression and the nervous wringing of her hands alarmed him. *What now?*

He led her over to a trestle table at the far end of the hall and motioned for a maid to bring them mead. Once it was poured and set before them, he said, "Well?"

"I have a question for you."

When women said that, it usually meant that they had

some grievance. After a heavy sigh and a long draw on his cup of mead, he flicked his finger. "Proceed."

"I haven't been wearing that slave amulet for some time, and you haven't mentioned my garments. Does that mean I am free?"

*Whoa! Talk about laying right into a man!* "What?"

"You heard me."

"Spit it out, wench. Exactly what do you want to know?"

"Come spring, when the weather clears, am I free to leave here?"

His skin went clammy, and blood drained from his head, making him dizzy of a sudden. He wanted to explode with anger at her question, and he wanted to ask, more softly, why she wanted to be free of him. "Why do you want to know?"

"I found out today that if I were to become pregnant with your child, it might be . . . it *would be* . . . a slave."

"Are you breeding my babe?" Pleasure welled in him in the oddest way. He should be appalled. Instead, he found that he liked the idea.

"No! Of course not."

Well, 'twas for the best, he supposed.

"But is it true? Would any child of mine be a thrall?"

*Thrall, thrall, thrall. Here we go again.* "I would treat any babe you bore as my son . . . or daughter."

"That doesn't answer my question. And, yes, I know it would be illegitimate since we aren't married. That's not what I mean. Would it be a slave?"

*Not if I could help it.* "Mayhap."

She flinched as if he had hit her.

"'Tis not so bad." He reached across the table to take her hand in his.

She slapped it away.

Now she was starting to irritate him.

"Free me. Today. Let's end this whole problem once and for all. Clear the air."

*And what then? You will leave me?* "'Tis not so simple."

"Make it simple."

"You do not give me orders."

"I beg you then."

"In all ways that matter, you are already free."

"Make it official."

"Then what?"

"I will make a deal with you."

He threw his hands in the air. "Another deal? Pfff! When have I benefited thus far from any of your deals?"

She ignored his question and went on her own merry way. "My birth control implant will work until next June, roughly six months. I'm willing to be your partner, in all ways, until then."

*All ways?*

"Well, not until June, just until the ice breaks in the spring and the first ships sail to Hedeby."

*All ways?* Her offer held appeal, he had to admit. Swive her silly for months on end. By then he would no doubt be bored with her anyway. Then send her away. He cared not about the loss of coin, her wergild, but for some reason, he cared about the loss of her. "What would you do in Hedeby?"

"It's where this whole nightmare began, and—"

*Nightmare? She considers her time with me a nightmare?*

"—if I am ever going to be able to return to the future, I suspect it will be from there."

He did not believe in her time travel theories, but he did not *not* believe either. If he sent her there, he would be taking the chance of never seeing her again. "And if the reverse time travel does not work?"

"I would find a way to live in this time."

"With another man?"

"Maybe. Later."

"Nay!"

"What do you mean, nay?"

"Nay, nay, nay! That is what I mean. I will not release you. That is my final answer."

She stared at him, dumbfounded. "Why?"

"Because"—*I love you*—" I have plans for you."

"What plans?"

*I have no idea.* "Big plans."

"I better be free in these big plans."

*Talk, talk, talk, that is all she ever does.* "Dost want to go tup a bit?"

She looked at him as if he had lost his mind.

He had. That and his heart.

Where would this all end?

## Joy to the world, really . . .

Another sennight passed in which Brandr evaded the wench's attempts to seduce him. In truth, he was enjoying her efforts and could not wait to see what she would try next. He was not fool enough to think he could resist forever, but it was fun trying.

He and Tork were riding horses side by side on the way back to the keep. They had been searching, to no avail, for the pack of wolves that had been harassing the henhouse at night. They would have to leave guards out that night.

It was a mild day for winter, but a light snow was beginning to fall. Pleasant, he realized. For a long time, he had not thought such days would exist for him again. Was it due to the maddening wench?

"You are smiling again," Tork pointed out

"And?"

"You are either in love, or you know of some jest of which you are not sharing, or you are gone barmy."

"None of those. I was merely thinking of that saga Joy told last night about her jumping out of the sky in a cloud of linen."

"It *was* an amazing story. Dost think there is any truth in it?"

"Hah! We would have to be daft to think so."

They both looked at each other and shrugged.

"Didst know she has been telling the women to demand their equal rights in the bedplay?"

"Yea. What is wrong with that?"

"Brandr! When a man is deep in the alehead, does he want to waste endless time bringing a woman to her peak afore diving in for his own satisfaction?"

"'Tis only fair."

"You have been around the wench too long. Since when do Vikings care about fair play in sex?"

"I always have."

"Me, too, but that is beside the point. It should be up to us, not something deemed a necessity. I wonder what she will come up with next?"

In the distance, they saw a sledge being dragged toward the keep carrying a huge evergreen tree the size of three grown men, one atop the other.

What was even odder was the sight they beheld once they rode across the motte and into the bailey. The tree was being dragged inside, intact. It had not been chopped into firewood, not that evergreens were good for the hearth; they burned too fast. And especially unsuitable were green, fresh-cut trees whose wood had not been seasoned.

Tork chuckled.

"What?" he asked.

"Wouldst dare to make a wager with me that your bed thrall has something to do with this?"

"Firstly, she is no longer my bed thrall."

"Not for lack of her trying. Or your wanting."

"I repeat. She does not share my bed. And, nay, I will not bet with you. The odds are in your favor."

When they entered the great hall, the wench was directing his men—*his* men, not hers—where to place the tree in a huge wooden tub of rocks and water, and how to anchor it to the wall so it would not fall over.

"What in bloody hell is this?" he said when he approached. "Who in their right mind plants a tree indoors?"

She smiled at him, an open, warm, loving smile . . . the first she had graced him with in many a sennight, certainly since he had refused her offer of a deal.

And his foolish heart twisted with joy.

"Not just any tree," she said. "A Christmas tree."

"A Christ tree? In a Viking hall?"

"Yes. Isn't that wonderful?"

"I can think of other words to describe it. That is not one of them."

"Really, Brandr," she put a hand on his arm, "it's what we all need at this time of year when so many people are suffering from SAD."

At first he could not think for the pleasure that shot through him at her mere touch. But then her words sank in. "I take offense, milady. My people are sad? Why? We have not been attacked in a long time. We have a roof over our heads, a warm fire, and food to fill our bellies."

"Not that kind of sad." She squeezed his arm and smiled.

He wished she would not touch him and smile and jabber on at the same time. He could not concentrate. He blinked through his confusion. "There are different kinds of sad?"

"I meant seasonal affective disorder SAD. That's where the long winter days with little sunshine make people get depressed. You have no idea how much sunlight affects people's moods."

"We cannot have depressed Vikings, can we?"

"You don't have to be sarcastic."

"And what has all this to do with trees shedding all over my keep?"

"More sarcasm! Listen, I figure by the marks I've been making in a piece of wood that it must be about December fifth . . ."

"What wood have you been marking?"

"Do you have to keep interrupting me?" She blushed. "The underside of the arm of the chair in your bedroom."

"You have been going into my bedchamber every day?"

"Yes! Would you stop harping on all these little irrelevancies?"

"Chopping up one of my chairs is irrelevant?" He was enjoying prodding her into a temper, immature as that was.

She made a clucking sound of disgust. "I love the Christmas season. The whole Yule season, especially all the weeks leading up to Christmas day. The tree. The decorations. The singing. The Christmas stories. The baking. The feast. Is it wrong for me to want to celebrate it here and share my traditions with your people?"

" 'Tis not wrong. In truth, we celebrate the Yule here, too, except we call it *Jul*, and it comes at the time of winter solstice, to mark the end of the long, dark days of winter. A reaffirmation that winter is not forever, and life goes on."

"Can't we combine the two celebrations? Except it would be an early *Jul* this year?"

He heaved a long sigh at yet another of her interferences in their everyday life. "As long as it does not disrupt our routine. No more havoc."

"It won't. I promise." And she nigh skipped off, no doubt to create more havoc. But then she skipped back, reached up, and kissed him quickly on the lips. "Thank you." And she was off again.

At that point, he decided, she could create all the havoc she wanted. That warm mood carried him through the day's work . . . until that evening when he entered his great hall, and his eyes nigh bulged from their sockets at the transformation.

### There are many different ways to celebrate . . .

Joy was in rare form that night, and she knew it.

She love, love, loved the Christmas season, and she was going to make sure all these primitive people enjoyed it as much as she did. Starting tonight.

Shifting from foot to foot in excitement, she waited for Brandr to enter, then rushed up to him. She wasn't surprised by his shock on first seeing the things she had done. It *was* an amazing transformation.

He was about to speak, probably to protest.

She wasn't about to let him rain on her parade, or Christmas cheer, so she put a forefinger to his lips. "Shhh. Don't say anything. Give me a chance to explain everything."

"You put a dead tree indoors and then placed lit candles all over it. That is an invitation to fire, if ever I saw one."

The eighteen-foot tree was beautiful, in her opinion, even without modern electric lights and fancy ornaments. "It's perfectly safe. Those twin boys, Brokk and Gandolf, have the job of watering the tree morning and night, and I've set buckets of water beside the tree in case there is a fire. Besides, it will only be lit at night, during the evening meal."

"How many bloody candles did you use? Have we any left? They must last 'til our next trip to the markets."

"Only fifty."

"Only fifty," he mouthed silently. Then, aloud, "And all that red ribbon and the crystal beads?"

"From your treasure room. Oh, don't get in a snit. I'll return them, good as new, once Christmas is over."

"A snit? I do not snit." Then he smiled, dimple and all.

Her heart turned over. She loved him so, despite his archaic views.

"I know for a fact that I did not have a copper star in my treasure room."

"Oh, that! I had your blacksmith cut the bottom out of a copper kettle and cut the shape. Then I polished it up a bit."

She thought he might object to her ruining a perfectly good kettle, but he didn't.

He laughed. "What am I going to do with you?"

She had a few ideas. "Just give me a chance to show you tonight. If you don't like it, I'll take it all down."

He agreed and let her lead him up to the dais, just as a group of children came in singing, as she'd taught them, "Jingle Bells," accompanied by actual ringing of cow and sleigh bells.

At first, there was a period of stunned silence, then all Brandr's people began to laugh and join in the singing. Like people everywhere, the Vikings welcomed an occasion to party.

"Unbelievable!" Brandr said at her side. But he was still smiling. Joy took that as a good sign.

"People!" Joy said, standing with arms raised to get their

attention. "Today is the first day of the Christmas season here at Bear's Lair, and the first day to celebrate your very own *Jul*. Yes, I know, it's early, but what better thing to do when the long, dark days of winter are still with us. This is what I plan to do."

She then told them how, during the next three weeks, she would teach them songs and stories from her time, like the "Jingle Bells" they had just heard. And she would welcome any of their stories and traditions, as well.

Waving a hand for the servers to bring in the food, she talked while they ate. First, she told them about St. Nicholas and Santa Claus, launching into a recounting of the famous "Night Before Christmas" story. They enjoyed it so much, banging their mugs on the tables, they insisted she repeat it five times and let her stop only when she promised to tell it again the following night.

Then she described how people in her time prepared their homes for Christmas, not just with trees, but decorating with holly and mistletoe. The old skald Alviss waved his hand and hobbled up to the bottom of the dais. "We have legends of the mistletoe, as well."

She smiled and sat down next to Brandr, letting Alviss take the floor. The old man rambled on about mistletoe being the golden bough, the plant of peace, and that when enemies met beneath it in the forest, they must needs lay down weapons and not fight until the next day. After the winter solstice, people placed sprigs of it over doorways and baby cradles for good luck.

"Mistletoe is equated with kissing in my time," Joy called out. "If you get caught under the mistletoe, you have to kiss whomever comes by."

"Well, there is that, too," Alviss agreed. "Baldr, not unlike your Christ, was a good and kindly god." He was speaking to Joy but also to all those in the hall, who were partaking quietly of their food and drink. "His mother, Frigg, goddess of love and beauty, went throughout the world urging fire, water, air, and earth to protect her favored son from harm. But Loki, the jester god, an evil one, to be sure, was jealous, and he found a loophole to Frigg's safe charms: the mistletoe. From its wood he fashioned an arrow and used Baldr's blind brother Hoder to pierce Baldr's heart. Thereafter, Frigg's tears became the mistletoe's berries. And some say that Baldr was thus revived to life, and thereafter Frigg deemed the mistletoe to be the symbol of love, and those passing under it should bestow a kiss." Alviss turned to her then. "See, we are not so unlike."

"Who says Vikings aren't romantics?" Joy remarked, reaching beside her on the table to lace her fingers with Brandr's.

He stared down at their linked hands.

She feared he would draw away from her, as he had been doing for weeks.

Instead, he squeezed her hand. "Well done, wench."

She tilted her head in question.

"It was a good evening for my people. Methinks we will enjoy your Christmas celebration."

"Thank you."

"Nay, thank you," he said, turning to look at her. Then, he stood, pulling her up beside him. "Come."

She knew without a doubt what he meant by that single word. Should she balk and ask for promises? Should she point out all the reasons why she should not? Should she expound again on the barbarism of slavery?

No, none of those. Not now. *Choose your battles,* Joy warned herself. *And seize the day.*

"Yes. Let's move this celebration to your bedchamber."

"Precisely." He lifted her still-laced fingers to his mouth and kissed them, one at a time, holding her gaze the entire time.

# Chapter 20

**Even Viking men can have their worlds rocked now and then . . .**

There was a roaring fire in his bedchamber hearth, much larger than the usual nighttime embers. Myriad candles had been lit about the room. A pitcher of wine and two silver goblets sat on a low table. A bed fur lay on the floor betwixt two chairs in front of the fire. All as Brandr had directed a house servant to arrange a short time ago.

He had known since this afternoon that he would be bringing Joy back to his bed furs. Her smile had been his undoing. Tonight's festivities, all her idea, had only reinforced his desire for her.

And desire it was, like none other he had ever experienced. Sex, of course, but more than that. It was a gentle yearning. A warmth that could grow white-hot in the throes of making love and glow with bone-deep heat that settled in the soul.

It scared him as no battle ever had.

Joy kept turning this way and that, taking it all in. "And you criticized me for wasting candles."

"All in a good cause."

She grinned at him, knowing full well what he planned. And not objecting, thank the gods.

He handed her a goblet of wine, then sank into one of the chairs, watching her. "I wanted enough light to see you," he said. "All of you."

She sipped her wine, still standing near the door.

He beckoned her forward with his fingertips.

After taking a few more sips, she set the goblet down and walked forward.

"Nay. Stop," he ordered when she was about to step on the fur. "Undress for me, sweetling. Slowly. Very slowly. And unbraid your hair." He rested one ankle on the opposite knee and relaxed back into his chair, cupping his goblet on his lap.

Without hesitation, she raised her arms and began to untwine her hair from its intricate three-way braid. Afterward, she combed her fingers through the wavy mass so it lay to her shoulders like a fiery mantle.

"I adore your hair," he said.

"It was the bane of my life growing up. Some of the meaner kids called me Orphan Annie."

"I do not know this orphan, but she must have been a beauty."

"Not quite." She toed off her leather half boots, removed her belt, then began to unlace the front of her gown.

"Slowly," he reminded her.

With a saucy grin, she turned and glanced back at him over her shoulder. Then, slowly, she let the gown slip down her arms to her wrists, where she held it, thus exposing her back down to her waist and the upper curve of her buttocks.

'Twas a beauteous sight. The red hair. The creamy skin of her shoulders and upper arms, which had the muscle shaping of a warrior, but then the feminine curve of her lower back, which was anything but manly. Without warning, she let the gunna drop the rest of the way to pool at her feet. Now she wore only thigh-high black hose. Her entire body, back view, was open now for his inspection, including delightfully plump buttocks.

His blood had already been thickening, but it nigh went to boiling when she bent over to release the ties on her hose, letting them, too, drop to the floor. "Oh, bloody hell!" he murmured at the lurching of his manpart. Not only was she giving him a view of forbidden territory, but her long, long legs appeared to have been shaven. For a certainty, he would explore that modern practice.

"Is this slow enough for you?" she asked, having straightened and turning slowly so that he had a full frontal view.

There was a dreamlike intimacy as she stood, vulnerable to his measuring inspection. High breasts, small waist, red curly hairs, long legs. For some odd reason, he noticed the flare of her hips and wondered what it would be like to have his babe nestled beneath, something she claimed could never happen.

The irony was that he had ne'er yearned to plant his seed in any womb, but now that he knew it was impossible, with Joy, he wanted it above all else.

Stepping forward, he cradled her face in his trembling hands. "You are so beautiful," he said before lowering his mouth to hers. He tried to let her know through mind thoughts and mere lips how precious she was to him.

She put her hands to his chest and raised up on tiptoes to better meet his kiss. Closing her eyes, she opened for him, kissing him back. He could feel shudders rippling through her body, matched by his own shaken composure.

"Slowly," he repeated again and helped her lie down on the fur, legs parted. While he began to remove his clothing, she watched closely, braced on her elbows.

"You like what you see?" he inquired at the slight smile on her face.

"Oh, yeah, but you're the one who's beautiful."

"What a foolish notion! I am too big and rough-edged."

"That's the beauty. You're everything a man should be."

He glanced downward, then lifted his head to wink at her.

"That's not what I meant."

As naked now as she was, he dropped to his knees at her

side. "You are not to move," he declared, "and you are not to speak."

"More orders?"

"For your good."

She laughed.

"For both our good, then. Now let me see all that I would. All the nooks and crevices you have hidden from me."

"I didn't . . ."

"Shhh! No talking. Just lie back and enjoy."

And she did.

And so did he.

Lightly, with fingertips and gentles kisses, he examined her face, which was less than perfect, seen up close. Tiny lines bracketing her eyes and mouth. Brows that were a little too thin. Lashes too light. One side tooth slightly crooked. But, with all her flaws—and he was sure he had thrice as many—she was more attractive to him than the most comely, younger maid.

Moving to her ears, perfect shells that harbored whorls and depths with many pleasure points, he soon discovered. When he wet them with his stabbing tongue, blew her dry, or tugged on the lobes, she sighed her delight.

Her arms and legs got his attention then. Every bit of them. He delighted in her shapely muscles and womanly curves. Even her hairless underarms and definitely her hairless legs were touched and checked and rechecked. He discovered the backs of her knees and the arches of her feet were especially sensitive, and so he lingered there.

Her breasts were already yearning for his ministrations. He could tell by their fullness. Even the areolas were puffed out. And the nipples, they were hard, rose-hued pellets, begging for his suckling.

She saw where he was looking and bowed her back in invitation.

"Not yet, sweetling." He skimmed her abdomen and waist and flat belly with his palm. Flicked a fingertip in her navel.

"Please, here," she whispered, taking his hands and moving them upward.

Even then, he withheld his most ardent attention. He lifted her breasts from underneath. He pressed her breasts together from the sides. He massaged the whole breasts with wide, sweeping caresses of his palms. Only then did he touch the tips. Just barely.

She let out a keening cry and panted for breath. Her legs went stiff, and her hands fisted at her sides. He could tell she was fighting an early peaking.

He could not allow that.

Leaning forward from his still-kneeling position, he took one nipple into his mouth, flicking it with his tongue, over and over and over, then laving it with the flat of his tongue, then sucking hard. His other hand was flat on her belly, holding her down as she shattered, thrashing her head from side to side. His mouth moved to the other breast, and under his palm he could feel the ripples of her woman pleasure.

She stared dazedly up at him. "You're torturing me."

"Nay, I am just whetting your appetite for the real feast."

She tried to laugh, but it came out as a gurgle.

"But I do not like to eat unless I know what food is being put before me," he said in a raw voice. All this holding back was having its effect on him, too, and not just his unruly cock, which was nigh to bursting.

Bringing several candles closer, he forced her ankles up to her buttocks, then spread her wide. Kneeling betwixt her legs, he got his first look at her woman parts.

"I'm going to get back at you for this," she grunted out.

"I can only hope," he said, leaning up to kiss her gently, and even that was an effort when he wanted to plunder her mouth hungrily and take all that she could give.

Sitting back on his haunches, he noted the glistening pearls of moisture on her fleece and in her female folds. "You weep for me."

"Weep? If I do, it's tears of pleasure . . . of anticipation."

"To be sure. Yours as well as mine. Now lie still whilst I look closer."

"Oh, God!" she moaned as he slid belly down on the furs

so that he was raised on his elbows on either side of her thighs. He was so close he could smell her woman musk of arousal.

He used one finger to trace a line from her curls, down to her back, then up the other side. His finger now wet, he inserted it inside to be clasped tightly. In and out he moved the appendage several times. Glancing upward, he saw that her eyes were shut tight, her lips parted, and her chest heaving with barely restrained enthusiasm for the coming of her second rise to ecstasy.

'Twas not difficult to find the nub of her woman's pleasure at the top of the cleft, which stood out, ruby flushed. He traced it carefully, vibrated it side to side, then leaned down to lick it with his tongue. Her eyes shot open, and she tried to close her legs to him, which he would not allow. Instead, he laved her several times more, then inserted not one, or two, but three fingers inside of her, just barely past his fingernails, with his thumb pressed below her nub of bliss. Then he waited to see what she would do.

She did not disappoint.

Holding his gaze, though her eyes were unfocused with her overwhelming need, she began to undulate against him. Rhythmic thrusts that drew his fingers fully inside and his thumb up to strum that other place. She was riding his fingers in the same way a man would ride her with his cock. In mere seconds, she began to convulse around his fingers, which he immediately withdrew.

"Wha-what?" she protested in a gasp of disbelief.

"Shhh. We will peak together this time, dearling." Placing himself at her woman's portal, he moistened the tip of his staff, then plunged in with a long-drawn-out groan of almost painful pleasure. Her muscles were clasping and unclasping him, but he could not dwell on that. With head reared back, he strived to bring himself under control. Which he did, barely. Then he thrust and thrust himself into her, unable to hold back. Forget long and slow. He was drawn almost against his will into wildly hard and short drives toward a peaking so powerful it shook him to the core and drained him to a boneless quaking of his limbs and thumping heart. He might have roared at one point.

Splayed over her, he could not speak at first. When he was finally able to raise his head, he saw she was equally stunned. "Did I hurt you?"

She shook her head, tears filling her eyes.

"I did hurt you," he said, thumbing away the moisture from her cheeks.

"No. I am just so overwhelmed. I've never experienced anything like that before."

"Nor have I, sweetling. Nor have I." He kissed the sides of her swollen mouth. Her jaw. The curve of her neck where the pulse beat strongly.

And he realized, to his amazement and embarrassment, that his member, still inside her, was beginning to grow again. Her eyes widened as she began to notice the same thing. Then she laughed. "You're kidding?"

*I am as amazed as you.* "Dost think you can keep up with me, or are modern women too weak to match a Viking?"

"Is that a dare?" She arched her hips up against his and then wriggled from side to side.

"A double-dog dare," he said, not really understanding what that meant, except that it usually prodded her into doing things she might not otherwise.

Pulling out abruptly so that he was kneeling once again, he took her by the waist and flipped her over. Her woof of breathlessness was soon cut short when he advised her to "kiss the fur." With her face pressed to the fur, he lifted her hips with her arse upwards, knees on the rug but spread wide. Then, before she could ask what he was about, he entered her once again. But this time, he was able to proceed in a more leisurely fashion, fondling her hanging breasts, nipping her shoulder with his teeth, and rocking in and out of her slowly . . . very slowly.

This time their peaking was just as powerful but with a more gradual buildup, each level of excitement raising their yearning to a sharper edge. His enthusiasm had never raged so strong or high.

She screamed . . . she actually screamed . . . when the
first ripples of her peaking began. Over and over she milked
his sliding cock, trying to keep him in. Inside she felt like
molten silk inflaming his staff like tinder. When he spilled
his seed, it was with almost painful, unending spurts to her
womb.

This time, he was the one spent and unfocused as he
rolled over onto his back, splayed to her curious eyes as she
leaned over him.

He reached up a hand to her face, caressing her jaw. There
was so much he wanted to say, but all he could manage was a
fierce whisper: "You are mine."

### Love means different things to different people . . .

Okay, they weren't the three magic words she wanted to
hear. But they weren't bad, either.

Joy stared down at this man who had become so important to her, the love of her life. Nothing had changed since
their conversation about babies and slaves, but she had decided to take each day as it came. Until the end. And there
would be an end, of that she was certain. The only question
was when and how that end would come.

He kissed her, a quick, teasing brush of the lips, then
stood in one fluid motion. For a man his size, he was easy on
the feet . . . and eyes. He tossed another log on the fire, then
stoked the embers with a poker.

Before he could turn around, she rose to her knees and
said, "So, is it my turn now?"

Startled, he turned to find her face level with his belly. A
very nice, flat belly with dark hair arrowing down to a limp
part resting over a nest of dark curls and tight balls. Even as
she stared at him, then licked her lips teasingly, she saw that
part of him move. Just slightly, but enough to show interest.
Which was amazing, after all the energy they'd both just
expended.

"Joy," he said cautiously, reaching for her.

She ducked and rose to her feet. "Uh-uh! My turn,

remember." Joy wasn't a big fan of oral sex . . . either getting or receiving. It was such an extremely intimate act, which should be reserved for a love relationship, almost, none of which she'd experienced in the past. But she had to admit, she'd enjoyed what Brandr had done to her, and she hoped to make him as equally happy.

"Stand still," she ordered and began to examine every inch of his body, starting with the back where she admired with caresses and kisses and just plain looking at his arms and broad shoulders with their planes of muscles. His back was pretty much hairless, but his underarms and legs were covered with curly black hairs, as was his chest and genitals.

When she stood once more in front of him, she caressed the strong tendons in his neck and nibbled at his flat nipples. When he attempted to take her in his arms, she shrugged him off. "Not yet, sweetie."

"Sweetie!" he mumbled. "Sounds like you think of me as a boyling."

She was down on her knees in front of him, where she chuckled. He was erect once again. "Hardly."

Cupping his balls, she tested their weight and couldn't help but notice his hiss of what she hoped was extreme pleasure. At least she assumed so, since he didn't shove her away. Then she ran her fingertips over the top of his penis and remarked, "I'm not the only one who weeps."

He smiled down at her, than jerked with surprise when she licked the bit of pre-come off the ruddy tip.

"Joy!" he cautioned.

"What?" she asked with sugary sweetness.

"You know what. By the gods, you do!"

She wrapped both hands around him at the base, and holy cow! Her fingers didn't meet her thumbs, so big was he. "Show me how you like to be touched."

He did, tossing his head back as she worked on him. His hands were fisted at his sides.

But when she took him into her mouth, all the way, then back out, sucking on the knob at the end, he roared out, "Enough!" Lifting her off of him, he walked them both the short distance to the bed, tossing her to the middle. He lunged after her and imbedded himself to the hilt before she could blink.

"Tease me, will you, wench? We shall see about that."

She tried to tell him she wasn't teasing, but his mouth was on her, devouring her with lips and tongue and teeth. Meanwhile, his hands were everywhere, caressing, pinching, tempting her to levels of excitement she'd never reached before. And the whole time he was plunging in and out of her, like a sex machine, wet, sucking sounds a counterpoint to her moans and his guttural sounds of deep, deep pleasure. Yes, that sounded corny as hell . . . sex machine . . . but it was the only way she could think of to describe what he was doing. Not that she was thinking much at all.

"Stop. Slow down. Too many things happening at once. I can't concentrate."

"Concentrate on this," he shouted and slammed into her so hard, practically to the womb, his pubic bone against her clitoris, that he moved her across the mattress and up to the headboard, where she imploded into one nonending orgasm after another. It was incredible. Blood drained from her head and lodged between her legs. Her lungs burned with heavy breathing. Her heart was going a mile a minute. And then she crashed into a million pieces.

She fainted then. Of course she did. What woman wouldn't?

When she regained consciousness, slowly, it was to find herself wrapped in his arms, her face on his chest, his big, rough hands making sweeping caresses down her back.

"That was amazing," he told her.

"I agree."

"Ne'er have I experienced anything like it."

"Me neither."

He tipped her chin up with a forefinger, wanting her full attention. Then, with an impossible air of arrogance, he repeated his earlier words. "You are mine."

"I love you, too," she said, wanting him to say the words.

But he didn't. Instead, he proclaimed, "I will not let you go."

"I'm not going anywhere anytime soon." She caressed his cheek in reassurance.

"You misread me, Joy. I will not let you go *ever.*"

Those were fighting words.

# Chapter 21

**Even Vikings got the spirit . . .**

Brandr was no fool.

He was a seasoned warrior. He knew when to retreat and plan new strategies for attack.

So when Joy nigh waged war on him, again, on his declaration that he would never let her go, by saying, "I beg your pardon! I *will* be gone by spring," he had said, "Whate'er you say, dearling." But what he had thought was, *Just you wait and see*.

He'd taken her mind off the subject good and well by reminding her, "I have not yet shown you the famous Viking S-Spot."

And then he had.

Afterward, she had been speechless, a remarkable and rare feat for her. In truth, she had probably forgotten her own name, let alone their piddling disagreement. He had been a bit speechless himself. Apparently he had not lost his knack.

As a result, things had gone smoothly with them in the days that followed. They made love by night . . . and during the day, too. Being frank of manner, she shocked him betimes with the things she said and did, which of course prompted him to say and do equally outrageous things. Like she with the honey icicle business, the icicle of which was not icy at all, not by a Norse long shot . . . *long* being the key word. Like him with the episode on the cobbler's bench. She had even invited him to shave her legs one evening in the bathing house. Sweet Frigg! He would never look at his sharpened shaving blade in the same way again.

His people were growing fond of her, too, or leastways they were fascinated with her stories of the North Pole, of which they were familiar, and strange characters like Santa Claus, a fat man with a white beard in a red tunic and braies, and reindeer who could fly, including one particular red-nosed reindeer, and elves . . . who could forget the elves? Vikings were a superstitious folk and loved the old tales of giants and dwarves and trolls and such. She fed into that hunger for fantasy. Which everything she said was, really . . . time travel fantasy.

So he should not have been shocked, but was, when he entered the kitchen now to find her baking mud balls in the bread ovens.

"What in bloody hell are you doing now?"

She smiled up at him. "Making baseballs for the children's Christmas presents. The little children *and* the big ones." She looked pointedly at him, as if he were a big child.

Vikings loved to give gifts, so he could not object to that, except, "Must presents require baking mud?"

"Yes. We needed something for weight in the center. So we improvised by gathering mud and mixing it with straw."

"Where did you find mud this time of the year? The ground is frozen."

"Behind the bathing house," she announced as if she'd just discovered the secret to . . . well, mud.

"Here's one that's already baked." She held out a perfectly round lump of a hard, claylike substance, not unlike the caulking used in wattle-and-daub houses. "See how Liv is covering it with yarn, crisscrossed over and over until it's about the size of a man's fist. Usually they're covered with thin leather, but I don't think we'll have time for that."

Liv grinned at him as she worked at her lackwit job, using a foot to rock a sleeping Erik in his cradle.

This was the barmiest thing he had seen Joy do so far, but for the changes she had made in Liv alone, he would grant her most any indulgence. "What does one do with a baseball?"

"Hit it with a bat. Osmund is making the bats out of hickory limbs. Isn't that great?"

"Just great!"

"Here, catch." She tossed a ball at him.

He caught it just in time.

"That's the way, except when you play outside, you would throw overhand, like this." She pretended to be throwing an object by lifting an arm over her head.

But he was more interested by something she said. "We are going to *play* outside. I like the sound of that. Except it might be rather cold." He winked at her, then turned to go back outside.

"What does he mean?" Liv wanted to know.

"Oh, Brandr was just teasing. He likes to play games with me, like 'Catch Me If You Can.'"

Brandr glanced back at her over his shoulder and gave her his *You will pay later* glower, but he was not really upset with her. He rather liked the teasing games she played with him.

"Hell and Valhalla, he is grinning again!" Tork observed as he was coming in, carrying several dozen thin saplings. "Have you no shame, Brandr? Brave Viking warriors do not go about grinning all the time."

Brandr ignored Tork's remarks and made his own observation. "I am afraid to ask what those are for."

"Hula hoops. Do you not know anything?" Then he demonstrated with one of the strips that had bound together into a circle. Putting it over his head and around his waist, he began to roll his hips in the most humorous fashion, trying to keep the ring from falling down, which it did, to Tork's disgust. "I must needs practice more."

Brandr made a clucking sound at the idiocy. "More Christmas gifts?"

"Yea, and Dar Danglebeard is cutting heavy sailing cord for jump ropes."

"Why would anyone need a rope to jump? Nay, do not answer that. I am sure that I do not want to know."

Sven the Scowler joined them then, and he was smiling. For the love of all the gods, Sven never smiled, especially since they had that fight over his snide words to Liv. Sven had a huge pile of holly boughs in his outstretched arms. "Merry Christmas!" he said as he passed by.

Brandr and Tork exchanged looks of wonder.

Mayhem, the woman was creating mayhem everywhere he turned. But he had to admit, it was a rather nice mayhem.

### The calm before the storm . . .

It was one week until Christmas, and the Viking household was in a full-tilt boogie, jolly Yule mood. Joy loved it!

Snow falling outside, warm fires inside, the anticipation of a big celebration to come. Everything that the holiday season should be, even if it was a thousand years ago.

There weren't that many children under age twelve. Only fifteen or so. But right now they were doing a grand job of singing carols to entertain the post-dinner crowd. The Vikings loved to sing, especially the livelier songs, like "Jingle Bells," "Here Comes Santa Claus," and "Rudolph the Red-Nosed Reindeer." But she'd told them the story of the Three Wise Men and the Nativity, and they joined in "Silent Night," as well. For some reason, they thought the song, "Joy to the World," was funny . . . because of its association with her.

But the lack of children . . . that's why Ebba's pregnancy was so important. Bear's Lair needed new life, the best way to heal after all the sorrow of the past. If only Ebba's baby wasn't to be a thrall.

But Joy wasn't going to think about that now.

One thing she would do, though, if she were to stay here—not that there was any chance of that—was to make sure that there were separate sleeping quarters for married couples. Oh, she knew that many of the huts and smaller longhouses had been burned down by the Sigurdssons and were yet to be rebuilt. That's why they were so crowded here. Even so, inside there should be privacy. She hadn't mentioned it to Brandr yet, because there were too many things on his agenda already. Plus it wasn't her place to recommend changes when she wouldn't even be here to help implement them.

Once again, she reminded herself not to go there. Not now. Not yet.

Brandr linked his fingers with hers under the table and smiled. "Why so pensive?"

"Just thinking about everything I have to do yet before Christmas."

"More?" he asked with mock horror.

"Yes, more." She squeezed his hand, as if in punishment, but she wasn't strong enough to do him harm. "Kelda and I are experimenting with a recipe for fruitcake. Our efforts so far, using honey instead of sugar, have been less than successful. Even the puppies wouldn't eat it."

"Well, I have all the Yule logs you requested."

"Good. Don't bring them in until Christmas Eve, though. It'll give the children something else to look forward to."

"You know that we Vikings have traditions related to the Yule log, too?"

"Really?"

"Yea. Every spark from the log is supposed to represent a new life born in the barnyard. Piglets. Calves. Chickens."

She brightened. "And babies. Human babies, too, I'll bet."

"I do not know about that."

"I do. It's a sign. Your home is going to flourish with new babies in the new year; I just know it."

He narrowed his eyes at her.

"Not me. I already told you that . . ."

"I know. I know. The birthing control device." He did not appear to like the idea of her implant for some reason, which was strange. Most men would relish sex without consequences.

Joy sniffed. "Don't you love the smells of Christmas? The clean hall. The pine tree and holly. Beeswax candles. The baking."

"I must admit, it is pleasant." He cleared his throat, then added, "I thank you, Joy, for the changes you have wrought here. There is a peace that has not abounded for many a time."

"That's Christmas spirit."

"There is that, but more."

She tilted her head in question.

"A Joy spirit."

"That's the nicest thing anyone has ever said to me."

"And for that you get tears?"

She laughed and swiped at her eyes. "I'm just happy."

He held her gaze for a long moment, then said softly, "I am happy, as well."

In Joy's book that was as close to "I love you," as he could get. With sudden insight, she told him, "I think that's why I was sent here. To make you happy."

He was startled at first, but then he grinned, dimple and all, and said, "Methinks there are a few other ways you can make me happy."

# Chapter 22

**Christmas visitors came knock, knock,
knocking on their door . . .**

He should have known. All good things end. But it was
shocking nonetheless to have the end come in the form of
a makeshift sleigh on the fjord, containing a woman and a
boyling of about four years, pulled by four men. All of them
frostbitten and nigh starving to death.

Tork was the first to spot them from the far exercise field,
not the one inside the bailey, where they had been practicing
swordplay. Quickly, he and his men ran to aid the visitors,
whilst Tork led other men inside to get blankets and ask Joy
and Arnora to prepare pallets for the lot, who would surely
be in need of care.

It turned out that these were the only survivors of a shipwreck that had occurred out at sea, near the mouth of Igorssfjord, six sennights past. They had been living in tents,
waiting for the fjord to freeze over so they could make their
way inland.

If the first shock was the arrival of the visitors, the second
shock came when they discovered that the woman was none
other than Dagny, Tork's divorced wife. The third shock was

that her betrothed was Einar Ericsson, who had formerly been promised to Liv. Still more shocking was the boyling with Dagny who very much resembled Tork.

Could things get any worse?

Well, yea, they could.

Joy developed an instant fascination for the monk who traveled with them, a man named Mendozo, Father Jacob Mendozo. He looked rather Arabic to Brandr, but he claimed some nationality Brandr had ne'er heard of: Mexican. Every time he checked, Joy was off somewhere in a corner conversing with the priest. And he did not think the God man was hearing her confession.

Right now, a day after their arrival, Brandr was sitting in a place he would ne'er in a million years choose to be: the far end of his great hall, acting as mediator betwixt Tork and Dagny.

"Fornicated with any goats lately, Torkel?" Dagny asked sweetly.

"None since you, dearling," he replied with equal sweetness.

"Why have you not come home in all these years?"

"I was waiting for you to leave."

"It is my home, too."

"Not after you divorced me."

"I had good reason."

"One mistake! Just one, and I was condemned for life."

"What if it had been me?"

"I would have killed the man. But I see you have found a new man. Do you not think he is a mite young for you?"

"I am only twenty-two to his twenty-four."

"Hah! You are twenty-six, almost twenty-seven."

"If you must know, Einar is not really my betrothed, not that it is any of your concern. We just made up that story to keep some of the shiphirds away from me. Some men still find me attractive. But mark me well, I could have Einar if I wanted."

"By the by, when did you plan on telling me that I have a son?" Tork stared bleakly at the other end of the hall where the boyling, Sidroc, sat beneath the Christmas tree, fascinated by the bright ribbons and crystal beads. The twins Brokk and Gandolf were with him, chattering away, no doubt relating all of Joy's Santa stories.

"If you had ever come home, you would have known."

"What kind of female illogic is that?"

If things weren't bad enough, Joy walked up and sat down beside him. He put his face in his hands, just knowing what would come next.

"Hi, Dagny. I'm Joy Nelson, a psychologist. I could help you two with marriage counseling."

"She comes from the year two thousand and nine," Tork informed Dagny snidely.

"Shut up!" Joy said.

Dagny's startled expression soon turned to one of admiration. She said to Tork, "I agree. Shut up!"

"One of the main reasons that marriages break up is a failure to communicate. Couples just don't listen to each other."

"See, dunderhead," Dagny told Tork. "That is the very thing I said to you on numerous occasions. You just do not listen to me."

Tork rolled his eyes.

"There is this one tried and true method that many psychologists use. It's called mirroring." Joy stood and made Tork and Dagny sit facing each other, almost knee to knee. "Now, let's start with you, Dagny. You tell Tork something that is really bothering you."

"You made love with another woman. That really hurt me." Tears welled in her eyes.

"Now, Tork, what you have to do is repeat Dagny's remark back to her as if you understand."

Brandr and Tork looked at each as if to say, "How can we escape?"

But Tork heaved a whooshy exhale, then said, "I believe what you are saying, Dagny, is that I hurt you by fucking the dairymaid."

"Exactly," Dagny said.

"Notice that I said fuck, not make love."

"Okay, okay, we are making progress. Now you repeat back what Tork just said, as if you understand."

"Tork, you are an idiot if you think that adultery is all well and good if you used your cock and not your tongue."

At the blush on Tork's face, she added with consternation, "Oh, good gods! You used your tongue, too."

"Not in the way you think."

"Go swive a goat, you big oaf!" With those words, Dagny stood and stormed off toward the kitchen.

Tork appeared confused. Then he stood, too, but not before slicing Joy with an icy glance. "Methinks it is time I introduced myself to my son."

"Well, that went well, don't you think?" Joy said to Brandr. "You can see how much they still love each other."

*I can?*

"Maybe we'll have a Christmas wedding here at Bear's Lair. Or a re-wedding, if you will. Ha, ha, ha!"

*That is not funny. Not at all.*

"Besides that, have you seen the way Einar keeps mooning over Liv?"

*What? I will kill him if he dares hurt Liv again.*

"Maybe we'll have a double wedding."

*What world is her brain residing in?* "Whate'er you say, sweetling." *I need a beer.*

**He popped the question, but it was the wrong question . . .**

Joy looked right and left to make sure no one was watching, then slipped down the corridor and into the second storage room, the one Arnora had shown her weeks ago.

Waiting there for her, behind some tall shelves, was JAM, a longtime SEAL, a member of her team. She had been shocked, absolutely shocked, when she had recognized him yesterday coming in with the shipwreck survivors. He'd been wearing a priest's disguise, which wasn't surprising. JAM had at one time studied for the priesthood, or so the rumors went. Quickly, he came forward toward her, giving her a quick hug. "Are you okay?"

"Fine. How did you get here?"

"It was weird. You just disappeared after that explosion in Germany, but there were no body parts found in the residue. Sorry to be so graphic. Then a couple weeks ago we got a signal from your GPS locator. Just a few blips and it was gone."

Joy knew just when that had happened. It had been when Brandr had discovered and removed the device behind her ear.

"That still doesn't explain how you got here."

"It's a long story, but a few years back, some of us SEALs had what I can only call an out-of-body weird experience. Torolf, Geek, Pretty Boy, Cage, and myself were on this reproduction longship in Norway, and suddenly, after a wreck, we found ourselves back in the tenth century, where we ended up fighting and killing this evil villain Steinolf. Then later we somehow managed to return to the future, bringing Britta with us. You know Britta . . . Torolf's wife? She was in one of the first WEALS classes."

Her mouth was gaping open. "How come I never heard about that?"

"Believe me, it's not something we ever talk about. If anyone found out, they would, first, not believe us, then, second, decide to put us in some isolation lab to dissect our parts."

"I guess so," she said hesitantly. "That still doesn't explain how you got here."

"Geek is the one who came up with all the clues." Merrill "Geek" Good was a genius. Why he was a SEAL and not a rocket scientist was a puzzle to everyone. "He took your GPS location, a current and past map of Germany, our knowledge about what had happened with us in time travel, and somehow with all the overlays, he came up with the theory that you had time traveled during the explosion."

"And you went to the authorities with that intel?"

"Hell, no! Only Geek and I know. We decided to go over to that reproduction Viking market town."

"Hedeby," she prompted.

"Right. Once there, we both got all kinds of—not sure

how to describe it—vibes. Geek left, and I hung around for days in a monk disguise." He patted his brown cassock with the hooded cowl and rope belt. "One day some idiot tried to rob me—a priest, ferchrissake!— by coldcocking me with the butt end of a pistol. When I woke up, I was on a longship leaving the Hedeby harbor."

"So, do you think people can just travel back and forth in time?"

"No. Not at all. I think God is involved and miracles and that there's a specific reason why these things happen. Does that make sense?"

She nodded.

"You figured out why you were sent back?"

She nodded again.

"Damned if I know why I was sent, unless it's to bring you home."

A moan of distress escaped her lips before she had a chance to catch herself.

JAM studied her closely. "Is it the brooding Attila the Viking Hun?"

She smiled weakly at his apt description. "Yes."

"He's suspicious of me, you know."

"What do you mean?"

"When I was in the bathing house last night, he came in. After staring me down for a minute or so—and, believe me, a naked guy staring at me in a bathhouse is not my idea of fun—he said something about my being the most muscular monk he'd ever seen. More like a warrior."

"Uh-oh! If he finds out who you are, he's going to consider you an enemy, no matter what I say. He might lop off your head."

"Not if I lop his off first."

"Don't you dare."

"Huh? Did you get motion sickness on your time travel trip and lose a few screws?"

"Probably."

"All we have to do is tell him that I'm a friendly, that I'm only here to take you back."

"You can't tell him that."

"Well, well, well, what have we here?"

Brandr was standing in the open doorway, taking in what he must consider a cozy scene.

*"Benedicat vos omnipotens Deus, Pater, et Filius, et Spiritus Sanctus."* JAM was making the sign of the cross in front of her face, as if he had been giving her a blessing.

But at the same time, although she was momentarily surprised by JAM's Latin, Joy burst out with, "I'm glad you came, Brandr. I can't find the candles that Father Mendozo needs for his church service tomorrow," she lied.

"They are right behind you."

She turned and laughed, or tried to. "Hiding in plain sight."

"Tell me true, what is going on?" Brandr stepped farther into the room. "And no lies."

Joy looked at JAM, and when he nodded his approval, she said, "JAM is one of the SEALs . . . a soldier from the future."

Brandr's hand went immediately to the sword in his belt sheath. "Are you carrying a weapon?"

JAM put both hands up. "No. I'm not armed. You can frisk me."

"Where are the others in your troop?"

"Back in the future."

Brandr made a scoffing sound.

"Hey, I think it's as unbelievable as you do, but it is what it is."

"Why are you here?"

"To bring Joy home."

"Over my dead body," Brandr said. "This is her home now."

"Whoa, whoa, whoa! We've had this discussion before, Brandr," she inserted.

He ignored her and asked JAM, "Are you a real priest, or just a soldier pretending to be a priest?"

"Uh, well, I studied to be a Jesuit priest before I entered SEALs, but I never took my final vows. I did qualify along the way to be a lay minister and deacon, that kind of thing. So, yes, I can do some religious services for you."

Brandr nodded. "Then you can perform marriages?"

"I suppose."

Joy figured Brandr was taking her advice about Tork and Dagny and Einar and Liv. *What a guy!*

"Then you will marry me and Joy on Christmas Eve."

"Whaaat?" she squealed. *The guy is a flaming idiot.*

Finally, Brandr gave her his attention. "What now? You were unhappy as a thrall. Now you will be a wife."

"You told me that a thrall couldn't be a wife."

"I found some loopholes . . . is that not the modern word you taught me?"

"You lied!"

"Nay. I just forgot some things."

"Like?"

"Son of a sword! Like I am the bloody jarl here, and I can bloody hell do whatever I want. And I want to marry you."

"Aaarrgh!"

"What is your problem?"

"Because you didn't ask me, you big lug. You told me."

"Oh. Well, then, will you be my wife?"

"No!"

He threw his arms up in the air in a "So there!" fashion. And JAM just continued to grin at the whole discussion.

"Why?" she asked.

"Why what?"

"Why do you want to marry me?" *Please, God, don't let him say it's because he likes to swive me.*

"To keep you here."

*That's just as bad.* "And that is the only reason?"

"What other reason is there?"

*Clueless! Men everywhere are clueless morons with the sensitivity of a rock.* With a grunt of disgust, she shoved past him and JAM, who was now outright laughing.

**Mayhap cluelessness is contagious . . .**

"I could give you advice," Tork told him that evening during dinner. "I have talents."

Somehow the seating arrangement left the men at one end of the high table and the women at the other end, both casting killing glances at each other.

"Those talents are gaining you great headway with your wife," he scoffed.

"She is *not* my wife anymore."

"She would like to be," Arnis piped up.

"Huh?" he and Tork said at the same time.

"I heard her tell Joy that you would swive anything with breasts. That is a compliment compared to swiving goats, I would think." That was Arnis's lackwit explanation.

"And she stares at you whene'er you are not aware," Erland added.

"And staring is good?" Brandr scoffed again.

"'Tis good when she stares with her heart in her eyes."

Everyone looked at Erland with surprise.

"I did not know you had such fanciful words in you," Brandr remarked after his teeth clicked together.

"Mayhap you should be our new skald," Arnis said, clapping his brother on the shoulder with great gusto. The two of them went off to get more logs for the high hearth, with Erland complaining, "Why is it that everyone makes mock of me when I come up with a perfectly good observation?"

"Arnis and Erland are wrong, you know," Tork said. "If Dagny stares at me, 'tis contemplating new ways to tear me down."

"Why should you care? Holy Thor! You have a face long enough to eat oats from the bottom of a bucket. Methinks you have feelings still for the wench."

"Love and hate are closer emotions than many people realize," said Father Mendozo, who was sucking up a great amount of ale for a priest, in Brandr's opinion. "Seems to me that the constant sniping between you two is a sort of foreplay."

Tork looked at the God man as if he had taken a walk down the barmy road.

" 'Tis like no foresport I have e'er heard of," Tork proclaimed . . . loudly. He was well into the ale joy tonight. They all were. "And, believe you me, my cock is going nowhere near her female parts. She threatened one time to cut it off when I was sleeping."

The priest laughed. "A Lorena Bobbitt, huh?" He went on to describe a woman who paid back her no-good husband in the ultimate way. On those ominous words, he ambled off toward the women, and Joy in particular, to discuss the Christmas service she was planning. Leastways, that was what he said. Brandr still did not trust the man . . . nor Joy, either, after catching the two of them huddled together earlier today.

Einar approached him then. The boy seemed nervous, and, yea, he thought of him as a boy, even though he had seen twenty-two winters. Some males matured at twelve or thirteen when they first went a-Viking, some matured when they were thirty, still others never matured. He put Einar in that middle category.

"Brandr, I would speak to you . . . in private."

Tork made to stand, but Brandr pushed him back down.

"There is naught you can say to me that Tork cannot hear."

"It is about Liv."

He sat straighter.

"I have a fondness for your sister. I always have had."

Well, that was good news, assuming Liv still cared for the boy. "Have you spoken with her?"

"I have . . . or I have tried, but she always has that bratling attached to her hip."

"Uh-oh!" Tork muttered under his breath.

"Bratling?" Brandr asked icily.

"I could forgive Liv for having the bastard, but really, Brandr, could she not put the babe aside now? 'Tis not seemly."

"Are you saying you would wed with her, if she got rid of Erik?"

Einar seemed startled that he gave name to the little one. "Yea. You do understand."

"What I understand, Einar, is that you are a weak, pale excuse for a man." Brandr stood. "If you cared for Liv, as you say, the babe would not matter to you. In fact, you would take it to your bosom, same as she does."

Einar stood, too. "You ask too much. There are not many men who would accept a woman who was thus soiled, let alone her child of shame."

"Uh-oh!" Tork said again, this time louder.

Although Einar was the same height as Brandr, his frame was thinner. Brandr barely restrained himself from knocking the fool to his skinny arse. The only thing that held him back was the recognition that he had felt the same way a short time ago.

"Let us be perfectly clear, Einar. Ne'er would I give my free consent for you to wed with my sister. She is too good for you."

Einar gasped at the insult and started to reach for the short sword in his hip sheath.

"Do not be a total idiot," Brandr warned. "I am this close to tossing you out in the cold. No trouble would I have in thawing your cold corpse next spring. But for the sake of the womenfolk here and their fine sensibilities and not wanting to spoil the Christmas festivities Joy has planned, I will let you go. But have a caution, you whoreson, and stay out of my sight."

Einar raised his chin haughtily and stormed off, swearing under his breath.

Suddenly, Brandr sensed that Liv was watching him. He groaned. Ne'er would he have the girl hurt. But Liv did something surprising. She smiled. Apparently, she was smarter in assessing Einar's worth than he may have expected.

He smiled back.

"Son of a troll! Do my eyes play me false?" Tork exclaimed.

"What now?"

"Do you comprehend what just happened here?"

Brandr looked right, left, and behind himself.

"To you, Brandr. To you. Do you realize that Einar provoked you in the extreme, but you did not fly into a rage? Not so long ago, you would be smack-dab in the middle of berserkness."

*Is it possible?* "You make too much of little."

"You have changed, my friend."

"Is that good or bad?"

"Very good." Tork patted him on the back. "And methinks you have the irksome, blathering, pushy wench to thank for that, much as I hate to give her credit for aught."

Brandr turned his attention to said irksome wench only to find her head-to-head with the priest, sharing some secret. They burst out laughing, and the lackbrain monk looped his arm over her shoulder.

" 'Tis a good thing priests are celibate," Brandr said, gritting his teeth.

"If you mean the good Father Mendozo, I must tell you that I asked him earlier if he did not like sex, if that was why he entered the priesthood, and he told me that he liked sex as well as any other man."

"You jest."

"Nay. Not this time. I said that I thought priests were supposed to be celibate, and he said he is not that kind of priest."

Brandr swore to himself and quickly downed half a cup of mead in one long swallow. "I am thinking about offering a special treat for the Yule feast."

"What? Boar? A hunt for wild boar would not come amiss about now."

"Nay, that is not what I have in mind," he said. "I find that I have a taste for . . . roast priest."

# Chapter 23

**Her clock was ticking . . .**

"He wants me to officiate at a wedding on Christmas Eve," JAM told her two days later.

"Can you do that?"

"Probably."

"Would it be legal?"

"Hey, we're in the freakin' tenth century. How legal are marriages performed by some Viking lawspeaker? At least I have some church credentials, limited as they are."

"You've got a point there."

"Look at that," JAM remarked suddenly. "Is that a pair of women's panties I see on that guy's head?"

"Unfortunately, yes," she replied with dry humor. "And over there is my bra . . . on the outside of that woman's gown."

JAM let out a hoot of laughter.

"So, who's getting married? It can't be Einar and Liv. That boy's turned into a real prick."

"Joy! Such language!"

"If you'd heard some of the crap he's been spouting about

wanton women who have babies after being raped, instead of killing themselves or the baby, you'd call him even worse. So, could it possibly be Tork and Dagny?"

"I suspect they're the ones and the reason for the secrecy. Brandr doesn't want to jinx their reunion, which is tenuous, at best. I did see them making out in his bed closet last night."

Joy smiled. It did her heart good to see things work out for the couple, especially since the little boy, Sidroc, was just warming up to his father.

"How goes it with you and Mr. Dark and Dreary?"

She grinned, knowing that's how she would have described Brandr at the beginning, too. They were still sleeping together and enjoying it immensely. But there was this big blinking elephant standing between them, which they did not mention, and that was his stubborn, ridiculous notion that he could keep her, against her will, by marriage or some other means. As if she would marry a man for any reason other than love. And that had not been mentioned, ever.

"The guy's nuts about you, Joy."

"I don't know about that. He likes sleeping with me, but . . ."

"Is there any chance at all that you want to stay here? Because you gotta know, it's your decision. I'm not gonna force you to go with me or even try to convince you that it's the best thing."

"You don't think I have an obligation to the military?"

"Hell, no! This time-travel crap goes beyond any Navy regulations. The rule book doesn't cover thousand-year black op trips. That would take 'boots up' to the extreme."

"Would *you* want to stay here?"

"Nah! But then I have no incentive, like you do."

"I would hardly call Brandr an incentive."

He arched his brows in disbelief. "I wouldn't mind staying here, in the past, for a while. It's interesting, if nothing else."

"And you think that you can go back anytime you want?"

"No, I don't expect to be able to dictate when and where

or even if it will happen. But I'm still a great believer in God and the power of prayer. Once I'm back in Hedeby, I'm pretty sure that eventually it will happen. And if it doesn't . . ." He rolled his shoulders as if to say it would be beyond his control.

"Then, are you saying I could wait until I'm ready to go back?"

"I don't think that's the way it works. Have you figured out why you were sent back?"

"I think so."

"Have you accomplished it?"

"I think so."

"Then your clock is already ticking, babe."

That's what Joy was afraid of.

### Beware of big men with big plans . . .

Brandr was making plans. Big plans.

And he was afraid they were all going to blow up in his face.

*Nay, I will not let that happen. I will succeed.* He was a seasoned warrior. He knew well and good that the best battles were won in the planning, so he would treat his pursuit of the wily wench like a military campaign. With him as the victor.

*Nay, nay, nay! That is not the way of it, either. We will both be victors. She just does not know it yet.*

"Arnora, did you find the gown yet?"

"I did, and it has been cleaned and aired out."

It had been his mother's wedding gown. A red so dark it was almost black and made of wool so soft it felt like silk. The garment had a gold link belt that hung low on the waist, with a matching linked torque to fit tight to the neck. There was also a ruby-encrusted head circlet, which would have been twined with flowers in the summer months. He had advised Arnora to use holly and mistletoe, instead . . . his own private jest. The raiment was completed with black velvet slippers.

"You are doing this backwards, Brandr," his stepmother said. "You should ask Joy to marry you before preparing the wedding."

"This is my way," he insisted.

"Barmy, if you ask me."

To Kelda, he said, "Make me a wedding cake."

"Whaaat? I doan know how ta make no weddin' cake. Do ye mean oak cake?"

"No, a wedding cake. And it should have many layers and be topped with frosting."

"Frosting? What is that?"

"Some sweet goop."

Kelda put both hands on her hips. "That is clear as pea soup."

"Use heavy cream, and mix it with a bit of sugar. I think there is some in the second storage room, locked in a special chest. Arnora will know for sure. Then ask Joy about frosting . . . sneaky like. Don't tell her why you want to know."

"Doan blame me if it is all a disaster."

"It will be wonderful, Kelda. I am depending on you."

Puffing her chest out with pride, she conceded, "I will do me best."

Next he asked Osmund if he would make an arched trellis, which could be decorated for the marriage ceremony. In lieu of a church, he wanted something to give a ritual note to the affair. "And a cross. Christians always have a cross or two. Make a cross, as well."

Osmund did not argue with him, as Kelda had, but the look in his eyes said, "Barmy, barmy, barmy!"

Then he took a piece of silver and a chain to the blacksmith with specific directions for his bridal gift. If this did not win Joy over, nothing would.

Now he needed to seek out the priest-soldier and get his cooperation. For that, he might need some reinforcements. Incentives, so to speak, to gain the priest's cooperation.

"Tork," he yelled. "Bring a jug of ale . . . or five."

## How do you say "dum dum dee-dum" in Old Norse . . . ?

Everything and everybody was really weird.

Joy was about to go down to the great hall on Christmas Eve wearing the spectacular outfit that Arnora had laid out for her. She'd asked Arnora why she was being given such a fine garment, and the old lady had just said that it was Brandr's gift. The gown had belonged to his mother.

Grateful that he would honor her so with such a priceless Christmas gift, Joy wore the gown but determined to return it before she left. Well, of course she would. How could she cart a valuable gown through time?

Which made Joy get depressed once again, thinking about going home when she really did not know where her home was now. But not today, she determined, shaking her head to rid it of unwelcome thoughts.

In the hall, also preparing to go downstairs, was Liv, who carried her sleeping baby on her shoulder. Liv was dressed for the festivities, too, her amber gown a perfect complement to her pale hair. It was amazing how Liv had gone from a reclusive, shy girl, not wanting anything to do with her child, to this gentle mother who chose never to leave her baby behind. Joy could only hope that Liv found a man someday who would appreciate her for the wonderful person she was.

"I am so excited," Liv said in a low voice so as not to wake the baby. "We have not had a feast like this since . . . well, since long ago. Our mother was alive then . . . mine and Brandr's. That was her gown, you know."

"I know, and believe me, Liv, I'm well aware it should go to you. I'll be returning it."

"Nay, 'tis Brandr's to give as he chooses."

They both gasped when they emerged from the stairwell into the hall. Candles and torches glowed everywhere, along with huge fires from Yule logs in the five hearths. The smells of holly and pine and good cooking permeated the air. Clean rushes scented with lavender had been laid on the floor that afternoon. Someone was playing a musical instrument somewhere. Probably a lute. Happy voices wafted over everything. It truly was a Christmas feast. A Viking Christmas feast.

"It is magical," Liv said in a hushed voice. "I wish Erik were old enough to see all the lights and hear the music. You must help us do this every year, Joy."

Joy nodded, although she doubted she would be here even one more year.

Then Brandr was there, standing before her with a huge dimpled smile on his face. "You are beautiful," he said in an awestruck voice.

"You don't look half bad yourself."

He wore all black: wool tunic, slim pants, leather belt with a silver buckle, even black cross-gartered boots. But all the black was edged with red and gold embroidery in an intricate bear design, like the Bear's Lair flag, which flew on their longships.

"How about me?" Liv complained in a fake whine.

"You always look pretty, little one."

"Little one? Hah! You will be calling me that when I am thirty."

"No doubt," he said, chucking her under the chin and giving the still sleeping baby a fond caress.

Then he held an arm out to each of them and led them across the hall and up to the dais, fielding greetings of "Good Jul" and "Merry Christmas" along the way.

Already on the dais, each in their finery, were Tork and Dagny, who indeed were dressed to kill . . . or to wed, along with Arnis, Erland, JAM, and a few others of Brandr's hersirs and their mates. Einar was at the far end of the hall, thank goodness.

"I just love Christmastime," Joy said, once seated, as the servants began to carry in platters of food.

"That is obvious, and contagious." Brandr raised their linked hands to his mouth and kissed her fingers. "Do you feel at home here, Joy? Nay, do not answer that. 'Tis just that you seem comfortable."

"Certainly more so than on my arrival. Nothing like being someone's present." She flashed him a teasing grin. *The only thing missing was a bow around my neck. Instead I had a thrall collar.* But she would not bring up that sore subject now.

The children began to sing some Christmas songs while everyone was eating, and their conversation was cut short. JAM exchanged a look with her at one point when the kids were leading the crowd in a rollicking version of "Rudolph," with one of them prancing around with a red puffy wool nose, pretending to be a reindeer.

She had to admit that the Vikings were adaptable, as historians had relayed, and they enjoyed a rowdy good time. They also loved gift giving, which would come in the morning.

After the main course but before the dessert, Brandr stood and raised his arms for silence. When all was quiet, except for the crackling fires, he said, "I have an announcement to make. Henceforth, there will be no thralls at Bear's Lair."

Shock held Joy speechless and motionless.

Murmurs rippled through the crowd. One man shouted, "Who will do the thrall work?"

He held his arms up for silence again. "Every thrall, man or woman, will be given a choice. They may remain here under contract to work for a given period of time, none to exceed five years. Those who choose not to work may leave come springtime, with no repercussions. I have been convinced that men and women work harder when under no yoke of slavery. I believe Bear's Lair will prosper in this new way."

Not everyone was convinced, but Brandr was a strong leader. He would show them that it could work.

"One last thing. From this point forward, no babies born at Bear's Lair will be thralls."

More murmurs of disgruntlement passed through the crowd.

"Now, resume the festivities. I will discuss all this with each of you after the Yule season."

With that, he sat down and reached for his cup of ale, taking a long draw.

She just stared at him. "What was that all about?"

Even though there were still grumblings, the music had started up again, and people were beginning to consume the plum pudding that Kelda had sweated over.

"Me. Adapting."

"You?"

"What? You thought I was so rigid in my ways that I could not change?"

"In a word, yes."

"See, we all learn something every day." He winked at her.

The wink was almost her undoing. "Did you do that . . . releasing the slaves . . . for me?"

"Not *for* you, but *because* of you."

"Oh, Brandr." Deeply touched, she put a hand to his cheek.

"Oh, good gods!" someone exclaimed to the right of her. It sounded like Arnis.

She looked to see what had caught his attention, then did a double take. Two men were carrying a huge platter on which rose a very large cake, at least two feet tall. A lopsided cake with white icing, sprinkled with black things that might be nuts, or dirt.

"*What* is that?" she heard Liv ask.

"A wedding cake." someone replied.

Brandr just chuckled and murmured something that sounded like, "Good old Kelda!"

"Dearly beloved," someone else said, drawing their attention to the other side of the dais where a holly and pine bough covered trellis stood with a crude cross on top. And JAM stood there in his priestly attire, his booming voice ringing out, "We are gathered here today to celebrate the union of one man and one woman . . ."

Joy smiled. The wedding. She turned to look at Tork and Dagny.

Who had turned to look at her.

In fact, everyone was looking at her . . . and Brandr.

*Whaaat?*

She jerked her head to the left. "Brandr, please don't tell me you did this . . . without consulting me."

"Yea, I did. It is to be a surprise wedding. Surprise, surprise!"

*I am going to kill him. I am really going to kill him this time.* "There is not going to be a wedding between you and me, surprise or not."

"You wear my mother's wedding gown and the torque my father gifted her. I honor you with this offer of matrimony. Nay, do not get your hackles up. Let me finish. More than that, I would be honored if you would marry me."

Tears were welling in her eyes, and she noticed that the hall was silent, everyone waiting for her answer. Could she be more embarrassed?

He turned her chair around so her back was to the crowd, and did the same to his own, a belated attempt at privacy. Then, taking her hands in his, he pleaded, "Be my bride, Joy. Please? Marry me. Be my helpmate, my lover, and the mother of my children."

She moaned and swiped at the tears rimming her eyes. "You don't make it easy to refuse you. And don't ever try to tell me ever again that you are not romantic."

"You have changed me."

"Why, Brandr? Why are you doing this?"

He exhaled loudly, as if trying to gain strength. "You came into my life like a lightning bolt, heartling, bringing sunshine where there was only darkness. If you leave, I despair that I can go on. The berserkness will come back, I know it will, like black, life-sucking quicksand."

"Don't play on my conscience. That's not fair."

"For the love of God," JAM yelled out, "tell the woman you love her."

Brandr blinked at her. "That goes without saying."

"It does not!"

He cocked his head to the side. "You do not know?"

"Know what, you idiot?"

"I love you, heart of my heart," he said simply.

And she was lost. Lost, lost, lost.

She fell into his arms, onto his lap, and wet his neck with her copious tears. She could no more leave this man than cut off a limb. It was crazy. She was a twenty-first-century woman. He was a tenth-century Viking. But they were meant to be.

A short time later, JAM said the traditional wedding vows over them. Out of nowhere, Brandr pulled out a heavy, etched, gold ring and slid it on her finger. She was handed a silver chain and medallion to slip over Brandr's neck.

"What is this?" she whispered.

"My slave collar."

"No way!"

"Yea way! The leather thong has been replaced by metal, and the amulet is silver, but the significance is the same."

She put a hand to the medallion and turned it over. "What do those runic letters say?"

"I belong to Joy."

### A new Viking tradition . . .

With a deep kiss and hearts singing, they both turned to JAM, who said, "By the power granted to me by God and the Navy SEALs, I now pronounce you man and wife." Then, with a chuckle, he added a loud "Hoo-yah!"

The Viking men thought that was a cue. Thus it was that a new tradition was born at Norse weddings, or at least those at Bear's Lair. A loud chant by Viking men of "Hoo-yah!" forever after accompanied horns of mead raised for the wedding toast.

Of course, that did not mean that the Old Norse rituals were abandoned. Brandr made sure he smacked Joy across her bottom with the broad side of his sword, just to remind her who was to be the master in this household.

No one believed that would be the case.

In fact, in their bedchamber that night, the bride was heard to say, "I've been thinking . . ."

And the "master" buried his head under a pillow.

# Epilogue

**Good-byes bring sweet sorrow . . . some worse than others . . .**

Even though it was springtime, the air was crisp as five of Brandr's longships prepared to make their way down Igorssfjord now that the ice had thawed. Two would be going a-Viking, and three would be for the markets of Kaupang, Birka, and Hedeby.

Brandr would not be traveling with his men. This was a time for rebuilding Bear's Lair. In addition, he had a new wife to coddle and hopefully to plant with the seed of his child as soon as her birthing control device wore out. Most important, ne'er would he leave Bear's Lair unprotected again, as it had been with the Sigurdssons. A strong hird of soldiers remained here with him.

"Make sure you bring back plenty of young hogs," he told Erland. "They will have all the spring and summer months to pannage amongst the acorn trees. By fall they will be fat enough to butcher, and our larders will be full once again."

Erland nodded, and they both exchanged "Godspeeds" with hands to each other's shoulders.

To Arnis, who would be a-Viking in Saxon lands, he said, "If you get a chance, go to Ravenshire where Lady Eadyth is a famed beekeeper. She is married to a Viking, Tykir's brother Eirik. Joy has it in her head to try beekeeping here. See if Lady Eadyth can give you some hives to start us off."

"Odin's teeth, Brandr! I am off to plunder, not do girling errands for your ladylove."

"I heard that," Joy said, coming up to them.

Brandr tucked her in to his side with an arm over her shoulder.

"You will do as you are told, Arnis. And besides, you will be the first to slurp up all the mead from their honey come summer."

He exchanged "Godspeed" with Arnis, too.

It was the priest-soldier's turn to say his good-byes, and Brandr was not surprised that Joy started bawling once again. It tore at his heart to see her so unhappy.

After about the tenth hug, Father Mendozo said to her, "Are you sure you do not want to return with me?"

She shook her head, to his great relief. "I'm just sad to see you go, knowing . . . well, knowing I probably won't see you again. Will you do me a favor, JAM? Will you go to my brothers and tell them that I'm okay? I'm sure they're worried about me, probably think I'm dead. My death on top of Matt's would be devastating to them."

Father Mendozo nodded. "Should I tell them the truth?"

"You can, though I doubt that they would believe you. I know . . . tell them to do some historical research, and see if they can find the name of a brave Viking warrior named Matthew Brandrsson. That should be proof enough."

He and Father Mendozo both turned to stare at her with furrowed brows.

"That will be the name of my first son," she declared.

Brandr squeezed her shoulder, too choked up to speak.

An hour later, he and Joy were the only ones left on the wharf watching the longships bearing the Bear's Lair flags disappear in the distance.

This was such an important turning point in Joy's life.

She was giving up so much for him, and he was not sure how to handle her pain. With care, of course. However, he did not want to do anything to upset her more.

But then she surprised him with the words:

"Let's go home, honey."

# Glossary—SEALs

**boondockers.** Heavy boots.
**BUD/S.** Basic Underwater Demolition/SEAL training.
**Budweiser.** The trident pin worn by Navy SEALs.
**CENTCOM.** Central Command.
**collateral damage.** Inadvertent casualties and destruction inflicted on civilians in the course of a military operation.
**Coronado (California).** The West Coast site of the U.S. Naval Amphibious Base and the Naval Special Warfare Center, where BUD/S are trained. The other SEAL training center is located in Little Creek, Virginia. Coronado is also home to the famous Hotel del Coronado.
**cover your six.** Cover your back.
**DOR.** Drop on request.
**FUBAR.** Fucked up beyond all recognition.
**Gig Squad.** A punishment inflicted during BUD/S where a SEAL trainee is forced to spend hours, after the evening meal and a long day of training, outside the officers' headquarters. doing many strenuous exercises, including the infamous duck squat.

**grinder.** The blacktopped area where PT takes place, along with the O-course, on the SEAL training arena at Coronado.

**high and tight.** Standard military haircut.

**Look and See.** Reconnaissance mission whereby the operators penetrate enemy territory, identify the targets, and depart without being seen.

**MRE.** Meal ready to eat.

**NSW.** Naval Special Warfare.

**O-course.** Obstacle course on the training compound, also referred to as the Oh-My-God course.

**PT.** Physical training.

**scruffies.** Lowest of the low in military training.

**SEAL.** Acronym for Sea, Air and Land, est. 1962.

**Sims.** Short for Simunitions, paint bullets that emulate live ammunition, down to short-range ballistics and cyclic rates of fire.

**snafu.** Situation normal all fucked up.

**SOCOM.** U.S. Special Operations Command.

**SOF.** Special Operations Forces.

**tango.** Terrorist or bad guy.

**UA.** Unauthorized absence, equivalent of AWOL in the Navy and Marines.

**WARCOM.** Warfare Command, as in Naval Special Warfare Command.

**XO.** Executive officer.

# Glossary—Vikings

**Althing.** An assembly of free people that makes laws and settles disputes. It is like a Thing but much larger, involving delegates from various parts of a country, not just a single region.

**Birka.** Market town where Sweden is now located.

**braies.** Long, slim pants worn by men, usually tied at the waist; also called breeches.

**drukkinn.** Drunk.

**gunna.** Long-sleeved, ankle-length gown for women, often worn under a tunic or surcoat or long, open-sided apron.

**Hedeby.** Market town where Germany is now located.

**hird.** Troop, war band.

**Hordaland.** Norway.

**jarl.** High-ranking Norseman, similar to an English earl or a wealthy landowner; could also be a chieftain or minor king.

**Jorvik.** Viking-age York in Britain.

**Jutland.** Denmark.

**karl.** One rank below a jarl.

**nithing.** One of the greatest of Norse insults, indicating that a man is less than nothing.

**Norsemandy.** Vikings ruled what would later be called Normandy. To them, it was Norsemandy.

**odal right.** Law of heredity.

**sagas.** Oral history of the Norse people, passed on from ancient history onward.

**sennight.** One week.

**skalds.** Poets or storytellers who composed and told the sagas, which were the only means of recording ancient Norse history, since there was almost no written word then.

**straw death.** To die in bed (mattresses stuffed with straw), rather than in battle, which was more desirable.

**Thing.** An assembly of freemen called together to discuss problems and settle disputes; forerunner of the English judicial system; like district courts of today.

**thrall.** Slave.

Keep reading for a special preview of
the next novel by Sandra Hill,

# Even Vikings
# Get the Blues

Coming soon from Berkley Sensation!

**Double or nothing . . .**

With a loud *whoosh*, Rita Sawyer's body went up in flames and she prepared to catapult through the fifteenth-floor window of the burning skyscraper. The whole time she pondered whether she'd have the time, or the inclination, to shave her legs before her date this evening with her ex-husband's brother.

Well, it wasn't a date exactly. Darron wanted her to meet the latest love of his life, Dirk Severino. *Darron and Dirk. Doesn't that say it all?* In addition, he was bringing along the "perfect man" for her. His words. Presumably heterosexual, and with a job. Absolute essentials for her as a twenty-nine-year-old veteran in the dating wars.

Darron was suffering major post-divorce guilt . . . on his brother Scott's behalf . . . and had made it his mission in life to find Rita a mate to make up for his hound dog brother's betrayal during Scott and Rita's short-lived marriage. To her embarrassment, after plying her with Fuzzy Navels last week, Darron had discovered that she hadn't been with a man in more than two years, not since the divorce. It was none of his business, of course, but Darron was a busybody from way back.

To be honest, she was still raw and angry over Scott's infidelity, whether it was one time, as he'd laughably claimed, or dozens, as she rightly suspected. Adultery was adultery in her book. She'd seen what it had done to her mother. Rita had suffered the pain herself.

She'd known Scott since kindergarten. Darron, too, who was the younger brother. She'd seen Scott at his worst, and it wasn't even when she'd caught him in bed with a fellow physician. Therefore, she shouldn't have been surprised when he'd turned out to be an adulterous snot when he grew up. Females had been drawn to his blond good looks from a young age. As if that was any excuse!

Actually, she had her own ulterior motive for meeting with Darron tonight. He was a top-notch financial advisor, and Rita was facing monumental money problems since her mother had died and left her with medical bills out the wazoo. It wasn't the long bout with cancer that had caused all the problems, but rather the experimental treatments not covered by insurance—for which Rita had gladly taken out loans—and the year she'd spent as a caretaker when she'd had no income. Unfortunately, it was all done in vain. Collection agencies now had her on speed dial. And, no, she still wouldn't accept alimony from Scott the Snot.

"Scene three, take two. Lights! Camera! Ready! Action!" Larry Winters, the director of this latest spy thriller starring Jennifer Garner and Hugh Jackman, shouted through his bullhorn.

Jennifer went sailing through the glass and the air with expertise, landing on a trampoline that looked like the roof of another building, from which she then front-flipped onto yet another rooftop, which was actually a padded platform. Of course, it wasn't really the fifteenth floor but rather the third, and it wasn't really a skyscraper but rather a set prop, and it wasn't really Jennifer Garner but rather Rita Sawyer, her stunt double.

"Cut!" the director yelled. "That's a wrap! Great job, Rita!"

Immediately, a technician began hosing down her flames while others were peeling back her flameproof wig, her two nomex jumpsuits, and her gloves. Still others wiped the flame-retardant gel off her face.

"Hey, Rita. Got a minute?" Dean Witherow, the producer, called out to her. "I have a couple gentlemen who'd like to meet you."

Noticing the two military types in the visitors' area, probably consultants on the film, she rolled her eyes. Folks were fascinated with her after witnessing some of her stunts, especially men who fantasized about what she could do in bed.

Being a proud lady of the SWAMP, as in Stunt Women's Association of Motion Pictures, she'd heard it all. One lawyer from Denver once asked, before they'd even gotten to the entree in a fancy Rodeo Drive restaurant, if she could do any kinky stunts during sex. Jeesh! And, yes, she could, actually. Not that she'd told him that.

After a quick shower in the doubles' trailer and a change of clothes to jeans and an Aerosmith T-shirt, she walked up and let Dean introduce them. "This is Commander Ian Mac-Lean and Lieutenant Jacob Mendozo. They're Navy SEALs stationed at Coronado."

*SEALs, huh? I've heard they can be kinky on occasion. They're certainly buff enough.*

But then she chastised herself. *Unbelievable! I am flippin' unbelievable. If I don't go ga-ga over Hugh Jackman, why would I be ogling these two grunts?*

Her eyes widened with interest, nevertheless. Like many others in this country, she had a proud appreciation for the good job SEALs did in fighting terrorism.

The one guy, the commander, was in his early forties, with a receding hairline that didn't detract at all from his overall attractiveness. He was too somber for her tastes, though.

Lieutenant Mendozo, on the other hand, was *whoo-ee* sex personified. From his Hispanic good looks to his mischievous eyes, he was eye candy of the best sort. And she'd bet her skydiving helmet that he knew his way around a bed, too.

*Rita Sawyer, get your mind out of the gutter.*

*Maybe I am suffering from sex deprivation, like Darron thinks.*

"Were either of you among those SEALs who got in trouble for riding horseback into Afghanistan a few years back? I saw it on CNN."

Both men's faces reddened.

"We don't talk about that," the commander said.

*Which means yes.* "Why so shy? It was really impressive."

"The Pentagon didn't think so," Lieutenant Mendozo explained with a wink . . . a wink his superior did not appreciate, if his glare was any indication.

"Heads rolled," the commander agreed with a grimace. "With good reason. Necessity might be the mother of invention, but in the case of SEALs, they well better be private inventions."

"What he's trying to say is that a SEAL scalp is a coup for many tangos . . . uh, terrorists. It's important that we stay covert. That episode in Afghanistan was a monumental brain fart."

*I'll tell you what would be a brain fart . . . me considering joining up with these nutcakes. That would be right up there with mistake number one . . . marrying Scott.*

"Well, it's been nice meeting you. Maybe you can—" she started to say.

"We have a proposition for you," Commander MacLean interrupted.

*Gutter, here I come.* She laughed. She couldn't help herself.

"Not that kind of proposition."

*Oh, heck!*

"I'm a happily married man. In fact, my wife would whack me with the flat side of her broadsword if I even looked at another female."

The lieutenant smiled in a way that indicated he wouldn't mind that kind of proposition.

But wait a minute. Did he say broadsword?

"Can we go somewhere for a cup of coffee?" the commander suggested.

*Or a cool drink to lower my temperature.*

Soon they were seated at a table in the commissary.

"So, what's this all about?" she asked, impatient to get home if she was going to make her "date." Now that her initial testosterone buzz had tamed down to a hum, she accepted that these two were here on business of some sort, not to put the make on her.

"How would you like to become a female SEAL?"

She choked on her iced tea and had to dab at her mouth and shirt with the paper napkins the lieutenant handed her with a chuckle. "You mean, like GI Jane?" she finally sputtered out.

"Exactly," Commander MacLean said. "It's a grueling training program. Not many women . . . or men, for that matter . . . can handle the regimen."

What a load of hooey! "Why me?"

"The WEALS program, Women on Earth, Air, Land and Sea, needs more good women who are physically fit to the extreme. With terrorism running rampant today, Uncle Sam needs more elite forces, and our current supply of seasoned SEALs is deploying on eight to ten combat tours. Way too many! So we're recruiting special people under a mentoring program. Bottom line, we need a thousand more SEALs over the next few years, and a few hundred more WEALS."

"I repeat, why me?"

The commander shrugged. "We want the best of the best. Men and women who are patriotic . . ."

*I do get teary when the National Anthem plays.*

". . . adventuresome,"

*Did they hear about my wrestling an alligator? Jeesh! Can't anyone keep a secret? It was an accident, for heaven's sake! I fell on the damn beast.*

". . . extreme athletes,"

*You got me on that one.*

". . . controlled risk takers,"

*That one, too. Stunt doubles take risks, but well-planned, safe-as-possible risks. But, boy, is he pouring it on!*

". . . intelligent,"

*I barely passed calculus, and how intelligent had it been to marry a serial adulterer?*

". . . skilled competitors who enjoy challenges and games,"

*Does he see "Sucker" tattooed on my forehead?*

". . . people who love to travel,"

*Yeah, like downtown Kabul is my idea of a Club Med vacation.*

". . . men and women with a fire in the gut."

*The fire in my gut comes from the enchiladas I ate for lunch. And from my continuing fury over Scott's adultery.*

"Only one in a hundred applicants makes it through Hell Week, you know."

*And you think I want to put myself through that?* "You've gotta be kidding."

Both men shook their heads.

"And my mentor would be . . . ?"

The sexy lieutenant gave her a little wave.

*Okay, I'm officially tempted.*

But not enough. She'd read about Hell Week. She'd watched Demi Moore get creamed in *G.I. Jane.* Who needs that? No. Way. She started to rise from her seat. "I'm flattered that you would consider me, but—"

"Plus there's a sizeable signing bonus," Lieutenant Mendozo added.

Rita plopped back down into her chair. "Tell me more."

And she could swear she heard the cute lieutenant murmur "Hoo-yah!"

## He was in the mood for . . .

Steven of Norstead, proud son of a Viking prince, handsome as a god, far-famed in the bedsport, well-tested in battle, was bored. Actually, more than bored. In truth, he was in a black, nigh unbearable mood and had been for some time.

"Who ever heard of a depressed Viking?" Oslac, his friend and comrade-in-arms, inquired, followed by a loud belch.

Steven belched, too, just to be friendly.

They were both deep in the alehead following a full day and night of debauchery . . . or at least multiple partners in his bed furs, if he recalled correctly. Not all at once, praise the gods. Not this time, anyway. But that other time! Good gods! Father Christopher had suffered a foaming fit when he caught him in the bathing hut with . . . well, never mind.

Vikings often practiced both the Christian and Norse religions, but it was no great loss when Father Christopher left them for an extended monasterial retreat, leaving behind Father Peter, who was less inclined to foaming fits and leaned more toward foaming ale.

But that was neither here nor there.

"I am not depressed, precisely. More like I carry a huge weight on my shoulders. All the time."

"Well, 'tis no small feat managing two vast estates—Norstead *and* Amberstead."

"And a fine job you do for me at Amberstead. Nay, 'tis more than that. I am only eight and twenty, and yet I seem to have lost my zest for life. I can scarce get up in the morn, with naught to look forward to."

"Mayhap you need to wed. Get yourself a wife and start breeding sons. King Olaf still claims you were betrothed at birth to his third daughter, Elsa."

He shot a glower at Oslac.

"What? She is not so bad."

"Oh, she is comely enough, but she talks constantly. About nothing. Blather, blather, blather. I would have to put a plug in her mouth afore tupping."

Oslac suggested something about the plug, which Steven should have expected. He had stepped into that one like a boyling unused to male jests.

"Whether with Elsa or someone else, you must wed at some point. Heirs are needed for Norstead and Amberstead."

He shrugged. "Time enough later."

"It's your brother," Oslac guessed.

He nodded. "Yea, ever since Thorfinn disappeared a year past—"

"Disappeared?" Oslac scoffed.

"Ever since Finn died, then." He cast a scowl at Oslac for the reminder. "We were in Baghdad. One moment he was laughing and telling me to meet him at the ship, warning me not to purchase any harem houris, whilst he conducted a final meeting with the horse breeder. The next he failed to appear, and all we found was a pool of blood and his short sword lying beside the road. Mayhap he is still—"

Oslac put up a halting hand. "Nay, Steven. You searched for sennights. A year has passed. He would have let you know."

"But there was no body," Steven insisted.

"The miscreants who took his life no doubt dumped his body elsewhere. Accept that he is gone and move on with your life. I know how close you were, but he is in Asgard now, my friend."

Steven sighed and drew another long slurp of ale from his carved horn cup.

"I must say, though, that Finn was always the serious one, especially after his wife left him, taking their infant son. And you were the lighthearted one, always up for a good time."

"Are you saying I have lost my sense of humor?" he inquired, not at all offended, though Viking men did prize their ability to laugh at themselves and all of life's foibles.

"Hah! You have lost more than that. Remember the time you and I fought off a black bear with our bare hands? Remember the time you tripped Eric the Bold when he was being particularly arrogant, and he fell into Mathilde Wart-Nose's big bosoms? Remember the time you brought that ivory phallus back from Hedeby and talked Seeba into inserting it whilst we watched? Remember the time we drank so much mead we decided we could jump off the roof of the keep into a hay wagon? Remember the time you tupped six women in a row and could still rise to the occasion?"

Steven just sighed deeply, again.

"Mayhap you should a-Viking."

"I did that last month. Brought two shiploads of plunder back from the Saxon lands."

"Boar hunting."

"Boring."

"Amber trading."

"I have too much amber already. Which reminds me . . . We must needs send several chests to Birka for trading afore the winter freeze over the fjords."

"Visit King Olaf's royal court."

"I will be going there for the yule season. A man can stand only so much of Olaf's bad breath."

"What we need is a good battle. Why is everyone so bloody peaceable of late?"

"I know. My broadsword will get rusty from lack of use. I will have the armor boy oil it and my brynja on the morrow."

Oslac poured them both more ale. "There are those pirates who are getting more daring of late."

"Or desperate."

"That, too."

"We should post extra sentries lest they strike afore winter."

Steven nodded. "'Twas a time when they only attacked longships that were poorly armed, and usually those farther south. Now they even stalk the inland fjords."

"Ever since Eric the Black was outlawed, pirates have become more than a menace. And others are following suit."

"Yea, 'tis is waste, too. Eric was a fine warrior 'til he and his men raped those girls at Sudeby and put a blood eagle on the mother for sport. Now he is a nithing, using his fighting skills to organize the pirates and train them to attack in fleets."

"Ah, look. Here comes Lady Inga, Rolfgar's widow. Mayhap she can lift your spirits . . . or leastways, your staff."

"She already lifted my staff. Three times last night she let me swive her. Or rather, she swived me, to be more accurate."

"Are you sure? *I* swived her three times last night."

He and Oslac exchanged glances of incredulity, then burst out laughing.

"Dost think she would consider joining us in . . . ?" Oslac then suggested something so outrageous that Steven, who thought he had tried everything that involved his cock, solitary or otherwise, was shocked.

But only for a moment.

Suddenly, Steven's enthusiasm seemed to be gurgling back to life. Not his mood though. But then, when had a good mood been required for a zesty bout of bedsport? A man's enthusiasm for sex play was a constant, especially the perverted kind.

"Oh, *Innnnn-gaaaaa*," Oslac called out.

Also from *USA Today* bestselling author

# Sandra Hill

# VIKING UNCHAINED

"Sandra Hill has truly outdone herself."
—*Night Owl Romance*

"Ms. Hill had me rolling with laughter with every turn of the page. She breathes life into her characters and makes the reader wish they were real. I dare say anyone who reads this story will come away with a smile." —*Coffee Time Romance*

"Hill goes a-Viking again! It's a blast!"
—*Romantic Times*

M448T0409